THE POISONER'S GAME

by Beatrix Conti

To those who can't stop writing and use other worlds to escape their own.

ISBN: 9798502792585

Cover design by: Beatrix Conti
Printed in the United States of America

CONTENTS

CHAPTER ONE

M.

Spring of 1877

Belgravia, London

Nothing good ever happened in London.

Escaping out of a window while my first ball of the season thrummed below had to be my worst idea yet. The letter in my reticule pushed me toward the ledge and a new wash of tears cloaked my eyes. Murder, the Poisoner, and a Duke had pushed me into a new storyline. Even now, the events of that time could have been pulled directly from a *Penny Dreadful* printed on cheap pulp paper.

I bit my lip until I tasted blood and moved forward. Everything would be fine once I reached the twisting maze in the garden. A loud creak sounded outside of the door and my heart beat grew to meet it. With one last check of the gardens, I tossed my reticule out of the window. It landed in the bushes below before sliding onto the stone pathway with a painful thud. I hoped I would fair better. Gripping the velvet drapes, I took a deep breath and planted myself on the window ledge.

Just as I had gained the courage to release the ledge I heard a voice. "Whatever are you doing?"

Bollocks. "What do you think I am doing?" I had no better response.

"Let me help you down."

The voice flirted with my memory. A handsome face with sparkling eyes. I turned my head to look at the speaker. A young man with tousled golden-brown hair watched me with an amused quirk in his brow. Without a pencil mark left on my dance card, I remembered him by his hand on the small of my back and his lips on the palm of my hand as the "Blue Danube" came to life. The feeling of gliding across the floor and belonging somewhere, if only for that moment, danced across the hollows of my heart with shimmering violins and answering woodwinds. A moment I was desperate to find again—hold onto and never let go. With a shuddered wince, I released the memory as it slid through my fingers until nothing remained.

I must have also released the ledge.

Air rushed past me and I couldn't even scream. I hit the bush, the branches splintering under my weight and piercing my hands. To my ears it sounded thunderous. My eyes remained shut for fear that the entirety of high society would be standing before me. I felt solid ground beneath my feet and forced myself to stand. Cracking my eyes open, I saw only the young man. His mouth hung open and he cleared his throat.

I brushed my hands down my worn yellow dress. With false bravado, I moved away from the bush. "I can take care of myself."

My knees trembled, and I turned toward the maze counting my breaths. I forced one foot in front of the other.

"My lady?"

I stopped and turned around. Hidden behind the thick brown clouds, I imagined that the stars laughed at my fate. They had given me quite a fate after all…murdered parents and lies.

"I am assuming you don't wish to leave this behind?" The young man held up my tattered reticule.

I didn't think my cheeks could heat further. With stiff legs, I walked back to the young man. The walk back seemed infinite and an edge of hysteria thrummed at my fingertips. My lips yearned to tell someone, anyone, that a murderer hunted me. A little voice whispered in the back of my mind, how did I know what my grandfather wrote held the truth? I thought he had died years ago after all.

Sticking out my hand, I stayed several feet away from the young man. "I'll take it now and be on my way."

He handed it to me after a moment of hesitation. "I didn't mean to look in it but if you're truly planning to run away, for why else would you be jumping from a window, I think you are woefully unprepared."

"I didn't ask you, now did I?" I growled at him, holding the reticule to my chest.

"My lady all you have is a book, a small money pouch, and little else. You could at least carry a knife for protection." He threw his hands into the air and shook his head at me.

I'd rarely been on the receiving end of someone's concerns. Especially not a handsome young man. I shook my head to clear it, I had taken several steps closer. Curiosity had rooted itself in my mind and it rarely let go easily.

"You won't try to stop me?" The words escaped my lips before I had a chance to stop them.

"Sometimes you need to escape," he responded and looked away. Something remained hidden within his words that felt all too familiar.

My feet ignored my brain and I took another step forward and into the light from the cast-iron lamp that hung on the side of the house.

The young man's eyes furrowed. "I know you."

My breath caught in my chest. A door opened, and I heard another man's voice. I dove for the bushes. Bollocks.

"Lord Alexander are you alone?" the new man asked.

His name sat poised on the tip of my tongue as I took a deep breath, tasting the scent of juniper. I stared at the brick wall of the townhouse, hoping the other man couldn't see me in the darkness and that Lord Alexander wouldn't give me away.

A long pause followed the man's question before Lord Alexander responded, "Yes. What is it?"

"His grace wanted me to relay that your informant has resurfaced in the Thames. Murdered."

"The Poisoner?"

Every thought in my head came to a crashing halt. The Poisoner. The man who murdered my parents. The man I was on the run from. It meant that my grandfather had told the truth. It meant I had to run. Escape.

"I'll leave you with this correspondence."

A door clicked shut. Writhing in the bush, I tried to push myself up. My corset dug into my sides and I realized I'd made a mistake. One of many that night.

Two firm hands encircled my shoulders and I found myself on my own two feet. My coiffure had fallen apart, and I brushed back a black curl from my line of vision.

"*Virtutem Forma Decorat*," Lord Alexander said as he pulled a sprig of juniper from my hair.

"What?" I asked in a breathless whisper. I knew the Latin words meant beauty adorns virtue.

Lord Alexander shuffled his feet. "It's a reference my mother always made when she saw juniper."

"Why?" I asked though I didn't know why I bothered.

"Something from a da Vinci painting." Lord Alexander shrugged. "Now, Lady Margaret, will you tell me why you're trying to run away?"

Sucking in a breath, I ran my tongue along the back of my teeth. "I'll tell you, my lord, if you tell me what you know about the Poisoner."

A thought entered my head, how did he know my name? For the first time, I felt the chill of the night run along my bare arms. This young man could work for the Poisoner.

Lord Alexander and I spoke at the same time.

"Are you familiar with the Poisoner?"

"How do you know my name?"

Lord Alexander's eyes narrowed. "I know your grandfather believed that your parents were murdered by the Poisoner. Is that why you're on the run?"

My mouth flopped open. "How do you know that?"

Lord Alexander pulled out a letter from his evening jacket. It had a crimson red seal—my grandfather's letter. With shaking fingers, I pried open my reticule and found the letter missing.

"Give that back to me, you miscreant!" I closed the gap between us and snatched the letter from his hands. He didn't fight me but only quirked a brow.

Looking me up and down, Lord Alexander leaned against the brick wall. The calm he exuded did nothing but increase my ever-growing anxiety. I didn't need his information, I needed to run. My plan for escape had been scrapped together within days of receiving my grandfather's letter. By no means was it a good plan, no, it wasn't even a decent plan, but I did not plan on getting murdered by the Poisoner.

"I am leaving, and you won't stop me." I took several steps back.

Lord Alexander shrugged. "Your choice..."

"Yes, it's my choice." It felt odd saying those words. Rarely in my life did the opportunity of choice present itself.

"But, don't you want to know who murdered your parents? Don't you want to know why?"

Why had been tumbling around my head for the last week with the power of a battering ram. It enticed me then like a pomegranate presented in the Underworld to the naïve Persephone.

CHAPTER TWO

M.
Clifton, Bristol
One week prior...

"You're coming to London." Aunt Emily didn't look up from her needlework.

I almost dropped my basket full of freshly darned socks and Rose screeched loudly enough for the both of us.

"Mama, you can't mean it?" Rose glared at me. "It's my come out, I don't need *her* to ruin it. Mama!"

Aunt Emily gave Rose a look she usually reserved for me. "My word is final."

I watched them both with suspicion. Often, I spent spring and summer alone in the country while the family visited London for the sitting of Parliament and the start of the season. I cherished that time strolling through Durdham Down, picking lavender that dotted the road, and swimming in the pond about an hour's walk from the city. If I had been asked if I wanted to go to London the answer would have been no. But no one ever asked me. They never did.

Rose pouted, with tears tickling the corners of her eyes. Aunt Emily's face softened, and she cupped Rose's chin with her hand. "Don't worry, my cherub. Everything will work out for the best, you'll see."

She looked me up and down, her mouth curling as if she smelt something foul. "Your role will be to be as unobtrusive as possible and to cater to the families' needs. If you so much as breathe out of line, there will be severe punishment. This season is important for all of us, even you."

I said nothing for I had heard similar pronouncements all my life. Yet, for some reason, I felt particularly small at that moment.

With the sharpness of a hawk with its eyes on a field mouse, Aunt Emily turned to me again. "You're still here, Margaret? Don't you have work to do."

I straightened and bobbed a curtsy. "Yes, my apologies, Aunt."

Scuttling out of the room, I softly closed the door behind me and leaned against it. My heart thrummed in my ears. I knew better than to question Aunt Emily, which meant I had to begin packing my bags. In the servants' quarters, I dropped off my basket. From a hook near the door to the gardens, I grabbed my sunbonnet. Though Aunt Emily always said, it would do little to lighten my complexion. Rose had either been born with the desirable peaches and cream complexion, or Aunt Emily's early implementation of veils, bonnets, parasols, and gloves, all utilized with religious intensity against the sun, had done their trick. Aunt Emily, like me, had been disgraced by a tanned-complexion which she worked tirelessly to absolve whether by washing her face every morning with ammonia or chewing on arsenic complexion wafers. I had only ever tried zinc powder. It did nothing to transform me into the English Rose of my imagination. Instead, I found myself left very much the same with unruly dark hair, too tanned skin, and strange grey eyes.

I walked out of Berkeley Square, past the High Cross in the College Green, and across the Bristol Bridge to Radcliffe. Above me and heading in the opposite direction, a flock of seagulls caught the wind to the Mouth of the Severn River and the sea. On the horizon, grey clouds threatened another rainstorm. For a moment, I allowed myself to be sucked into the hum of the city as servants went about their tasks in the shadows cast by the towering white Georgian terraces and the faraway sounds of the docks. Past Somerset Square, I found the largely abandoned glass factory that had once produced the famous Bristol Blue Glass.

Using a key hidden beneath the numerous rose bushes, I

pushed open the door. Sun shone hesitantly through the dusty windows. Hulking metal machines, which I had no name for, lay dormant on the factory's floor. Miriam's family, the Jacobs, had once been the most predominant family in glass-manufacturing in the area until her grandfather, Issac Jacobs fell on hard times. Her mother's marriage to Miriam's father, as a wealthy Jewish heiress from Amsterdam, had revived the family's connection with trade but they had never touched glass again. All except Miriam.

"Miriam?" I called.

"Over here!"

Miriam's head was bent over a delicate dessert bowl made of a royal purple glass and gilded with burnished gold on the rim. Before her, on a table, stood a copper engraving wheel. I only knew the name for the many times Miriam had tried to coax me into working with glass. I feared even touching the delicate works of art would cause them to turn to dust.

"What do you think?" Miriam asked as she held up the bowl for my inspection.

Like her grandfather and great-grandfather before her, Miriam had a way with glass. She had engraved a delicate rose pattern to the sides of the dessert bowl.

"It's lovely of course." I watched the light reflect on it as though it were a sprig of lavender and once again remembered that my summer had been ruined by my family.

"I've been telling Tate that we should re-open the factory. We once sold items like this to Queen Victoria." Miriam set the glassware on the worktable and sighed wistfully.

I scuffed my worn-leather shoes on the floorboards, twisting my dress in my hands. "I am going to London."

"What do you mean? Are you running away?"

The thought crossed my mind for the briefest of moments as it so often did. "No, the family has *invited* me." Invited seemed not at all like the correct word.

Miriam's face scrunched in confusion as she opened and closed her mouth several times. "Actually, this might be perfect."

"What?"

"Mame wants me to have a come out of sorts in London as well." Miriam pushed strands of white-blonde hair out of her blue eyes.

"I thought she wanted you to marry into the Alexander or Jessel family?" I asked slumping onto one of the stools.

"Yes, of course, but she knows I am not budging until I've seen more of the world. Even if the only world she'll allow me to see is London. It's so unfair that Lionel has traveled to the Far East and I can't even go to the docks."

Often, Miriam and I had talked about our yearning for adventure. Miriam taking the full-forced leap, while I stood two steps back. I wanted to be like her, but something always held me back.

"I doubt I will be having a come-out. It seems I am just to be the specter to their activities."

Miriam rolled her eyes and cleaned off the glass bowl with a cloth. "They truly are the worst."

I sucked on my cheeks as my nails dug into my palm. "I suppose so, but it could be worse. I should be lucky to have their Christian Charity."

"Cockamamie and you know it. They and their idol worshiping charity can toss themselves in the Thames when we get to London."

Tension eased from my chest and found its way out of my body in the form of a choked laugh. "I did sound rather too much like Aunt Emily, didn't I?"

Miriam imitated an overly-exaggerated shudder. She put away her tools, while I busied myself watching the street below. Across the way from the factory, I saw a man with a bowler hat. At first, it didn't concern me as he looked like one of the many men going about their business from the small factories to the shops that filled the street. However, he didn't look away and his eyes seemed to bore into mine.

"Miriam, do you see that man below?" I asked, turning to look at her. She came to my side and when we both returned our gaze to the street, he was gone. "Never mind then."

"Would you like to come to mine for Shabbat dinner?" Miriam asked as we left the factory. She held her precious glassware boxed and wrapped in cloth.

My stomach grumbled out a plea for agreement. "I would but we leave tomorrow and I need to pack."

"Bubbe made fresh gefilte fish and bought challah from the bakery."

Again, my stomach seemed to make out a mangled plea, but again I shook my head. I doubted I would be able to eat anyway as my stomach equally rolled with anxiety. I hadn't been to London since I was a small child during a time I didn't want to remember.

CHAPTER THREE

A.
HMS Alexandra
Malta Naval Base
Some months prior...

A knock sounded on the door to the officers' quarters which I shared with four other lieutenants. I had just begun to take off my uniform for the night. The other men would be out carousing in the streets of Malta finding whatever wicked brew they could and soaking in the good weather that rarely graced their motherland. Normally, I would join them, but I had the expectation of a promotion hanging over me.

Re-buttoning my white shirt, I responded, "Enter."

A young midshipman of maybe fourteen nodded in the doorway. "Lieutenant Rocque, Commander Hornby has requested your presence in his quarters, if you'll follow me."

I flexed my hands, my heart hammering as I composed myself at once glad I had not joined the rest of the men. Tossing on my blue naval jacket and making sure that I looked as sharp as possible, I followed the midshipman. Gas lanterns hung along the hallway of the ship, which ever so slightly rocked in the harbor. We had arrived in Malta in March after Sir Geoffrey; my longtime leader and mentor had been promoted to Commander-in-Chief of the Mediterranean Fleet. For the past few weeks, we had been listening to whispers of aggression from the Russians against the Ottomans. The Balkan uprisings had heaved the unrest of the area into full focus with the brutal retaliation by the Turks. Disraeli wanted something to be done about it before his rival Gladstone embarrassed him again with another pamphlet like the "Bulgarian Horrors and the Question of the East." With the signing of the "London Protocol," the Royal Navy had the job of retaining a threatening presence in the Mediterranean.

Once we reached Sir Hornby's door, I excused the midshipman and straightened the cuffs of my sleeves before giving the door a firm knock. The door opened, and Captain Fisher exited, he gave me a once up and down which neither held kindness nor malice.

"Captain," I nodded as he held the door for me.

Moonlight shone through the four glass-paned windows at the back. A lantern hung above Sir Hornby, highlighting the weathered cracks in his face. It seemed like only yesterday that I had been foisted into his care. Motherless and practically fatherless.

***

May 20th, 1869
Hamoaze, England
The Devonport Dockyard

"Your name, lad?"

I looked up from my muddy shoes, wishing I hadn't stopped to throw rocks into the estuary. I had realized too late I was standing on nothing but mud banks. At least, my crisp uniform remained spotless. Clearing my throat, I stared up at the man with deep lines around his eyes, a receding hairline, and thick sideburns. Perhaps, his sideburns had stolen the hair from atop his head.

"Lord Alexander Rocque, sir," I breathed out, trying to refrain from the mumble I was always punished for. "I am the third son of the present Duke of Auden."

"Please sit, cadet." Commodore, Sir Hornby, indicated to the seat in front of a large desk covered with an assortment of maps and papers. He sat across from me and shuffled through the papers looking at me over their crisp edges. "Your age, cadet."

"Thirteen, sir." My chest expanded. Everyone always expected me to be fourteen because of my height.

Sir Hornby didn't look up. I deflated once more. "Your training?"

"Two years at the Britannia Royal Naval College in Dartmouth, sir." My heels knocked lightly against the sides of the chair. The mud didn't budge.

"You enrolled when you were eleven years of age?"

"Yes, sir."

"Yet, you received a first-class passing grade in studies, seamanship, and conduct."

"Yes, sir." I swallowed. "I passed to the rank of midshipman and spent a year on a training vessel."

"You'll be the youngest member of this squadron." Sir Hornby's golden insignia flashed in the beams of sunlight streaming through the window. "You'll have to pull your own weight."

"I'll pull six times my own weight!" I was immediately embarrassed by my childish and impassioned response.

Sir Hornby smiled. "Report to Captain Hopkins for your assignment, midshipman. We leave at dawn tomorrow."

***

Sir Hornby sat behind a table that had already been cleared and shined. He held only a letter. To the side of the room, his trunks were packed and ready for their removal to his home on land. Only since January had the HMS Alexandra become home and yet I still missed the HSM Liverpool which had carried us around the world.

"Commander, you requested my presence?" I asked keeping any emotion from my voice.

"Yes." For a moment Sir Hornby said nothing else and I felt a tinge of anxiety with every passing moment. With a deep sigh, he folded up the letter in his hand. "You're not going to like what I have to say. Please, take a seat, Alexander."

Sir Hornby had only called me Alexander two times in the eight years that I had known him. Once when I had almost gotten myself killed roughhousing in the crow's nest and a second time when my father had bid me stay on the ship for Christmas my first year in the Navy. I sat with reluctance, any expectation withering away and leaving nothing but nausea in the pit of my stomach.

"The Duke of Auden requests your immediate return to London." Sir Hornby regarded me with a pitying expression that made my hands clench. We had never once spoken at length about my father and we never would. I wondered what he'd think if he knew the truth.

With a coldness that surprised me, I responded, "Is there to be a funeral?"

Sir Hornby's expression didn't change. "His grace didn't say."

Of course not. At least I could be certain that neither of my older brothers had passed, for surely that would have reached the papers across Europe long before a letter from my father reached me. I hadn't seen my father in two years and hadn't seen him beyond a crowded ballroom in four years. Nothing good ever came from his summons.

Before I could respond saying I wouldn't go, Sir Hornby cleared his throat. "You'll have to go. I have no sway over the Duke and his whims, neither does the Royal Navy. You know your father." What he didn't say was that my father never made requests but only demands. No one had ever told him no.

I swallowed my pride, the numbness of a little boy trying to claw its way inside of me. "Did he say anything else?"

Sir Hornby thought for a moment and then unfolded the letter again to scan it. "He wrote that you should 'pay your respects' to your mother."

Every fiber of my being stilled. The little boy inside me heard a woman scream and saw the glint of a knife like the eyes of a wolf. Blood dripped down his chin.

I took a breath.

CHAPTER FOUR

A.
London
One week prior...

My father's house never changed, or it hadn't since my mother's death. I sometimes wondered if my life would be different if that day had never happened. A bitter memory of hope, warmth, and contentment threatened the edges of the stark foyer before me. At one time one could not find a room that didn't smell of lavender and fresh flowers. Now, just like me, they were banished. The Butler, Mr. Griggs, who had known me since birth, looked me once over with little kindness reflecting in his eyes.

"I will see if his grace is in, my lord." With that, he turned and stiffly walked down the hall.

"Pleased to see you again too, Griggs," I muttered.

My teeth ground together as I paced the foyer. I hadn't even been given the courtesy of relinquishing my hat. It would be the ultimate insult for my father to now refuse me, but I wouldn't let him. Not this time. After what seemed like just enough time to be rude but not enough time for one to make a fuss, Mr. Griggs returned to the foyer and indicated that I follow him.

"I know the way." I stopped once we entered the hallway lined with my ancestor's faces. As a child, I felt their eyes follow me so much so that I wouldn't venture down the hall until my mother and I had thoroughly examined each portrait together.

"But, my lord." Mr. Griggs puffed up with a weighty sense of protocol, for he still used the proper honorary title while holding me in contempt. I wished I could tell him to call me first lieutenant as it was something won through grit rather than birth.

"This is my family home is it not?" I raised a brow, knowing Griggs could little refuse me though we both knew the truth.

Griggs gave me a shallow bow and left me alone in the hallway. Outside my father's study, I stopped to listen to the murmur of voices.

"Your grace, the Queen's coffers have suffered a particular blow in the Indian markets this quarter," a male voice spoke, coming from behind the partially closed door.

"If the Royal Navy could manage to avoid crashing clippers in the Suez Canal, we'd have a better chance," murmured my father. "You may leave." Hearing his voice straightened my spine like nothing else would.

The door opened and a man exited. He stopped in front of the door, fumbling in his pockets. A flame blazed across my eyes as he lit a cigar, highlighting the white scar across his face. Smoke tickled my nose as it drifted down the hallway, following his retreating figure. He never even looked my way.

With what some might call bravery and others might call foolhardiness, I pushed open the door without knocking. A study materialized. On one wall, a bookshelf reached to the ceiling and was crammed to capacity. Plastered on the other wall were maps of shipping routes and ship schematics, covered with unfamiliar symbols and a messy scrawl. The maps depicted land and ocean routes, anything from the Suez Canal to the Port of Hong Kong. Built for purpose and out of place in the grand house, the room lacked any display of wealth.

I moved toward a large, sturdy oak desk in the center of the room. Behind the desk sat my father, his face hidden in the shadows. I could only hear my muffled tread over the carpet. My father's harsh presence encircled me like a chill across the moorlands in Yorkshire.

"Would you care to tell me what this business is about?" I asked my father before my courage escaped me.

Just like the stinking fortress, he never changed either but for several more lines etching themselves into his forehead. He didn't stand upon my entrance but lazily swirled his brandy in his crystal snifter. However, I knew my father well enough not to let my guard down.

He leaned forward into the light. Sharp and hollowed features scrutinized me to my bones. His eyes were pure metal. With a head full of steel-grey hair and dark slashing brows below a lined forehead, his face revealed little kindness. From cravat to evening jacket, his impeccably tailored suit was midnight black. Several silver rings adorned his fingers.

"Don't let your youthful impatience lead you to rudeness, first lieutenant," he responded while he shuffled his papers.

The cut felt deeper than I wanted it to and much deeper than I wanted my father to realize. I pushed onward. "What does this have to do with my mother?"

"I have information regarding the Frenchman," he pulled out a piece of paper from his stack, "you so resolutely believe killed her." He said the last part with a tinge of sarcasm and dismissal. The paper that might have meant something or nothing at all disappeared into the stack.

I held back my response waiting for his answer before I said something that would send me on the first ship back to Malta or worse, without any answers. Capturing the Frenchman had been part of my waking nightmare for the last nine years. It didn't surprise me that my father held the information as a bargaining chip, he knew I wanted nothing more.

"But I will not give you this information unless you do something for me first. Something of importance to this nation and the Queen."

I wanted to tell him I had been doing important work for the Queen stopping the Turks and Russians from all-out war, but I said nothing. Taking the seat across from him, I leaned back and affected a bored expression. My father didn't realize he'd taught me well. A fire blazed in the hearth, flickering across my father's face.

"Tell me then."

"You'll be tracking a man known as the Poisoner. He's been hidden on the continent until a few weeks ago when we intercepted his correspondence." My father opened a drawer in his desk and pulled out several letters.

Everyone within the international trading community had heard whispers of the Poisoner, a man of the underground who had used a diverse set of brutal tactics to control certain unsavory markets. At one point, several years ago, the Royal Navy had tried to intercept him in India with little success. Nobody lived to talk and if they did they ended up dead days later.

"Why do you care?" I asked, pushing my luck. "Isn't the Poisoner the C.I.D.'s case?"

"Yes, yes of course. Howard Vincent, the Director, is about to retire into politics, and I don't want the case to slip into," my father sighed loudly, and took a swig of his brandy, "imbecilic hands."

I made one last push forward. "But, why do you care?"

"I am a man of business, and the Poisoner is bad for business." If my father were a man to shrug he would have.

"Why me then?" I asked. I wanted to ask to add why take me out of my career, why make direct contact after so long, and why was it so important?

"There's a girl."

"I don't follow."

My father sighed as if I should already know the answer. "The correspondence we intercepted is between a young woman and the Poisoner. I need you to charm her, seduce her if you must, but you need to gain her trust and her access to the Poisoner by attending society events without calling attention from anyone but other silly young ladies. You have your mother's coloring after all." The latter might have been a compliment from anyone else.

"What's her name?" I gritted out.

"Lady Margaret Savoy."

CHAPTER FIVE

M.
London
One day prior...

The train stopped at Paddington Station and a porter helped me down from the car as the others piled our luggage on a trolley. On the platform, the station expanded before me. Wrought iron arches in three spans supported the beautiful glazed roof that filtered in grey light. Signs read Dining & Tea Room, Bookstall, General Offices, Telegraph Room, and Cloak Room. Voices mingled, bouncing off the ceiling in a cacophony of rough sounds like the seagulls that pealed loudly at the docks in Bristol. The scent of unwashed bodies, cloying rose perfume, and bustling elbows crashed into to my senses. I twisted my hands uncertainly, wishing for Miriam's presence.

"Margaret, Margaret! We are leaving, hurry up," Aunt Emily's shrill singsong voice cut through the noise. I followed Aunt Emily's slight figure weaving through the sea of black. She led a railway worker pushing our trolley of luggage out of the station's large arch entrance on Praed Street.

The Clarence, a sleek black coupe with four large wheels and pulled by two horses, waited for us with the family footmen. The coachman opened two small doors and handed us into the carriage by way of a small step. As we took off a horrible growling sound followed us like that of a wounded dog or pig. I understood why Londoner's commonly called the Clarence, the Growler. I gawked out the window, everything felt too unfamiliar.

Thunder rumbled in the distance; rain on its way. The gray

sky swirled in turmoil playing with the coal-infested clouds as if the heavens had eaten something unpleasant. The townhouse, my home for the next months, sat in a crescent row of Georgian architecture. Each townhouse looked much like the last with white stone facades of symmetrical form with classical touches, much like I imagined debutantes were supposed to look at a ball. Individuality on Grosvenor Square either came with the size of the estate and pocketbook, neither of which my family had in excess.

We had only just settled in when Aunt Emily called me to fetch her the mail. I slumped down the stairs, a grand list of tasks already overcrowding my travel weary mind. On the sideboard in the foyer from a delicate silver tray, I picked up the mail and leafed through it. As I came to the bottom of the stack, I found a letter addressed to me in an unfamiliar hand. I slipped it into the pocket of my apron that covered my serviceable grey frock. Delivering Aunt Emily's letters, I rather forgot all about the letter in my pocket until well past midnight when one shouldn't be reading things best left to machinations of Gothic novelists.

I sat down on my creaky bed, rubbing my temples. A sharp corner dug into my thigh and I pulled out the forgotten letter from my apron pocket to toss it onto the bed. After finishing my nightly rituals, I dipped my frozen feet under the covers and wiggled into the bed picking up the letter. It was as normal as any letter before it, with a neat, straight scrawl that looked rather scientific in its precision. The card had little weight and I opened it with my silver letter opener.

Dear Margaret,

You are in danger.

I re-read the words, my heart ticking in my throat. Danger? From what? I looked around my room, thankful for the light cast by my lamp and for the drapes across my window.

Your parents were murdered by a man called the Poisoner. You either must leave London or find the answers for yourself. Do not trust the Duke.

With fondness,

Your grandfather – Heman Claxton

I didn't even realize my hands had begun to shake until I tried to re-read the letter. The words blurred before me and I set the letter on my lap, clasping my hands together. Murdered. No. I had only been six when my parents passed. First, my mother in a carriage accident and then my father a week later from a heart attack. Until that moment, I had thought that my maternal grandfather had passed around the same time. That thought gave me pause as I considered the letter with a slower heartbeat. It had to be one of Rose's pranks. She didn't want me in London after all and what better way to scare someone than with ghoulish threats of a burgeoning mystery. Yet, I didn't sleep well that night and instead had dreams of the man in the bowler hat who had watched me in Bristol.

I pulled at the sleeves of my worn yellow ball gown if one could classify it as such. Pinching my cheeks failed to create a soft blush. I glared at myself in the mirror, brushing back my dark curly hair that only seemed to mutiny and create flyaways. I scanned my room and noticed the letter crumpled on the floor. I wish I hadn't for, perhaps, I wouldn't have found myself hanging out of a window only several hours later. On the back of the letter, I found something I hadn't noticed before. The words struck me to my bone and to a past I had little wish to remember.

P.S. If you don't believe me, don't forget you witnessed your father's murder.

As though a sharp blade impaled my chest, everything in the room stilled as I tried to remember how to breathe.

***

London

December 24th, 1867

First, just a few delicate snowflakes drifted through the crisp winter air, until slowly the icy works of art dusted the ground. The scent of burning wood clung to the air, as it escaped the chimneys of the shops along the stone road. Their glass-paned windows reflected the glow of candles that gave some warmth to the cold December air. The square darkened with each closed shop, frost coating their gloomy windows.

I stood before a small hearth holding my nanny's hand and watching the fire turn pitiful in its ashes. A large oak desk, laden with papers, quills, and harried in its organization stood in solidarity in the middle of the room. In the front of the room, a massive grandfather clock stood with an owl upon its mantle —its eyes seemed to be staring at me. I shuttered pulling at my nanny's hand, she didn't budge but instead shushed me.

Under his wire-rimmed spectacles, my father's eyes and his long skeletal fingers leafed through some papers. His shoulders were hunched in concentration and his foot beat an anxious tune. Again, I pulled at my nanny's hand.

"I want to go home."

"Soon, lamb, we're waiting for your father. You can have a nice cuppa warm milk with peppermint if you practice your patience. That's a big word, do you remember it?"

I nodded solemnly, and we continued what would be a vigil of my father's death. The dark shadows of my remembrance seemed to dance maniacally around the walls, closing in ever so silently. My father clenched the papers with whitening knuckles as if to wring something out of them. He took out a piece of paper and began writing. The clock chimed, and I jumped squeezing my nanny's hand.

He sucked in ragged breaths that cut off as he gripped his chest, his bleary eyes widening in pain. My father slid from the chair, his weak hands grasped at the desk and sent papers flying into the fire, which flared to life. My nanny rushed forward, leaving me standing alone with the ticking of the clock behind me. His skin turned yellow, his eyes glazed over, and suddenly my father was still. Too still.

"Papa!"

***

I dropped the letter and dashed for the porcelain water basin. I dry-heaved, my temples ablaze with pain. Murdered.

Danger. Both repeated in my mind on a loop. Down the hall and what felt like miles away, I could hear Rose complaining to Aunt Emily about her shoes.

"They're much too big. My feet could escape at any moment."

Escape. I needed to escape.

CHAPTER SIX

A.

Lady Margaret watched me under her eyelashes and hadn't yet moved from her spot several feet away. She bit her lip as her eyes darted around the dark garden. The letter I had pulled from her reticule made no sense to me, unless her grandfather didn't know she was in league with the Poisoner. Or, perhaps, she wasn't involved at all. My father had the evidence and he didn't have any reason to lie to me. Yet, why had the letter writer told her to not trust a Duke? Which Duke? It couldn't be my father.

The girl still hadn't moved but instead had retreated several steps back. Catching her climbing out of a window had not been in my plans. My only goal for the evening had been to dance with her, flirt just a bit perhaps, and then find my next in for gaining her trust one step at a time. I had agreed to meet a member of the C.I.D. outside in the gardens at just the moment Lady Margaret appeared. No coincidence, perhaps.

"Who are you?" she finally spoke as she inched closer, her reticule clutched to her chest.

"First Lieutenant Alexander Rocque III and lord by the happenstance of birth." I gave her a dramatic bow.

She notched her chin in the air, but I could see her shoulders shake whether from cold or fear I couldn't tell. "Why are you interested in the Poisoner?"

While I had not been given a cover story neither had I thought this was how I'd begin the case. It should have been a simple reconnaissance mission, but I could already tell it had gotten more complicated, so I lied. "I work for a small unit in the

Royal Navy that deals with criminality within the Empire's trade networks. The Poisoner has been on our list for some time."

Lady Margaret's brow furrowed, and she mumbled to herself, "So, he is real."

"Pardon?"

She looked at me again, her stance had weakened, and her arms now hung loosely at her sides. "Nothing."

"It seems to me, my lady, that you have found yourself tangled in something you shouldn't be involved with?" I leaned against the brick wall, mindful of the door and that we weren't quite in the best location for this kind of talk.

"I suppose so." Lady Margaret had re-entered the light cast by the illuminated ballroom just above us. "I didn't believe any of it was real until..." She ended her train of thought by glaring at me.

"Until what? You clearly believed it enough to run away."

"It doesn't matter." Her face turned grey at whatever thought had crossed her mind. "You said you had answers. About my parents?"

Her hopeful expression looked all too familiar and my cheeks felt hot. "Not exactly."

Lady Margaret retreated several steps once more and watched me with wary suspicion. I didn't quite understand her reactions but thought that maybe she played a game of damsel in distress. Only one of us would win the game and I planned on being the victor. "I have no information but perhaps we can help each other. I find the Poisoner and you find out what happened to your parents."

"I don't see how I could help you as I don't know anything," Lady Margaret said. I looked for the lie, but she seemed to be telling the truth, at least something of it.

From the maze, we could hear the loud laughter and drunken slur of several men close to our location. Lady Margaret, like a frightened deer, skipped toward me and I almost imagined she would have used my body as a human shield if she had to.

"We will need to find a better place to speak. Somewhere

more private."

Lady Margaret nodded in stuttered agreement, watching the maze with wide eyes as the laughter inched closer. "We will need a proper introduction. Not like our dance." Her eyes flicked to mine as quickly as they flicked away.

I nodded. "Consider it done." Over the hedges of the maze, I could just make out top hats bobbing in our direction. "You've been gone from the ball too long. Can you make your way back to the ballroom alone?"

She nodded, and we parted ways. This had not gone to plan. Not at all.

***

M.

In the hallway mirror, my wide grey eyes stared back at me through a mess of dark curls peppered with sprigs of Juniper. Even my typically olive complexion looked ashen. I could not return to the ballroom in this state or my reputation, insignificant as it might be, would be destroyed. As best I could, I searched my hair for lost pins. But for a few curls, who refused to cooperate, I eventually managed to arrange the mass back into place. In the foyer, I found a footman.

"Excuse me?"

The footman stared at my rumpled outfit with a suggestive smirk. That was the first time, but not the last time that I decided I was going to kill Lord Alexander. I wouldn't have fallen if he hadn't scared me.

"Could you please fetch my cloak; the name is Savoy."

He nodded to me and minutes later returned with my cloak. In the ladies' retiring room I relaced my corset and bodice. The crushed bustle and the wrinkled satin were beyond a quick repair and I covered myself with my cloak.

At the edge of the ballroom, I sat down next to Aunt Emily who snorted awake.

"Where have you been, girl?" she slurred drunkenly. "You know," she covered a burp, "he was supposed to come tonight.

Won't now." Aunt Emily swayed in her chair, and I pushed her upright. "The Duke frightens him, I think."

"Uncle Matthew is still in Somerset." I watched her reach for her flask under the chair. Yet, I wondered if it was the same Duke my grandfather warned me about.

"You don't understand." She sat up, taking a swig from her flask. She focused on me again. "Where have you been, girl?"

"I went to get my cloak, Aunt. I was chilled." The ballroom sweltered with human body heat.

She gave me a look, pouring spirits from her flask into a glass of punch. "You're an odd pigeon." She nodded as if agreeing with herself. She said nothing more of my disappearance and never would.

CHAPTER SEVEN

A.

Before I could speak to Lady Margaret again, I needed to find her grandfather. If he knew the Poisoner, perhaps, he was my lead rather than the lady in question. With the help of C.I.D., I found the records of residence for Mr. Claxton and left my calling card for an introduction. It took several days but I finally received a response inviting me to visit.

The sun glared cheerfully down at me, too cheerfully, and I squinted it away with disdain. A large brick townhouse towered above me, in Queen Anne's style. White masonry surrounded each of the four sash-windows in contrast to the red brick. I walked up the wide staircase to the front door, mentally preparing myself for anything. I gave the door a swift knock.

Framed in the doorway stood a plump middle-aged Indian man with a salt-and-pepper mustache and a full head of hair. He wore a long white tunic over loose white trousers and brown Oxfords on his feet as his only Western accouterment.

"Ah, you must be Lord Alexander Rocque?" The man leaned out, looking right then left down the street, before returning my gaze.

"Yes." I handed the man my calling card. "I assume you were expecting me?"

The man looked over my calling card, scanning the streets again. "Yes, please come in." The man stepped to the side allowing my entrance, but almost caught my coat in the door as it closed.

"My name is Arjun Manda. I am the agent of the estate." He looked around the foyer, his eyebrows coming together.

Rushing back and forth with the disposition of a harried rabbit, he straightened perfectly straight doilies and brushed at invisible specks on the wooden table. The house was dark but clean with several frames covered in diaphanous black fabric, indicating the death of a loved one. To my right was a forest green parlor, filled with exotic imports from the Orient. On the sideboard, I noticed a worn photograph shoved haphazardly in its frame as if it had been recently removed.

"My lord?" Manda asked, leaning over my shoulder. "Ah, yes, that is Mr. Claxton and the East India Trading Company in Bombay many years ago."

"May I?" I asked as I picked up the photo. Manda nodded. My gaze came to rest on one face in particular—my father. Involuntarily, my grip tightened around the frame. I set it back in its place, my jaw strained and a pounding headache forming. My eyes watered from their lack of sleep.

"Manda, could you inform Mr. Claxton that I have arrived?"

"Of course, my lord." His eyes narrowed, yet he turned up the stairs before I could confirm.

The minutes ticked by, allowing my mind, once more, to wander to the grey eyes that seemed to haunt it. I had told Lady Margaret I would give her answers, but honestly, I didn't have any. She was somehow involved with the Poisoner, which she either machinated of her own choice or was another victim. I didn't know which and that worried me.

"Lord Alexander, the master will see you now. If you'll follow me." Manda beckoned me up the stairs.

The hollow echo of sound traveled through the space and for the first time I noticed the lack of other servants bustling about. Following Manda into a dark room, the musty smell of flesh, sweat, and blood hit my nose.

"Manda, would you draw the drapes, I have a wish to see my guest," croaked a dilapidated voice. The speaker remained hidden in the depths of a large four-poster bed surrounded by heavy navy velvet drapes, which cast dark shadows across his face. Besides the bed, sideboard, and washstand, the large room was empty.

Manda drew the drapes, as hacking coughs came from the bed. "Sir are –?" Manda began, but the man, who I assumed was Mr. Claxton, interrupted him.

"I am quite well, Arjun. Now, stop your infernal mothering and get Mrs. Watts to bring the tea." A veiny, liver-spotted hand stuck out from the shadows and gave a dismissive flick. "My boy do come closer. My sight is not what it once was," the voice requested after intervals of wet coughs into a blood spotted handkerchief.

Dust motes floated through the air, which reeked of death. I sucked in my cheeks at the familiar scent, doing my best to block my memories of war. I cringed without realizing it extended past my mind and through my body.

"Don't worry Lord Alexander, I am not contagious, not since '72. The doctors say I may have cancer. My doctor told me he would have gone his whole life without seeing cancer if not for me." Mr. Claxton laughed. I noticed his accent, which lilted with an unfamiliar tinge, but I decided it was a symptom of his illness.

"My condolences, sir."

He watched me through glazed eyes, his skin waxen and stretched over his sharp facial features. Yet, he exhibited a startling awareness, though he was in his seventies with barely a hair on his liver-spotted head. Propped up against pillows in his night robe, his shrunken figure seemed more stooped.

He cleared his throat. "I believe you are here to investigate my daughter and son-in-law's murders." The man's eyes narrowed. Perhaps, he had sent Lady Margaret the letter after all.

I had looked through the records of their deaths and had found nothing that would lean toward the conclusion of murder. "To be blunt sir, there is no evidence."

"Do you believe everything you're told, boy?" Mr. Claxton laughed, losing to a violent cough. He took a sip of the water by his bedside. "The story goes my daughter died in a carriage accident, and five days later her husband died of a heart attack. Rather convenient, I would say. They loved their daughter, they wouldn't have left her."

The image of my own mother filled my mind, her soft hair that always smelt of lavender and her warm eyes always laughing. "Some things are out of our hands."

"Always such a pessimist, Henry," Claxton tutted, suddenly mistaking me for my father, who went by his middle name rather than Alexander. I doubted he meant someone else. "Do you remember when you thought I'd never get the shipment to China? I proved you wrong, didn't I?"

My father wouldn't explain the "shipments" nor explain how he happened to know the grandfather of the woman he had me track. The fact that they had a connection sent alarm bells ringing through my head. I'd have to listen carefully for when he cracked his knuckles, his only tell I'd ever caught. My father had many secrets, most he would take to the grave.

Mr. Claxton's eyes focused on me once more. "What if I told you I had evidence they were murdered?" He leaned back into the pillows, his reed-thin arms folded across his chest.

I stilled as he returned to the present. "I'll take the bait, continue."

"I had my man, Manda, compile a record of the events that transpired before the..." he pierced me with his eyes... "murders." He pointed to a box next to his bed, filled with correspondence, loose paper, and other items of writing.

I crouched down to look at the first page. "*Dear Mr. Francis.*" I stood up and faced Mr. Claxton. "Who is Mr. Francis?"

"He was my daughter Esther's first suitor. He was a great man of business, with his connections I might have been able to go home and end my association with the East India Trading Company." Mr. Claxton waved his hand through the air. "She was a beautiful girl."

"Home?"

"India of course. I still don't miss the bloody heat." His eyes seemed far and away.

"You're from India?"

"Oh, yes. My father was a British officer and my mother..." Mr. Claxton shook his head and rubbed his eyes. "There's no use dwelling on it. After I had agreed to the marriage, Esther eloped to Gretna Green with the Earl of Stanhild."

I looked through the letters again most of them addressed *"Dear Dada or Dear Mame."* Each written in the same elegant looping cursive.

My father, her grandfather, and the Poisoner somehow all had business ties. But in what? The East India Trading Company had dissolved many years ago. And, how did a murderer and crime boss like the Poisoner get involved?

"What evidence of foul play did you find in these correspondences?" I looked at the crate again, my fingers itching to leaf through the papers.

"A few years into her marriage, my daughter came to me. We hadn't spoken since her elopement, but she was pregnant. Esther wanted me to be in my grandchild's life and I wanted that too. Everything was fine—perfect—after Margaret was born." Mr. Claxton coughed into his handkerchief.

"But it wasn't perfect?"

Mr. Claxton shook his head. "My daughter and her husband had gotten involved in some sort of organization, or cult, I am not sure. It's when the reign of terror began. Their greenhouse was set ablaze. *Besiyata Dishmaya*, my daughter was not in it." The first words were unfamiliar to my ears, but he gave me little time to dwell on them. "Over several months it became clear they were being blackmailed. Perhaps, the cult was targeting them or something more. The blackmailer, who didn't give a name, told them to give him money, both from Stanhild's coffers and my own. We sent the money, but it wasn't enough."

"What more did he want?"

Mr. Claxton gave me a shrewd look. "I don't know, boy. He killed them, just like that. Pour me some more water. The pitcher is on the sideboard." He pointed to a glass pitcher and sighed loudly, a darkness clouding his face. "Stanhild and I came up with a plan for his fortune, so if something should happen, that his private capital would go to Margaret."

"You believe the blackmailer was the murderer?"

"Undoubtedly."

I took his glass from next to his bed and filled it with fresh water. He grasped the glass from me with trembling hands. He took a large gulp of water, before setting it down on the side table.

"Do you know the name of the organization?" I asked.

A look of perplexity overcame Mr. Claxton's face. "I can't remember. Maybe there never was one. Forgive my feeble mind, boy. I became bedridden shortly after the funerals. I was supposed to take in the girl, but I had to give her over to the care of my other daughter, Neta." Again Mr. Claxton looked confused and I wondered how reliable his information could be. "No, Emily. She's quite cross when I call her that. My little seedling." He yawned, showing me a mouthful of rotting teeth. "I missed the girl's funeral. She brought such a light to my life. Funny little thing. Always asking questions. She was so young, only seven."

My heart skipped a beat. "Pardon me?"

"My granddaughter, Lady Margaret Savoy, died of tuberculosis about a year after her parents died."

"Sir, your granddaughter is alive."

"Of course, my granddaughter Rose is alive." Mr. Claxton chuckled and coughed again.

"No, sir. You misunderstand me. Your granddaughter, Lady Margaret, is alive."

He froze, the blanket falling from his hands. "No, it cannot be."

"She is alive, sir. I've seen her. Spoken with her. Danced with her," I trailed off.

Mr. Claxton's breath came out in heavy pants. "But, Emily." With wide eyes, he stared at me, his mouth agape.

As I rested upon his grey eyes, a spark of recognition reflected in their rheumy depths. With surprising agility, he pulled me down so that we were face to face. His skeletal hands gripped my wrists, bruising them, and his eyes held me with a crazed intensity.

"Esther? Esther?" he yelled, looking around the room. "My dear, my beloved daughter, forgive me. Forgive me." Twisting his hands around mine, he continued, incoherently mumbling as saliva foamed at the corners of his mouth. "I was selfish. My life's work was not worth your life. We know him. There was *ra* in his heart, I should have seen it. Richard loved you more than I did." He grasped my hands even tighter, and I swear I heard my wrist bones crunch together.

"The code!" He released my hands and tried to stand as his bed covers twisted around his legs.

I tried to settle Mr. Claxton back into the bed, but he became frantic, waving his arms and legs, landing blows on my head.

"I must hide it. I must save them. Doc—." He convulsed, his shoulders shaking and his long fingers reaching for me. "My fault. My fault. Save her. Save her." He collapsed into the bed—silent.

Manda, and whom I guessed was Mrs. Watts, ran into the room.

"You must leave, the master is unwell," Manda flung at me, as he and Mrs. Watts rushed to tend to Mr. Claxton. "Take the damned papers with you."

I secured the box under my arm and left. From then on, two sets of grey eyes haunted me. If Lady Margaret's grandfather hadn't sent the letter, then who did?

CHAPTER EIGHT

M.

The days after the ball spun by me in a blur of anxiety. I hoped that Lord Alexander, the Poisoner, and the mysterious Duke had already forgotten all about me and that in the grand populace of London there was, indeed, another Margaret Savoy. She would be better suited to facing this unknown than I could ever be.

Curled up on a chair in the back parlor like a cat without a spot of sun, my mind dwelled in the murky bog of better left alone thoughts. The afternoon tea sat before me, but I did not drink it. Instead, I warmed my uncommonly chilled hands on the fine china glass. Rose's numerous dresses lay at my feet like a flurry of fallen birds.

The clearing of a throat interrupted my thoughts. Our butler, Buxley, stood in the doorway to the parlor, his nose notched in the air at just the right angle.

"My lady, you have callers…" Buxley said, clearing his throat again as if also surprised by the unfamiliar utterance.

The last part of whatever he said was lost to time as something crashed above us followed by a wail of rage from Rose. At first, my mind dismissed his words, and I nodded thinking that he had offered more scones. I set my cup on the coaster and picked up the hemming once more.

Buxley bowed and left.

What did he say? The hemming needle shot through the pad of my thumb and a droplet of blood threatened the sanctity of Rose's muslin dress. Slumping back into the chair, I sucked on my injured appendage with my eyes fixed to the door.

The door creaked open. I removed my thumb from my mouth. Lord Alexander walked in with quiet stealth and a casual perusal of the room. A black walking-suit fell comfortably on his lithe form, and his hat remained in his hands, indicating a short visit. Next to him stood a petite woman at just below five feet. Below her hat, decorated with beautiful jade plumage, her hair was pure white. Not a single wrinkle graced her face but for laugh lines around her deep brown eyes. She looked me up and down without any expression.

My hair fell in disarray around my face, my loose bun barely kept the strands of curls together. Only a few shades lighter than bombazine-black, my dress was already too heavy for the spring weather. I shuffled my feet covered in worn leather shoes that had seen better days beneath my skirts. But Lord Alexander noticed and quirked a brow, before sitting across from me after the older woman. I did not want to dwell on what they might have thought of me, or the wish that the other Margaret Savoy would take my place.

An obstinate silence filled the room. Sunlight gleamed directly across his eyes, and he didn't even squint. In his presence, I felt wholly too much like a mouse. My tongue rolled along the back of my teeth to keep myself from liberating a batch of nervous rambling. Why couldn't he speak first? My tongue pressed against my lips again. Courage welled in me to speak only to splinter apart as the sound of Rose's voice reached my ears.

"Buxley? Buxley, what do you mean, 'Margaret has a gentleman caller?' You must have misheard. Direct me to him immediately."

I avoided Lord Alexander's eyes and instead stared at my poorly befitted feet. I folded up Rose's dress and cleaned up my sewing kit—bracing myself for a tirade of epic proportions. The older woman tilted her head toward the door and then whispered something in Lord Alexander's ear.

"I am sorry, Miss Rose, but the gentleman asked for Lady Margaret, and she said she would receive them."

After no more than a few seconds of silence, Rose

wrenched open the door to the parlor. "You must be mistaken, I will see that your imbecility is remedied."

Lord Alexander stood upon her entrance. Rose's in-door toilette, made of Sicilienne in the shade *aurore du Bengale* and trimmed with India embroidery and rosettes of velvet, better complimented Lord Alexander's attire. I only knew the name of the pale salmon pink color, for the many times Rose had butchered its pronunciation to the French seamstress.

When she saw Lord Alexander, her cherub face flushed pink. She looked like a delicate china doll. I could not help myself but remember her cracking open the head of my very own china doll years ago, laughing as its smile split in half.

Coming out of her momentary surprise, and giving me a perfunctory glare, she walked up to Lord Alexander. Brushing his arm, she cooed, "My lord, I am sorry for this mishap. You know how servants can be." She smiled as if they shared some great secret. "Our Butler is getting old in years and must have misheard you. I'll direct you to my parlor."

She walked to the door, expecting him to follow. "Margaret, you should be working on the dress, I have another that also needs mending."

The older woman, who had been completely ignored, cleared her throat and stood. As she stared Rose down with a look of contempt, she seemed to gain height. Rose tilted her head deferentially. I wanted to be like this woman. She looked down at me and I bolted to a stand as well.

"Miss Rose, Lady Margaret, may I introduce you to my Aunt, Lady Ildwoors," said Lord Alexander.

Rose turned beet red as she curtsied. "My lady, I do most *sincerely* apologize."

"Of course, dear." Lady Ildwoors' voice sounded like the touch of rich royal purple velvet. "Your cousin has agreed to join us for a ride through Hyde Park. Please give our regards to Lady Wellmont and we will be on our way."

Rose glared at me, her eyes daring me to leave. I paused, stuck between two worlds, the one I knew and the one that would mean certain rebellion. Other Margaret would have been ready for whatever consequences followed a leap away from the known. I didn't believe I had the pluck. I nodded to Lord Alexander and his Aunt. Rose gave me a calculated look. She huffed off in search of Aunt Emily to quell my small uprising—I had rebelled by saying nothing at all.

In the open landau, Lady Ildwoors gave me a long look, not calculating like Rose's but rather inquisitive like I was not as she expected. "Today is the day to see and be seen. We want all of London to believe you two are romantically attached isn't that right, Alexander?"

I felt the blood leave my face and gripped the leather seat. Lord Alexander's mouth flapped before it transformed into a straight line. "Lady Margaret, I decided that the only way we could meet in public without too much attention, or rather the worst sort, would be for us to be romantically attached if even in the briefest way. It's not like we can invent an old acquaintance. People will talk either way and I'd rather not endanger your reputation."

London scenery passed by in varying shades of grey and muted green. The brownstones, the smoke in the distance rising from the factories, and the storefronts with glistening windows surrounded us on all sides. Before I could say anything in response, Lady Ildwoors stopped the landau in front of a hat shop. She looked between us with the briefest smile that I almost missed, and Lord Alexander definitely did.

"Excuse me for but a moment, I am going to pop into this shop." With the assistance of a footman, she left us alone.

"What in God's name do you mean, Number Three? I will go no further with you until you tell me why we need *this* cover story?" I insisted as authoritatively as possible, the tone tripping out my mouth like a novice ice-skater in winter.

"Number Three?" Lord Alexander chuckled.

I clenched the bottom of the seat as I leaned forward. Lord Alexander cocked his head to the side. From the other end of the carriage, he leaned forward with his elbows resting on his knees.

A foot between us, I leaned back first and immediately regretted my retreat.

"At least, treat me with some information and respect, or you will not coax me to help you."

Lord Alexander sighed. "I apologize, Lady Margaret. I fear we have started off on the wrong foot."

"You have given me no feet beneath me by not discussing the plan. If you don't tell me the full of it, I will..." I narrowed my eyes, waiting for his answer as I didn't really have anything I could threaten him with. I could feel my courage deflating with every passing moment and hoped he would answer soon. "I will never stop calling you, Number Three."

"Perhaps, I like when you call me Number Three." Lord Alexander wagged his eyebrows in my direction.

The very core of my being regretted my petulant nickname.

The smile faded from Lord Alexander's lips. "Please, trust me, if only for the time being. I will tell you everything after that. I promise you on my mother's grave." He gave me his hand.

I shook my head, and his hand disappeared. "I don't trust you. I cannot trust that you won't kill me then toss me into the Thames. I don't even know if your mother has a grave to be sworn upon. Perhaps you work for the Poisoner."

"My word is my honor, something I highly value, even if you don't." For the first time, he frowned at me as if genuinely insulted. "I'll tell you what you need to know. I won't, however, tell you everything you want to know. We need each other, don't we?"

"I can take care of myself, my lord," I responded curtly. "And my *sensibilities* can withstand more than you know."

"My lady, though that may be true," Lord Alexander ran his hand through his hair, "you are out of your depth."

With that, I glowered at him, realizing I could not push him further. Lord Alexander remained stoic in his silence. He tried to wear me down with his hard gaze, which I was not willing to break.

Before we could say anything more, Lady Ildwoors returned without a hat box or any purchased items.

"Anything interesting happen while I was gone? No good hats today," Lady Ildwoors said with an innocence I did not quite believe. I wondered what Lord Alexander had told her.

The clip-clop of horses' hooves against the cobblestone and a choir singing "God Save the Queen," reverberated through Hyde Park at the height of calling hour. Both Lord Alexander and Lady Ildwoors responded to greetings from the passersby in similarly situated carriages. The river Serpentine meandered along our side, and rowing teams powered through the water. Gentlemen took a gentler pace rowing their ladies, who protected their dainty visages with white lace parasols. Rotten Row paralleled us across the Serpentine, where the jauntier tried their hand at racing horses.

"What is the schedule for the day, Number Three?" I asked, crossing my arms over my chest. "Suppose I had plans..." I did not. The truth remained that I wished to stay out of the Wellmont's path as long as possible. Only punishment would greet me when I returned.

Lord Alexander ignored me and waved to a young man around his age on a dapple-grey gelding.

"Rocque, old chap. Never thought I'd see you..." the young man trailed off as Alexander gave him a dark glare.

"Norbell." Alexander nodded at the rider. "Let me introduce you to Lady Margaret Savoy and to my aunt, Lady Ildwoors." The carriage pulled to a stop, and Lord Norbell reined in his horse. The horse snorted and tossed his head, before quieting, its feet left dancing.

"What a pleasure it is to see two such," he took in my outfit, his smile fading, "beautiful ladies." Norbell doffed his hat to both of us, preening all the while. He showed his dandy outfit and lovely horse to the best light, as he turned it around.

"Oh, you, flatterer." Lady Ildwoors fluttered her lashes up at him while fanning herself, rolling her eyes so only I could see. I liked her even more.

"The pleasure is ours, my lord." I smiled at him from beneath my straw hat. Fancy, if for its blue ribbon and the fake flowers that decorated the brim.

"Rocque are you coming, to..." Lord Norbell tilted his head as if indicating to something down the road and then mouthed out the word, "club?" I averted my eyes and quieted a chuckle.

"No." Lord Alexander shook his head, his hand grabbing mine and I fought the urge to wrench it from his. "Norbell isn't there somewhere you need to be?"

Norbell's eyes widened and fastened to our hands. "Ah, yes, Rocque. My ladies." Norbell turned his horse and rode off.

"That boy thinks women cannot read lips." Lady Ildwoors tsked after Lord Norbell.

A laugh escaped from my chest, partially from the humor and partially the stress.

Lord Alexander looked between both of us and smiled. "Norbell means well. By tomorrow all of London will know we are attached at least informally. He's quite the gossip."

My mouth went dry and I opened my reticule in search of a mint. All of London would know. The countless voices which surrounded us came to a deafening crescendo in my head. A part of me pretended I could hear my name bandied upon their lips. I looked for Lord Norbell in the crowd, spotting him speaking with a group in a landau.

A young man with silver blond hair and around Lord Alexander's age rode toward us on a large bay gelding. He pulled his horse to a stop in front of us, watching us with blue eyes below barely visible brows.

Lord Alexander greeted the man with a wide smile. "Trent."

The man grinned in return, his eyes moved to mine, and he quirked a brow at Lord Alexander. However, more delicate than Norbell.

Lord Alexander turned toward me. "This is Captain Trent of the Metropolitan Police. Captain Trent, this is Lady Margaret and my Aunt, Lady Ildwoors."

The man doffed his bowler hat to us. “Pleased to make your acquaintance, Lady Margaret, and Lady Ildwoors.”

“Likewise, Captain Trent.” I inclined my head toward him as did Lady Ildwoors.

Lord Alexander and Captain Trent watched each other as if silently communicating. Lord Alexander looked over at me, holding my gaze before looking back to Captain Trent. Out of the corner of my eye, I noticed Lord Alexander lightly touch Lady Ildwoors hand.

“Oh, Lady Margaret, look, Mute swans.” Lady Ildwoors pointed to the banks of the Serpentine. “Or, possibly they’re Whooper swans. I can never tell the difference. My husband was quite an ornithologist.”

While Lady Ildwoors pointed out other bird species that inhabited the banks, out of my periphery, I noticed Lord Alexander pass a slip of paper to Captain Trent.

“If you’ll excuse me, my ladies.” Captain Trent fixed his sharp gaze on me. He nodded to Lord Alexander, “Rocque,” and then rode off again.

A strange encounter, but I didn’t think much of it as we moved onto the next person eager for an introduction. Throughout the rest of the morning, we met more than a few older lords that flirted outrageously with Lady Ildwoors, acquaintances of Lord Alexander, though none greeted as genially as Captain Trent, and several clusters of shimmering debutantes who took me in with calculating eyes.

“We’ve accomplished our mission. I believe it is time you take me home, so I may have a cool glass of lavender lemonade.” Lady Ildwoors licked her lips, fanning herself. “London is now your acting chaperone.”

Lord Alexander signaled to the coachman to turn us around. We made our way out of Hyde Park in the late afternoon. Warm golden light gleamed through the green leaves of the trees that marked the pathway. The pomp and circumstance of the park disappeared as we joined the traffic and the swell of disgruntled profanities.

CHAPTER NINE

M.

We left Lady Ildwoors in a posh neighborhood close to my own. I thought our misadventure had come to an end, but we once more turned toward Hyde Park. A gust of wind knocked my bonnet from my head and into Lord Alexander's lap. I reach for it, but Lord Alexander stopped me.

"Allow me."

I froze, the voice of my late school marm filled my head, screeching at me to stop him. *"Lasciviousness leads to expulsion from heaven, most especially for a young lady with little to recommend her."*

"Lean closer," he said in a gruff voice. I complied, and the schoolmarm quieted. He put my bonnet upon my head and tied the bow beneath my chin.

His thumb just barely caressed my chin as he stared into my eyes, before sighing and leaning back. I wondered if I detected a slight blush on his cheeks. The thought made my own face flare. He must have been in the sun too long. I pulled my bonnet down, further shadowing my face.

"You should not have done that."

"Perhaps not."

He gave me his profile as he stared out of the carriage, shadowed beneath his hat, the white scar etched on his chin stood out in contrast to his rather honeyed-skin. Like a crow staring at a shiny bauble on the street, I watched Lord Alexander. He did not behave how I expected him to behave and never would. He had been rather kind.

We continued to ride in silence, reaching Hyde Park, and

the Marble Arch at Cumberland Gate. The arch, made of Carrara marble and discolored from London pollution, looked more like a wilted sugar sculpture in a confectioner's window than triumphal. However, we passed the park altogether. My gaze darted to him and the door of the landau. Could I jump? The distance between the park and the carriage increased as we traveled through the thick deluge of London traffic.

"I thought we were going to Hyde Park again?" I watched him again, now as the crow that had been swiped at by the cat. I should have learned by then to trust no one.

Lord Alexander shook his head at me. He sat with the ease of a fat cat in the sun, while my temper kindled to life. I needed answers, even if I didn't yet realize that they would mean life or death.

"Does this look familiar to you?"

A great Queen Anne style brick home, two-stories high, with windows covered by curtains, rose before me. I looked at the street sign, "Baker Street." A memory bubbled to the surface, but it left as quickly as it came.

I looked back at him. "Should I?"

Lord Alexander's eyes narrowed for a moment. "I am not certain, yet."

"My Lord, what exactly are we doing here?"

"Would you like to stop for an ice at Berkeley Square?"

"No."

Asking him for answers felt like running into a brick wall that formed on all sides. I wanted to hate him. Again, I wondered if I should have taken my grandfather's first directive and run rather than try to find answers where there were none.

"You, Number Three, are the most unmoved of all the men I have ever met. For you to think I will continue to let you deceive me is another notch to your absolute arrogance. I am not your average 'miss,' who would let you, with your good looks manipulate me any further. You owe me some answers." I shoved my finger into his hard chest.

My heart pounded, as my words sank into my brain. What

have I done? My anger disappeared. I'd never yelled at anyone. He truly would throw me into the Thames. There was nowhere to hide, and for a moment I wondered again if I could escape through the carriage door. I didn't even know yet with certainty that he didn't work for the Poisoner.

Lord Alexander laughed from his belly. "I cannot possibly take the medal for 'most unmoved' man. I could name at least twenty that far surpass me. Not even my handsome visage can live up to that lofty title." He wagged his eyebrows at me and the fear faded.

I ground my teeth. "For your information, I said, 'good looks,' Number Three.'" I growled, taking some pleasure in the freedom my anger brought.

"Think what you will of me, m'dear," Lord Alexander cocked his head, an almost melancholic smile appearing on his lips, "your words will not be the worst I've heard and will never be close to the truth." He looked out the window of the carriage.

"Then prove me wrong, my lord," I whispered too low for him to have heard.

A sort of pity welled in my stomach without so much as asking my permission first. I searched for the truth he spoke of as if it could be revealed in his face. He had a straight nose, but for a small bump as if it had been broken in fisticuffs.

Yet, I didn't need to discover his secrets, I needed to protect my own. As I came up with more insults to add to my growing list, the landau lurched forward sending me tumbling unceremoniously into Lord Alexander's lap. My nose smashed against his firm chest. Sandalwood and an, altogether, undeniably masculine scent emanated from his form. The fine linen tickled my nose, and the sound of his steady heart echoed loudly in the silence, though I was the only one likely to have heard it. Quite a wonderful scent I decided, only to stop breathing all together at the direction of my thoughts.

"Sorry," I stammered.

I looked at anything but him. Lord Alexander lifted my chin to look at him, and I found an indiscernible look in his gaze.

His head leaned forward, and I automatically narrowed in on his lips, as they came closer, closer, and closer. Instead, he moved me back to my seat. My heart dropped, and I scolded its foolishness —I didn't want to kiss *him.*

We stopped in front of the townhouse. I fought the urge to run out of the landau up the stairs and hide in the depths of my bed. The frigid air hit my cheeks.

Lord Alexander stopped at the landing. "Will you be at Lady Westerly's ball at the end of the week?"

I nodded fixing my eyes to his lapel and avoiding his eyes at all cost.

"We will talk then."

For the first time, I looked up. "You've already lied once to me, my lord."

"I wouldn't call it lying just the omission of truth for the time being." He cocked his head at me as if willing me to believe his words.

"That is the definition of a lie." I had to still my eyes as they threatened to roll back in my head at his statement.

"Well, then, this lie has a time limit that expires at the ball." He bowed to me with a half-smile and entered the landau.

CHAPTER TEN

A.

Nothing seemed to add up in the way I had first expected it to. Either Lady Margaret was incredibly skilled at lying or telling the truth. She had none of the traits of someone I would expect to correspond, let alone work with the Poisoner. He was well-known to leave behind a string of stunning women around the continent from opera singers to the wives of diplomats. No one would put Lady Margaret in league with those women with her tanned complexion, freckles, and misbehaved hair. Yet, when her grey eyes sparked with anger something about her look became regal. I shook my head. Get your head out of the gutter, man.

I reviewed the facts; Lady Margaret received a letter from someone who could not be her grandfather as he believed she died as a child warning her about the Poisoner. My father intercepted correspondence between Lady Margaret and the Poisoner, proving they were in league with each other. Neither of those facts could be true together, meaning I needed to find the lie first from my father.

The sound of voices coming from the closed door to my father's study, stilled my pacing. My mind tumbled through carefully laid paths to approach my father, none of them seemed quite right.

The door creaked open, I stood at attention to the side of the room. A fair-complexioned Persian man dressed in a silk patterned shalvar, a long tunic that reached past his knees, exited the room. A sarband turban covered his head, made of thick maroon fabric and interwoven with golden stitches. His dress reminded me of those I'd seen worn by the locals while stationed in the Gulf. His groomed beard traced his jawline and transitioned into a thin mustache with pointed tips His dark eyes took in my presence, but ultimately ignored me.

He gripped my father's right hand and with his other hand held my father's elbow. In a soft voice, he said, "*Motevajjeh am.*"

Both my father and the man inclined their heads, eyes shut, and their right hands to their chests.

My father responded to the man as they stepped away from each other, "*Be salamat.*"

The man inclined his head once more and bit his index finger briefly. I remembered it to mean, "God forbid," a widespread practice among the merchants whenever Navy men debarked. He looked at me again and turned away.

I watched the man until he rounded the corner, wondering what journey my father had sent him on. My father only ordered and never made requests.

"Alexander, enter. I do not have all day." My father's gruff and commanding voice brought me from my thoughts.

I nodded and entered the study. My father sat behind his desk and shuffled his papers together. He rolled up a map and put away the little statuettes of ships, people, and battalions, sweeping them away with a negligent hand. I noticed the word, "*Afyūn*," the Persian word for opium, inscribed in black across the top of one of the papers before my father added it to the pile.

He looked up at me over his gold octagon spectacles. "Speak up."

I cleared my throat, as he continued to organize his desk. "There have been some developments in the Poisoner case."

My father stilled his hands, but only for a moment. "Yes?"

"Who is Heman Claxton?"

My father didn't skip a beat. "A man of business, he ceased his activities fourteen years ago when the Poisoner left for the continent and has been a recluse ever since."

"What activities?"

My father paused watching my face judiciously. "He was

involved with the Indian cotton trade in the early '30s, but his background before then is unknown. In the 1840s, he focused his attention to," he paused again, "shipping and made smart, but risky investments." My father cracked his knuckles against the desk, which told me that there was a lie embedded in what he just said.

"Investments?" He didn't answer. "You know Mr. Claxton."

"That is none of your concern." He returned his gaze to his paper.

"It seems as though nothing is ever, 'my concern.' You brought me out of the bloody Navy, out of my career, to run errands for you."

My father stood, shook out the paper and put it on the table. "There are things about this case that you do not need to know. I gave you your objectives, and I expect you to follow them." Silence filled the space. "Or did the Navy teach you nothing? You were only to have contact with the girl. Gain her trust and her connection to the Poisoner."

I watched him, clenching my jaw and holding my fist at my side. We said nothing for minutes.

"It's of no significance now, Mr. Claxton is dead. He died within hours of your visit yesterday." He opened another newspaper, this one in French.

"He's dead?" I whispered, once again assailed by guilt while none burdened my father.

"Yes." He barely looked up from the paper. "Mrs. Watts, his housekeeper, quickly confessed. My men found a bottle of blue mass in her possession. It was only a matter of time before his mind began to leave him."

"I think it already had." I swallowed back a painful lump in my throat.

My father's eyes followed the trade routes on a map of China. He pinched his nose. "What did he tell you?"

"He believes, I mean believed, that Lady Margaret's parents were murdered."

"Of course, they weren't. The old fool had spent too

many years infused with mercury." My father's knuckles cracked loudly in the quiet space.

"But it's a strong lead..."

My father interrupted me, "No. I need you to investigate the girl not the ravings of a demented old man. Perhaps, the Poisoner killed Mr. Claxton to protect the girl and whatever information the man could have divulged if you hadn't been enraptured by his sad story." His steely eyes pierced me with doubt.

"As you wish, your grace." I gritted my teeth, but I wasn't ready to give up the lead just yet. No matter what my father said.

He relaxed in his chair upon my pronouncement. "Mrs. Watts wouldn't tell us who commissioned her to do it, but I think we can both guess who it was. She was taken into police custody yesterday evening. I've recently found out that she hung herself using the bed sheets in her room. It wasn't suicide. Her neck had been broken before she was slipped into the noose." My father looked me straight in the eyes as if daring me to refute him. "We have not told the family the cause of his death, and neither should you."

"Fine. I would like to see the correspondence between the lady and the Poisoner. It'll help me with the case."

My father cracked his knuckles again. "I do not have it at the moment but once C.I.D. returns it, you can have it though I doubt it will give you any information."

Part of me didn't believe the documents existed but I left my father to his lies, wishing only for escape. I settled on my horse, deciding om a ride to St. Katharine's docks to clear my head. The idea that the sea was only a ship away could soothe any encounter with my father. But tonight, the salt air tinged with coal did nothing to alleviate the gnawing in the pit of my stomach

My father's mistrust of women, or rather his remembrance of my mother, clouded his judgment. I wondered if it would cloud mine.

CHAPTER ELEVEN

M.

He didn't even answer my questions. A rake of the first order, I fumed, stomping into the townhouse and passing a startled Buxley.

"Margaret?" Rose glided up to me with Aunt Emily trailing behind. "You better have a good explanation for mother, about where you've been."

Aunt Emily ushered me into the back parlor and slammed the door behind us. With my eyes closed, I took a deep breath and emptied my thoughts.

"We didn't take you in, allow you into our esteemed family, for you to play loose like, like a common prostitute," Aunt Emily rained down on me as she had for the past thirty minutes.

"Aunt Emily, I didn't do anything outside the bounds of proper behavior," I whispered for what must have been the one-hundredth time as my cheek throbbed and a slight buzzing sound filled my ears.

"No one asked you to speak." Rose pushed me and walked to Aunt Emily's side.

"You must think of your cousin's reputation. What has she done to deserve this cruel behavior?" Aunt Emily fell onto the settee, and Rose handed her a fan.

Rose shook her head at me, a gleam in her eyes. "What are we to do with you? Mama, what do you think? We can't let Margaret fall into moral shambles, now can we? Our good Christian duty just won't allow it."

"You're right as always, my cherub," Aunt Emily beat her fan at a furious pace, her cheeks flushing.

Rose, impatient of my beratement, and most likely hoping for more, spoke, "We could always send her away—."

But, Aunt Emily stood. "No, no that does not suit the plan. Buxley, Buxley, come here," Aunt Emily called out the door. "Bring the rod, immediately."

#

Days later, dressed in black from head to toe and wearing bonnets with black crepe veils covering their faces, Aunt Emily and Rose entered the foyer. Whenever Aunt Emily returned from an outing, she went to her parlor for a smoke on her elegant glass pipe. I counted on getting Rose alone.

"Maggie, little dear. Why ever are you skulking about in the hallway, like a common thief?" Rose stopped near the door to her room, pulling at her black lace gloves.

"Where were you today?"

"Not that it's any concern of yours," Rose glared at me, "but, we were at grandpapa's funeral."

"Did I hear you correctly, godfather?"

"No, I said grandpapa, you dolt." Rose rolled her eyes and tapped her foot. "Sometimes I think you have wool in your ears."

I gritted my teeth. "Rose both of our grandfathers are dead and have been dead for many years."

Rose covered a small smile with her hands. "You really don't know? Well, isn't this grand."

"What?" I regretted the word the moment it slipped from my lips.

"It was Mama's father, Grandpapa Claxton. He passed away a few days ago."

"You're lying."

Her hand extended out catching the soft flesh of my cheek in an abrupt slap.

"Don't raise your voice at your betters, you brat. He could not bear to look at your dark face. He told Mama he never wanted to see you again and that you were a disgrace. Especially, after your father's shameful gambling ruined the family's reputation," Rose hurled at me, stalking me until my back pressed up against the opposite wall. "The polite thing to say would be, 'I'm sorry for your loss.' Really, where are your manners?"

No surprise entered me upon her pronouncement that my grandfather never wanted to see me. No shock came from realizing my worst imaginings of people were often accurate. Cruel beasts with swords for tongues and iron hammers for fists circled me in London and could not be escaped even within my own family. Yet, faint memories of my grandfather had trickled into my mind, suffused with a warm glow since I received the letter.

"I'm sorry for your loss." My tongue stuck to the back of my throat. I swallowed but to no avail.

Since I was old enough to carry a feather duster, I'd worked for the family to earn their "Christian charity." My life had been like choosing between Scylla and Charybdis for as long as I could remember. But, then, escape seemed impossible and too perilous to even imagine.

I caressed the worn cover of *The Iliad*. Every yellowed page was covered in annotations written in my late father's hand. Some comments were so academic they made my head spin, while others made me feel like I knew him even if I could barely remember him. The Greek Gods and Goddesses comforted me, even if they were as cruel as the mortals who surrounded me. Their stories reminded me of a better time. When my father passed I memorized every story, so that I could tell them to myself.

In the hallway that led from the kitchen, the housekeeper had tacked up a thorough list titled, "The Modern Householder's List for the Kitchen." The list featured items from a patent digester to a bottle jack – all the elements needed to keep the kitchen in working order. New linoleum outfitted the servants' hall to keep down the noise.

"Good morning, Mrs. Riley, do I smell saffron buns?" I picked up Poppy, the calico cat, from her resting place on the kitchen chair before I sat down with her on my lap. Max, the hound, must have already been outside, for Poppy barely lifted her head in my direction.

"Aye, milady that it is. Always were your favorite, weren't they?" Mrs. Riley said with a smile, before setting a warm bun before me with a cup of Earl Grey tea.

The servants sat around me, greeting the early hours of the morning with groans and grumbles. Though they were not hostile toward me, I had no place in their rigid hierarchy. At least not in Aunt Emily's Panopticon, where a thousand eyes watched your every movement. Then, more than ever, they seemed to be watching me and hoping for any misstep.

"Have you seen Samantha?" I sipped my tea and hid a cringe as Mrs. Riley's gaze focused on my bruised cheek.

Mrs. Riley shook her head. "Dearie, she snuck out in the wee hours of the morn to see her Charlie. If you're wantin' to interrupt her," Mrs. Riley trailed off with a wink. "If they weren't engaged Mrs. Kimble would have that girl's head."

I blushed and considered my empty cup of tea, the leaves had gathered together at the bottom to form smoke like spirals. Burning maple syrup, like the scent that floated through the air in a cloud of smoke from Aunt Emily's pipe, hit the back of my nose. Its thick richness and sickly quality held me enraptured in a trance-like state. Yet, the scent wasn't there, but oozing out from the alcoves of my mind.

"Dearie, did you hear me?" Mrs. Riley's voice broke me from the grasp of the memory.

"Pardon, no." Though the scent left my nose, a sticky sweet residue remained, clouding my mind.

"I chopped up some comfrey leaves for your bruises." Mrs. Riley offered me a small brown package.

I swallowed a lump in my throat, wondering if I had a mother she'd have offered me something similar. If I had a mother, would I have bruises? But, I couldn't dwell on thoughts of what could be, false hope never did me any good.

"Thank you."

Mist clung to the cast-iron lamp posts that lined the street, their flames flickering in vain through the grey dawn. I packed the damp comfrey leaves on top of my hands, wrapping them with cotton fabric, as a hiss of pain escaped my lips.

Outside, a black carriage pulled to the front of the house. A man, his top hat blocking his face, exited, walking toward the front door. Ordinarily, I wouldn't notice a visitor, but as the sun had just peeked over the brownstones, I couldn't help but wonder who he'd come to visit. Aunt Emily and Rose were not ones to rise before the clock struck eleven. Yet, by luncheon, I had all but forgotten the guest's presence within the house, until he happened upon me.

"My lady?" a deep male voice said from behind me. "Allow me to introduce myself, I am Dr. Francis."

I set down the feather duster, my hands trembling and took in a shuttered breath. Turning around, I performed a deep curtsy if not just to look at my feet and avoid his eyes. The man wore a black Newmarket coat. His blonde hair shone like spun gold in the sunlight streaming from the window and his blue eyes sparkled. He looked to be my father's age if he had lived. Yet, there was something about him. Something about the way he watched me, as if he looked straight through me, but pierced my core in the same instance. An aura of confidence emanated from him. A circling thing that closed in around my own existence until I had little space to move. As quickly as the invasive presence intruded upon me it departed, leaving me unsure if I felt it at all.

"Pleased to make your acquaintance." I nodded.

"I am an old friend of your family." He smiled, his teeth white and straight. "I grew up with your mother and aunt."

"My mother, you knew her?" I leaned forward, hope pounding in my chest. My family would never speak of her but in thinly veiled insults for her elopement, supposed wild temperament, and large ego. I had never believed them.

"Oh, yes we were quite close at one time. I could tell you about her, I am certain your Aunt doesn't have many kind things to say." He leaned in to whisper in my ear, "I am quite sure your Aunt was jealous. Your mother was as kind as she was beautiful."

I breathed in his words—starving. "Please tell me more," I

paused, embarrassed by my outburst, "if you have the time?"

"Of course, dear. I am sure she'd want you to know." He smiled at me again. "You will. You look..." he stopped a darkness settling over him.

For a moment, a flash of pain flickered but it disappeared once more behind his handsome exterior. Not a natural pain, but a twisted thing like the gnarled branches of a dead tree, black and rotten through, petrified by time to remain in that state. With a suddenness that caught every inch of me unaware, he smiled, a warm lightness seeping into his tone. He appeared at once like nothing more than a man with honest intentions.

"Oh, Dr. Francis, there you are." Aunt Emily glided in breathlessly, wringing a kerchief in her hands and a strange sentimental smile affixed to her face. "The tea has just arrived."

"It seems like it will have to be another time, dear." Dr. Francis shrugged before a serious expression overcame him. "Emily told me you've come into the crosshairs of a Lord Alexander, I know of him through my contacts in the Navy. He's nothing but a rake, who'll break your heart. What's the freedom in that?"

He bowed to me as my heart hammered in my chest. In the dark depths of that space, something stirred and woke an uncanny thing that stared me in the eyes as if it knew me better than I knew myself, without a care to time, condition, or place. Grotesque grey lips parted, and with a sound no louder than that of a dead leaf falling, it spoke to me.

"Run."

But, from who?

CHAPTER TWELVE

M.

On the night of the Westerly's fancy dress ball an insistent, perky, and unmistakable knock sounded at my door. It wretched my gaze away from the catastrophe in emerald silk that covered my bed.

"Come in."

Rose glided in, her dress floating around her frame and bouncing with each step. She spun around for effect, swan down circling her neckline, and her skirt cascading into diaphanous silver-white silk.

"Oh, how marvelous. Your dress came."

I stared at her. "I beg your pardon?"

What had Rose done? Her merciless punishment had already worn me down, and I didn't think I could withstand more. Even for her, the stamina of the assault was unnerving. A certain darkness had fallen over her since we'd arrived in London. She wasn't only angered by my excursion with Lord Alexander, and that terrified me the most because I couldn't discover its origin. It seemed that the semblance of safety I'd created over the years could come crashing down at any moment. I smoothed my expression, trying to hide my tumultuous thoughts from her predatory gaze.

Rose smiled and tilted her head in cunning fashion and arrayed a gloved finger upon her chin. "Well, my dearest cousin, I thought the dress Mama ordered was much too plain for you, my already plain relation. Mama let me design you a new one. It's your first fancy dress ball after all."

"You did what?" I restrained myself from screeching.

Rose smiled maliciously at me. "I just wanted to give you something special. But if you do not like it, I guess you will just have to stay home. We can find an uncouth American heiress to take it back with her." She left as quickly as she came.

Moments later, Samantha entered to find me pacing the floor. I am surprised that flames didn't sprout from the top of my head. I fell face first, speaking into the bed, "What am I going to do?"

Damn and blast, Rose! I pounded my fist into the mattress. Fancy dress balls had only just fallen out of fashion so that even if one were invited to one, they would not dress for the occasion. To arrive dressed in the style of Marie Antionette's court would mean certain ridicule. But, I had to go. I had no other choice. Though I rebelled against the thought, I needed answers more than I needed my dignity.

"We shall make the best of it." Samantha smiled solemnly as if she were about to read my obituary. My social obituary.

Once she finished, my untamable dark hair had vanished beneath a profusion of sculpted curls woven with dark green ribbons into a pouf hairstyle. The bruise that marred my cheek had been hidden beneath a fine powder. With quick hands, Samantha fastened my leather high-heeled shoes. I didn't dare bend over, even if I could. I pulled on my pair of long white gloves, wincing as they snagged on my rough hands

Luminescent fabric cascaded over the hoop skirt in the same emerald green that I imagined graced the hills of Scotland. It parted below the waist to show layers and layers of ruffled white lace. Scandalously low, a barely-there lace ruffle surrounded the square neckline. Lace cascaded off the ends of quarter-length sleeves. The tight bodice made my waist look impossibly small especially with the added exaggeration of the pannier.

I would stand out like a weed in a sea of lilies. A married woman could have worn the dress, or even the most daring unmarried miss, and by daring, without a care to her reputation. I jolted to a stop as I prepared to leave, my hip swinging to one side as the pannier slammed into a hutch.

"I don't even know where I end, and this blasted dress begins," I muttered, realigning the pannier and my skirts.

"If the ladies of Marie Antoinette's court survived twenty years with the fashion, so may you survive one night," Samantha tsked, a smile growing at the corners of her mouth.

"They chose their lot." I turned to face her, just missing knocking over a vase in the hallway. "I have been subjugated by enemy powers."

I didn't have a choice but to bring the abominable pannier for leaving it behind would have meant drowning in yards of silk. I had no wish to embody the likes of Ophelia from *Hamlet*.

Rose and Aunt Emily waited at the foot of the stairs. They had allowed me to accept my invitation and by the time I reached them they could do nothing to stop me. An unbecoming red flush crossed Rose's face as she folded her arms over her chest.

Aunt Emily glared at Rose and whispered something in her ear for a moment, before turning to me, "Hurry up, girl."

Rose watched me, her face ashen.

***

At the top of the grand staircase, above the swirling figures of dancing couples, Lord and Lady Westerly welcomed us to the ball. The attendees dressed mostly in the usual ball attire, but for a few poor fools, like me, dressed in full costume, mingled below. I searched the crowd, through the bobbing ostrich feathers, pastel dresses, black suits, and the fluttering fans for Lord Alexander.

"Ah, Lady Margaret—you know you look quite a bit like your dear mother, God rest her soul. We went to finishing school together, did you know?" Lady Westerly rambled, before flushing, "But of course, my dear, you would not know that."

She patted my hand sympathetically. I forced a smile to curve my lips, even as everything in me wished to curve inward.

"I am glad of your attire, dear. In New York, people are saying Mrs. Vanderbilt is about to host the fancy dress ball of the century." Lady Westerly looked blissfully around the crowd. "Lord Westerly believes it is the end of the fancy dress ball," she leaned in whispering conspiratorially, "but the Americans cannot have all the fun."

Aunt Emily humphed from behind me, hopefully too quiet for Lady Westerly to hear. I smiled and nodded. "Lady Westerly, thank you. Perhaps, you are right."

"That woman lacks class," Aunt Emily whispered loudly as we descended into the ballroom leaving our hosts behind. "How she ever caught an *Earl,* I will never understand." I turned my ears away from her jealous pronouncement to take in the ballroom.

Light shone from antique candelabras that would have been at home in Thornfield Hall, especially during a most magnificent thunderstorm. The decorations, I believed, were used to create a gothic ambiance as if we should have expected to be in a moldering mansion on the edge of a dark moor with a ghost haunting our every step. A young man tripped in the darkness and poured a glass of punch down a lady's bodice. Perhaps, the effect was too potent.

I looked around the ballroom and spotted Lord Alexander leaning on a Corinthian pillar. Next to him, a beautiful lady traced down his arm with her fingertip. She fluttered her fan as fast as her eyelashes. Lord Alexander took her hand and kissed it before smiling at her. It seemed that what Dr. Francis had told me held some truth.

Humph.

I caught his eye and beckoned him with my fan. He turned away from me and returned to his ladylove. I narrowed my eyes and I considered all I had imperiled to be here. He risked nothing. If he wanted my cooperation again, he would have to lay siege.

I pleaded a headache to Rose and Aunt Emily. They'd forget about me soon enough. I wandered through the ballroom in search of some punch—a nasty watered-down substance available only at high society balls. I skirted the edge of the dance floor and saw Alexander dancing with a new young woman. He appeared everywhere, circling all corners of the ballroom, flirting with matrons and maidens alike. I would not go home empty-handed again.

Peeking into the card room, I backed away as smoke filled my eyes. In the banquet hall rows upon rows of empty tables greeted me. They would remain that way until dinner. I realized the ballroom was not quite as big as I had imagined. Wishing for anything but having to watch Lord Alexander flirt his way through every skirt in the building, I decided to search a little farther back in the hallways.

"Lady Margaret," a voice called my name from down one of the side corridors. I went toward the sound.

Rough hands fell upon my side, shoving me away from my course. My heel caught, and I fell flat on my back into a room. My head slammed into the hardwood, only half-cushioned by a rug. A scraping sound and the warning click of the heavy wooden door barely passed through my awareness.

Rose.

Yet, as I lay there, letting my thoughts reassemble, I realized Rose could not be the culprit. Her torments never left the family home.

I rolled onto my side, a rush of blood coming with me as I propped myself up on one elbow. With careful slowness, I picked myself up and fluffed out the back of my crumpled but fixable gown. The faint outline of furniture filled the room, but other than that, darkness. I stared at where I thought the door might be located, expecting it to swing open at any moment and let in a stream of light. Putting one foot in front of the other, the tips of my toes sacrificed for anything that might have laid before me, I reached the door and clenched the cold doorknob.

It didn't budge.

I pounded on the heavy door. "Hello? Can anyone hear me? Hello? Please, I'm trapped." After all I went through to be there, I found myself locked in a room. It seemed like some sort of cruel irony.

My voice cracked as I released what might have been my twentieth plea for assistance. A tingling sensation spread over the palms of my hands. I slipped my gloves off rubbing my hands together. No one knew I was here. What if no one found me? My stomach clenched uncomfortably as it imagined the food the other guests would enjoy while I remained trapped: the watery potatoes, over-sauced meats of questionable origin, and the multitude of utensils by which to eat them.

My vision had adjusted somewhat to the darkness. Searching with my hands, I made my way around the room. I glided my fingertips over picture frames, bookshelves, stopping only when my fingertips grazed soft velvet. Curtains? I pushed them open. Luck finally graced me with her presence.

With the moonlight shining through, I pried open the window and leaned out. I could not be climbing out of another window. I scanned the area and saw that, though I was on the first floor above the garden level, the ground was not impossibly far away. I rationalized that I would land in the bushes at worse. It was rather a best-case scenario, but I had done it before after all.

Below, I could see the light spilling out of the garden level windows. The faint murmuring of voices tickled my ears. If someone noticed me escaping from the window a fancy dress would be the least of my worries. I waited a few more bated breaths, but no one appeared. With one last breath of confidence, I left the rest up to fate.

My dress snagged against an open cabinet as I prepared to swing my legs over the ledge. It must have been the hand of God stopping me. In a moment of clarity, brief as it might have been, I realized that the weight of my dress alone would have pulled me down to the ground faster than my bones could withstand.

I took off my cumbersome pannier and retied my billowing skirt so that the length did not deter me. I glanced at my hands, they still hurt. Scooting myself onto the wide window ledge, I swung myself over. My torso remained firmly planted on the ledge.

Strong hands encircled my calves. My breath stopped. Pulling at the ledge, I kicked at my captor. The rough stone bit into the circulation of my fingertips. My blood rushed to meet gravity's pull. I wormed further onto the ledge, my captor's hands not a bit loosened.

"Lady Margaret."

My foot connected with something hard and angular. A yelp, manly, but a yelp, all the same, stopped my second kick.

CHAPTER THIRTEEN

M.

I risked a glance over my shoulder gasping out, "Alexander?"

My fingers strained as they clung to the inside of the ledge. My brain registered that I had made a miscalculation.

"Damn and blast, Margaret." Alexander rubbed his jaw, having released my legs and standing a safe distance away. "I did not expect to find you hanging from a window yet again."

"You scared a year away from my life," I babbled while holding onto the ledge. My fingers ached, bringing forth the startling image of falling to Lord Alexander's feet and breaking every bone in my body. I was an idiot.

"Still your feet. I am trying to keep you from falling to your death," he growled out at me. I glanced over my shoulder again, watching Lord Alexander inch toward my legs as if he were hunting a fearsome beast.

"Well, pardon me," I replied, still hanging on. My fingers begged for retreat. "I have been trapped in this room for hours with no aid. What was I supposed to do?" Stop talking to him, Margaret. Get back into the room.

"Wait for someone to let you out." Alexander sighed deeply

"Would you have done that?" I huffed, finally pulling myself back into the room, and leaning out to look at Alexander.

"Of course not, I am a man." I rolled my eyes at his pronouncement. "In any case, I have been searching for you for quite some time."

"Is that true?" I narrowed my eyes at him. "You seemed

quite occupied with the other ladies." I leaned out of the window. In any other instance, I might have felt like Juliet looking down on her Romeo. A senseless love story.

"I have a reputation to uphold." Lord Alexander looked up at me from beneath his top hat.

"You've found me, congratulations." I gritted my teeth, ignoring his statement. "Since I am not 'allowed' to rescue myself, come up and unlock this door."

"That, m'dear, might be a problem if anyone unsavory is lurking about." He looked up at me, arms outstretched. "You're going to have to jump. I'll catch you."

"What? No. You'll drop me." I backed away from the window, gripping the soft velvet curtain like my life depended on it.

"I won't drop you. You have such little faith in my abilities," he tutted up at me, arms still outstretched.

I looked back into the darkened room, peering at the door and hoping my gaze could force it open. My stomach grumbled, and a cool breeze filtered across my cheeks. The floorboards creaked outside the door and my heart leaped out of the window deciding my course of action.

Looking at Lord Alexander once more, my tongue decided on a petulant response before my brain had signed off. "Fine, but if you drop me, Number Three..." I tapered off. I didn't really have anything I could threaten him with yet again.

I turned back toward the room casting my eyes about before I threw all good sense to the wind. My gaze fell on the shell of metal boned fabric. "Wait, we cannot leave this behind."

I picked up the pannier and hoop, tossing both out the window. They careened toward Lord Alexander's head, but he leaped out of their path. He looked up at me with horror, as he stepped around the ladies' undergarments that splattered the ground. I wished it had smacked him in the head. He deserved it.

"When you're ready, m'dear. There's no one about."

I swung over the side of the window again and called to him, "I'm not light."

"I'll catch you. One, two, three," Lord Alexander said,

seeming further away than before.

On three, I released the window. I shut my eyes as the frigid night air flew past my face. Humph. I jolted to a stop with Lord Alexander's arms, warm and firm, around me.

"You're light as a feather, m'dear," I heard him say, even over the blood pounding in my ears.

Looking up at him through my lashes, I caught his half-smile. "You better not have looked up my skirt."

Alexander looked down at me and laughed, as he gently set me down. "There's no way to see through all those ruffles, m'dear."

Heat rose to my cheeks. To distract myself, I walked to a shadowed alcove leading from the house, stepped into and re-attached my crumpled pannier and hoop.

Lord Alexander came over, "Would you like to check the room now?"

"I thought we could not do that, which was why you had me jump?" I shook my skirts out, a defensive wall building within me.

"Yes, but now we can see your wayward captor before he sees us," he said like he believed I fell into the room on my own accord. "There should be no harm in casually walking by."

I didn't fully believe him. "As you wish, Number Three," I responded coolly, but he ignored my tone.

Lord Alexander offered me the crook of his arm. "After you, mademoiselle. Interesting costume." He held the door open, and we entered the house.

"Interesting costume?" I cringed inwardly and glared at him. Curse Rose and her Machiavellian ability to make my life hell.

"You look quite lovely tonight, I mean." Lord Alexander watched me with bewilderment. "Truly."

"Thank you," I mumbled, not wishing for his pity. Any of the beauty I had felt while wearing the dress deflated like the volume in my now sagging hair.

Once returned to the first floor, we looked for the door to

the room I was trapped in.

"There should be three doors in this hallway," Lord Alexander began, rubbing the nape of his neck, "you came out of the last window. It would be the third door."

Following his gaze, I walked to the third door and tried the knob. "It's locked. Why would someone shove me into a room and then lock the door?"

For the first time, Lord Alexander took me in with sincere consideration, his eyebrows scrunching together. "You've answered your own question. Someone wouldn't simply do that. You were put in this room for a reason." He crouched and looked closely at the floor near the door.

"I thought I heard someone call my name. That's why I came down here." I remembered as I felt the knot on the back of my skull.

"Most assuredly then, it was premeditated," he said looking covertly down the hall. "I am not letting you out of my sight for the remainder of the evening."

I rubbed my arms, looking about the hallway, a sudden fear climbing up my spine. In an instant, I remembered the possible danger Lord Alexander had threatened. At the other end of the hall, we heard the creak of the floor and heavy tread scratching the carpet. Lord Alexander pushed me into the far corner of the hallway, his body in front of me, and his back to the intruders. The shadows of the curtain acted as cover and left us almost undetectable to the two men who entered the hall.

"Let us check on the girl, right? I 'aven't 'eard a peep from 'er in a while," said one voice, followed by the rattle of keys.

"Maybe, if you 'ad not wanted a bite to eat, we wouldn't 'ave been gone so long," replied another.

I held my breath. Lord Alexander's motionless form surrounded me like a shield. The door creaked open. "Bloody 'ell, she's gone. She's gone. The master's gonna kill us."

"We 'ave to find 'er." I peeked around Alexander to see the second man enter the room.

"This were supposed to be easy. Right. Keep the girl locked

up, the chuffin' master would rescue 'er from us. That's it and," one of the men exited the room, "gain her trust."

The other one followed, both men were dressed like house staff, but their forms looked more honed for physical labor. "She could not 'ave got far. Let's return the keys before the nobs find out."

"Oi, what's that?" One of them started walking toward us.

Lord Alexander pressed further into me and whispered in my ear, "May I kiss you?"

I looked up at him, his hot breath on my neck, and leaned forward. "Yes."

At first, all I noticed was the new and strange sensation of our lips touching. For some reason, I imagined kissing as a small peck on the lips. Something that lasted seconds and barely left an impression. In the first moment, the realization that I could feel and taste the softness of the inside of his mouth overwhelmed my confused thoughts. Yet, moments later that all disappeared. My back against the wall, his hands on either side of my head, while my hands bunched up in his jacket compelled my mouth forward.

The pressure of the kiss was unlike anything I had ever experienced. My breath caught in my chest and my head tilted forward without my permission. With hesitance, I kissed him back, and my arms looped around his neck. An action, which, at the time, I didn't wish to consider.

At Casterton, the girl's boarding school of my youth in Northern England, Mr. Wilson, with the help of Miss Temple, caned one girl and forced her to wear the "sinners' dress." They had caught her talking to a boy from Cowan Bridge unchaperoned. We called the dress "the hag," and shuttered at the thought of being forced into its brown scratchy folds which rubbed the skin raw and let the chilly air seep into the bones. If the vile Mr. Wilson, who threatened the girls with hell and damnation daily, could have seen me then.

"Leave it. Cor blimey. Some bloody lovebirds. Let's keep movin'," the man further down the hall called to his companion, who followed his lead.

The men's voices disappeared down the hallway. Lord Alexander's lips left mine, and a chasm of physical distance explored the space left behind. I imagined his fingers, which wrapped around my upper arms, left behind a red brand. He released me.

I stared at him. My ears burned like hot coals. Lord Alexander stared back at me and cleared his throat several times. I let my hands fall away from him with the shock at what I had let myself do or what I had let him do to me. It was wrong to even consider.

"This is much worse than I thought, Number Three." I was proud my voice came out firmly without a hint of breathiness, even as I realized the double meaning behind my words.

"You're in danger, more so than I believed." Lord Alexander looked me over. He looked unruffled, which attached a barb of embarrassment to the edge of my heart. "You're under my protection now."

Any other time and I might have let myself believe his words. Lord Alexander grabbed my hand to pull me along behind him. Pain shot through my hand, a slow scalding burn, and I couldn't conceal the yelp that escaped my lips.

Lord Alexander stopped in his tracks. "What happened? Are you hurt? Did I hurt you?"

I shook my head, backing away. I didn't want him to see, but most of all, I couldn't bear his pity. Lord Alexander gently pulled me toward him and took my gloved hand. He opened the curtains. The moonlight streamed in, and he pulled my gloves off with the most intimate care. My smaller hand, resting in his broad one looked almost delicate in the forgiving moonbeams. I looked away, up at the ceiling—waiting.

Once the glove left, snagging on my calluses as it went, my hand felt clammy to the air. Nothing, no gasp, no mumbled breath filled with pity or muttered tsk—nothing. I looked at Alexander, taking in his hooded eyes and his sphinxlike expression. He took a deep breath, a tick forming in his jaw.

"How did this happen?" he gritted out.

I could not tell where he directed his anger. Black and blue bruises marred my knuckles and the palms of my hands in many straight lines. In some areas, the skin had broken and barely scabbed over. My other hand told the same story.

"My aunt." I paused trying to discern his feelings. "My aunt was angry that I went out with you or really at all, without her permission. This was my punishment."

I aimed for nonchalance. Quiet reigned for a few minutes, my hand warm in his, an all too unfamiliar moment of human contact.

"Where else?"

"My other hand and my left cheek." Thankfully, cosmetics covered that bruise, which painted my face with black and blue brush strokes.

Lord Alexander nodded with dark eyes, and with a cautious tenderness, he slid my glove back onto my hand. "I am sorry. This won't happen again."

A deranged laugh escaped me. "You cannot stop it, Number Three."

He tilted my chin up, his thumb tracing my bottom lip and catching my breath in the palm of his hand. Resolute in his stance, I decided not to refute him again and ignored the sinking sensation in the pit of my stomach. The same feeling, I had at the first ball—nothing good ever happened in London. At any moment, I expected a gust of wind to crash through the windows, the curtain left to violently play with the wind, and a flash of lightning, perfectly placed, to slash across the black sky. But, I wasn't in a Gothic novel.

"Lady Margaret, you are under my protection now," he said with the surety of what I assumed was ignorance.

There was no escape.

Lord Alexander put my hand on his arm as we walked back to the ballroom. "I'll make your excuses to your aunt and our hosts. Then I am taking you home. It's too dangerous here."

We entered the ballroom and searched for my aunt. She

disappeared into the wall with her taupe colored dress. Aunt Emily's eyes widened as she caught sight of us as if she searched for something more.

"How are you here?" Aunt Emily whispered, her hand trembling slightly as she gripped her flask.

Wondering if she had fallen senile in the time I'd been gone, I spoke slowly, "I came with you and Rose, my lady."

"I know that." She narrowed her eyes. "Where have you been?"

"The ladies' retiring room, I was feeling quite faint. Lord Alexander has graciously offered to lend me a carriage to return home. I do not wish to interrupt the evening, but my faintness has not abated," I pushed out my words with one breath.

"The ladies' retiring room, you say?" Confusion marred Aunt Emily's face, creating thin lines between her brows. She searched the room once more, her frown deepening.

"Yes." I nodded my head empathetically, my nails biting into my palms.

Aunt Emily retired her scrutinizing gaze and sat down in her chair, as if infinitely weary. "My lord, I hope you'll dance with my daughter?"

"May I offer Lady Margaret the use of a carriage to your residence, Lady Wellmont?" Lord Alexander took a step forward.

Aunt Emily took a delicate sip from her flask, her eyes clouding. "I'll allow it if you dance with my daughter."

"Agreed. Thank you, my lady." Lord Alexander bowed to her, his eyes hard and cold.

CHAPTER FOURTEEN

A.

Damn her beautiful eyes and damn my own. My mind hopped back and forth between wanting to kiss her again and following my own better judgement. Danger like black pitch—sticky, odious, and inextricable—had ensconced Margaret more than I could have imagined. The Poisoner hunted her, prowling on the very edges of proper society with the audacity, and willingness to cross the line even at so public a place as a ball. I needed to find something, anything before he made his next move. If he hadn't already.

She stood off to the side, clutching her green cape around her shoulders like a shield. My gaze sought her gloved hands, fastening to them as my chest tightened. Whether or not I laid the lattice of bruising along her flesh, I held the blame for putting her in danger. If I hadn't grabbed her hand, I might have never known.

"Alexander?" she asked, her eyes widening. "I mean, Number Three, will you—I must know."

"Please call me, Alexander." I wished to call her Margaret.

She nodded haltingly, eyes narrowing, and I regretted my push forward into familiarity. Her grey eyes held me, and I had to fight myself to let her mind remain at ease, even as mine tumbled.

My family-crested carriage pulled to the front of the townhouse, and I extended assistance to Margaret. I followed behind her, making sure that no eyes followed us.

"Why haven't you tried to contact your grandfather?"

"How do you know that?" I didn't benefit her with a

response as I had come to know she disliked uncomfortable silences, I waited. She rewarded me shortly. "I thought he was dead. Finding out he was alive... I didn't know what to believe. It's too late anyway."

How had both grandfather and granddaughter been led to believe the other had died? And why? I wanted to tell her the truth but telling her the truth would also reveal that she'd never get the chance to know him. I didn't know if I could wait.

I went back to the conversation held by two men in the corridor, imagining that the Poisoner had orchestrated Margaret's entrapment. "Who told you he died?"

"Aunt Emily. She's little more than a drunkard." Margaret rolled her eyes skyward and flexed her hands. With a steady breath, she looked me in the eyes for the first time since leaving the ballroom. "I am not involved with the Poisoner by any choice of my own. Still, I doubt that Aunt Emily, excuse my lack of a better word, knows bollocks."

The repetition of lies that shrouded Margaret's every move created a tension in my own shoulders and, yet again, I could not shake the feeling I was three steps behind. A part of me was relieved I didn't need to tell her the truth nor my involvement in it. Mostly my involvement.

"It might not be your choice, but the Poisoner has singled you out. I need your assistance in finding out why," I swallowed, "and then we can go our separate ways."

I should return her to her home. Find the answers and leave her uninvolved from danger, including me. I couldn't believe what my father said about her collusion with the Poisoner. Again, my suspicion that the letters didn't exist settled in my gut.

She nodded, her eyes glistening like silver bullets in the night. "Then let us begin, my lord. Who is the Poisoner?"

"I don't know or rather no one knows his true identity."

She narrowed her eyes. "Fine. What is my connection to the Poisoner? If he really isn't just a Spring-heeled Jack."

"He is real, my lady. I did not create him to scare children on Lavender Lane. He's connected to your grandfather and thus you. We don't yet know if he killed your parents, but it wouldn't be outside of the realm of possibility."

"Well we can't just ask him can we." She cleared her throat. "I found out he died. It must have been after he sent me the letter."

"Who told you this?" I didn't correct her assumption even though my suspicions leaned toward the letter being a fake. If her grandfather hadn't known was alive until just days ago there was no way he wrote the letter. Then who did?

"My cousin," Margaret put a hand to her cheek, "after my aunt and she returned from the funeral. It was by my own foolish curiosity I learned the fact."

Quickly, I looked down at my notes before speaking as my cheeks flushed. "I met your grandfather." I didn't tell her when I met him. "The brick house on Baker Street was his."

Margaret sat up, her lips trembling and cheeks red. "You used me."

"I wouldn't call it that," I rubbed my hands down my thighs. "I needed to see what you knew without my influence."

She sat back again, arms folded over her chest pushing up her bosom, as she looked out the window. "Why is that, my lord?"

"Herman Claxton, your grandfather, was led to believe you died of tuberculosis at the age of seven. I needed to confirm he hadn't lied to me."

"Bollocks." Her eyes swam with unshed tears, and she clenched her hands together.

"Why would I lie?"

"Why wouldn't you?" A spark of admiration filled me to find another jaded soul.

"I can prove it." I opened a compartment on the side of the carriage, pulling out a letter and a diary. I handed both to Margaret.

She held the leather diary. First, her gloved hands reverently caressing the cover. She opened it and scanned the contents. After a few minutes, she looked up. "This is my aunt's, where did you find it?"

"Your grandfather gave it to me." I catalogued the identity of the writer. "Do you know who the man with blue eyes is, by any chance? She writes about him quite a bit. Seemed to be in love."

"My Uncle Matthew, most likely. He has blue eyes. Though this diary is quite old." She continued to scan the pages. "Why is my aunt's diary important to you?"

"It was in the box of files your grandfather gave me, though I initially thought it was an accidental placement." I leaned closer to her, before thinking better of it.

"You don't anymore?" She looked up from her reading.

"I don't doubt your Aunt told him you were dead." I swallowed the rest of my words, realizing that they came out harshly.

Margaret's eyes hardened, and a small frown marred the space between her dark brows. "I am sure she did it out of spite and nothing more." Her nominal reaction surprised me as I had expected the womanly expression of tears, or, at the very least, a provoked gasp.

"But you were only a child?" I murmured in unchartered waters.

My vision of motherhood stringently held by my own mother's gentle kindness clashed with the image of Lady Wellmont's cold eyes.

Margaret shrugged as we passed through the shadows and placed the diary on the seat. She looked at me directly and calmly folded her hands on her lap. "Why did you speak with my grandfather?"

"Part of the case." I didn't tell her that I believed there was a connection between my father and her grandfather. "As you know your grandfather believed that someone murdered your parents. I believe that someone was the Poisoner."

Her eyes shut, and she blinked hard. "I still can't believe it. They died of natural causes under tragic circumstances," she said the words with the familiarity of a much-repeated sentence, one my own father would agree with.

"I might agree with your grandfather. Your parents' deaths follow the Poisoner's pattern." I swallowed, even away from my father it was difficult to disagree with him. "I want your help in figuring out your family's involvement with the Poisoner. Please, read the letter."

She looked at me with suspicion but pulled out the letter and read it. Her face didn't give much away as she read, but for the increased furrow of her brow. She finished, smoothing the letter against her knees. "This is from my mother to my grandfather."

"Yes, she believed that she and your father were in danger —that you all were."

"You believe it was the Poisoner?" Margaret closed her eyes. "But, why?" she whispered.

"I don't know why, and worse, I believe he has unfinished business concerning your family and you specifically." Moments of silence passed, as Margaret's eyes moved back and forth behind her closed lids.

"I'll help you." She nodded though her eyes remained closed.

"Thank you." She didn't have a choice. "Though I am not happy that you are in danger," my father's face came to my mind, "I know what it is like to have answers withheld."

She turned away from me to look out the window. "Where are we going, Number Three?"

"I can hear your stomach growling from a mile away. I decided we should stop at my Aunt's house for some supper. You know you're taking this quite well." The carriage pulled to a stop.

Her face gave nothing away. "She won't mind, your aunt, I mean?"

"No." Probably too elated. While she had played down her excitement in front of Margaret, she'd been pestering me with questions since their first meeting.

In front of the familiar classical structure, I helped Margaret from the carriage. I missed Aunt Bita, more than I thought. It seemed like months ago since I had returned at my father's bequest. I had thought, if only for a moment, that we might have changed after seven years. Nothing had changed—except Margaret. For some reason she fascinated me, and I didn't want to dwell on what that meant.

"Don't you have to return to the ball?"

"Your cousin can wait." I barely had any intention of dancing with the spiteful girl.

A butler with an emerald green waistcoat, a direct confrontation to the customary black, opened the door. He nodded to us both. "My lord, my lady, her ladyship is in India if you'll follow me."

"India?" Margaret mouthed.

"You'll see, m'dear."

Exotic knick-knacks covered every available surface, in a flurry of rich palettes and vibrant shine. Home, it called to me. My gaze took in a golden Egyptian cat; a silver Celtic Cross; a Turkish rug; a Chinese tea set; an ebony wood sculpture of a man with an elongated head; a jar with a collection of bronze coins, and the list that, if continued, would have filled a museum. A smoky scent, like that of cloves and some other spice, swirled languidly through the air. Aunt Bita. Breaking my focus, a little dog with long pure white and black fur, a stout face, long ears, and a smushed black nose, skidded into the room.

"Jun-ko." I picked up the dog with one hand, rubbing his head. The little dog licked my fingers, his curled tail wagging feverishly. I pointed the dog in Margaret's direction. "He's friendly. Come, give him a pet."

She walked forward and scratched him behind his ears. "He's a funny looking dog. I've never seen the like."

I set Junko down, as we followed the butler. He ran in front of us and then behind us, back and forth, herding us to our destination. "He's a Japanese Chin. My aunt and her late husband brought him back from Japan a few years ago. A diplomatic gift."

We reached the parlor. Against my better judgement, I

leaned forward and whispered in her ear, "Welcome to India."

An assortment of brass statues: one of a man with four arms in a ring of some sort, a golden chest with dancing figures, and a brass elephant sitting with a turban atop its head, were arranged on the top of a shelf. On the walls, cotton tapestries hung like scrolls, where images of colorful people with elaborate turbans posed. Tropical flora filled the room in a cascade of green, and I imagined during the daytime, beautiful blossoms would bloom. Pushed against the wall, a long day bed with a pleated crimson-orange seat pillow of silk stood. To the left of that, toward the covered window, a bench hung from the ceiling. In the middle of the room, a low square table stood, surrounded by large square pillows. A tray with a tall bronze teakettle and a smoking stick in a dish of sand were centered on the table.

Margaret leaned into me. "It reminds me of the scent of a Synagogue." She blushed. "My dearest friend Miriam is Jewish."

Sitting on the floor with her knees tucked beneath her, sat Aunt Bita. Her pure white hair peeked out from beneath a jewel-tone yellow turban with a large ruby gem in the front.

Aunt Bita's eyes widened when she saw Margaret and she picked up Junko. Standing, she seemed even smaller than before. More frail and delicate.

Arms outstretched she reached for me. I bent down, so she could plant a kiss on each cheek. "Alexander, my favorite nephew. It means something since I have more than one." She pinched my cheek.

"How are you, Aunt Bita?" I am sure you remember Lady Margaret?"

Aunt Bita placed her hand on my arm, and I felt myself relax. I hadn't cried to her since I was thirteen when I had been exiled to the Navy, yet something in me wished to do so again

"Yes, yes, I'm old, but not blind." Aunt Bita squinted at Margaret and held up a hand. "Wait. Jane-e-e?" she called in a clear, demanding tone.

Jane flurried into the room, her light-ash hair slightly askew.

"Bring my pince-nez," Aunt Bita directed toward the woman.

Jane nodded and left as fast as she entered. In mere seconds, she returned with a pair of round gold spectacles, which she wiped off with a cloth before handing them to Aunt Bita. Affixing them to her face, Aunt Bita dismissed Jane, who curtsied before exiting the room.

"You're as pretty as I remember. Has anyone told you, you look like..." I agreed with Aunt Bita's assessment. But, Aunt Bita paused her perusal of Margaret's face. "No, it can't be. Excuse the ramblings of an old woman."

She moved to lounge on the daybed, Junko curled up in the sleeve of her kimono. "Come, come, darlings, sit down. I do so hate craning my neck." She gestured with her hand toward the bench. We sat at her command, and a moment of panic consumed me as the swing jolted back. For a moment, I was back on a ship.

Aunt Bita petted Junko's head, gazing at me with clear and knowing eyes. I knew what she thought. Margaret looked at me with confusion. The Aunt Bita she had met a week ago had nothing in common with the woman in front of her. That woman was merely a facade to hide eccentricities.

"Thank you for having us, my lady," Margaret whispered. She had a white-knuckle grip on the swing as well.

Aunt Bita sat up, upsetting Junko, who jumped down to hide under the daybed. "Now that you've come to my home, you must call me Aunt Bita. It's not every day my young Alexander brings someone to my home." She gave me a side-eye. "Never, in fact." Clapping her hands together, Aunt Bita gave me a look before speaking, "Who are your parents again, dear?"

Embarrassment I rarely felt assaulted me. "Lady Margaret is the daughter of the late Earl and Countess of Stanhild." Aunt Bita's eyes widened, but she smoothed her expression.

"A lovely name—stalwart. Though your mother's name was Esther if I am correct?" Margaret nodded to her, and she continued, "If that had been my name, I never would have changed it. I was horribly misnamed, 'Prudence,' as an infant. What an atrociously boring name. When my late husband, Henry and I were in Persia, in '53, a year after Amir Kabir's execution, I heard the name, 'Bita,' and knew it had to be mine. It means 'precious,' in Persian," Aunt Bita mused, a soft smile lighting her face.

"I've always thought my name was rather boring too, but I am used to it. I don't even know what I would change it to. My middle name is Admina. It's quite odd and I've never heard the like." Margaret smiled at Aunt Bita, as Junko peeked out from under her skirts.

Aunt Bita caught my eye with a frown. "Oh, nonsense. You are younger than I was when I changed mine." She noticed something, but she was unlikely as my father to tell me what.

"Aunt Bita, there are things we must discuss," I murmured, putting an end to our small talk. "We also haven't had a chance to eat."

She stood, and we followed suit. "The truth comes out. You didn't really come to comfort a poor, lonely old woman." Aunt Bita dramatized, hand to her heart as if she were about to faint. She leaned conspiringly toward Margaret. "He always did love my cook's Moroccan lamb cutlets. This boy used to eat me out of house and home during his summers away from the academy."

I shrugged my shoulders. The truth was neither my father nor myself could bear to be in the same room after my mother's death. He always blamed me. Perhaps, I blamed myself.

Aunt Bita glided from the room and through one of two doors down the hall, urging us to follow. A footman helped us to our seats and waited in the doorway for Aunt Bita's command.

"Bring up two dinner plates and a spot of Darjeeling." Aunt Bita dismissed with a delicate hand. "Darlings, what is it we need to discuss?" She rested her chin in her hand. Junko's head popped up from her lap.

Margaret looked to me.

"Aunt Bita, we need your help with a delicate situation."

"Delicate situations are my forte."

"I need Lady Margaret's aunt to accept my courtship or rather fake courtship of her, so I may use her knowledge for my case."

"Did she not accept it last the time? Why ever not?" asked Aunt Bita with a frown.

Margaret shook her head marginally, pleading me with her eyes. I spoke again, "Perhaps, she doesn't trust me."

Margaret relaxed. "I should really like to help Lord Alexander, so that we may both be on our way."

I swallowed back a barb of pain at the thought.

Aunt Bita pouted. "What a disappointment. Are you sure it can only be fake?"

Margaret and I avoided each other's eyes. I still saw a gleam in Aunt Bita's eye, which I should have given more credence. We nodded with equal determination to leave it at that.

"You could never ask for a better procurer of a respectful ruse." Aunt Bita smiled overly long at me.

I narrowed my gaze on Aunt Bita. "Thank you."

We stared at each other in a contest of sorts, for so long that Margaret needed to break the silence.

"Thank you, Aunt Bita. You have been ever so kind yet again," Margaret said.

"You're welcome." Aunt Bita stood, and I followed. "Well, darlings, I must excuse myself, but I would have a word with you first, nephew," she paused, smiling at Margaret, "alone. If you'll excuse us."

Out in the hallway, Aunt Bita shoved her pointer finger into my chest. "Alexander, this girl is not a dock doxy."

I pushed her hand away. "I never said that she was, nor would I... She's..." I trailed off as Aunt Bita's eyes lit up.

"Ah, I see." She grinned a secretive smile. "How did an innocent like her get caught in one of my brother's webs?" Aunt Bita's eyes narrowed as if she had thought of something, but if she had, she didn't share it with me. "Or, is that what you're trying to discover?"

"You'll help us?" I breathed out, wishing to escape whatever net she'd cast. I could never forget she and my father had similar, particular talents.

"Of course, darling." She pinched my cheek as she returned to the dining room. "I quite like the girl, already."

CHAPTER FIFTEEN

M.

I stood in the center of a vast chessboard, white and black towers looming above me into a never-ending sky. A giant hand picked me up, tying me to the black pawn. The rope dug into me, rubbing at my flesh as I pushed against it. The ropes seemed to tighten with each tug, lashing around my chest and wrenching the air from my lungs. Loud and booming laughter filled the infinite space and the hand snaked out to grab the pawn, lifting me and placing me on the board. Over and over again, black and white raced past me at a dizzying pace. My head swarmed, and my stomach heaved. The sound of a war drum pounded in my ears and the taste of blood filled my mouth. I looked up to see the white queen sliding toward me.

***

I woke up with a start, propping myself up on my elbows as I pet Poppy. Her head tilted as she watched me with gleaming green eyes. I must have woken her too. My head throbbed, and I dropped myself back against the pillow, staring at my water-stained ceiling. Even now, in the light of day with the darkness of the previous night departed, I found myself afraid of Alexander's answers.

I imagined skeletal fingers winding around my wrists and I had to force myself not to look down for the fear that I might find blue bruises encircling them. The Poisoner, who'd ripped away an entire life from me, evoked the image of Thanatos—death personified. My father once read to me Hesiod's *Theogony*, which described Thanatos with "a heart of iron, and his spirit within him as pitiless as bronze: whomsoever of men he has once seized he holds fast: and he is hateful even to the deathless gods." I wondered if we even had a chance.

Around half past seven in the morning, many hours from the proper calling time when Alexander and his aunt would pick me up, I readied for the day. Uncle Matthew would be arriving tomorrow. A shudder passed through me, as I imagined the entrance of my Uncle's blustering presence pushing through my already fractured existence. In Bristol, I had ample space to avoid him. During the Summer months, I'd spend every waking moment outside, resting my feet in the clear streams, or running through the fields of lavender and startling the bleating sheep. I had even come to miss the smell of wet wool. Sometimes, I could even escape punishment for returning home with darkened skin and my hair caressed into a state by the wind. London may have had a million more nooks and crannies than Bristol, yet, none of them would help me escape Uncle Matthew.

I began to organize Uncle Matthew's office in preparation for his return. As I cleaned, Aunt Emily entered, glaring at me. She unlocked a drawer in Uncle Matthew's desk and slipped in an envelope. She left the room as quickly as she came, slamming the door behind her. While polishing the desk, I noticed that Aunt Emily hadn't fully shut the drawer. I pushed it closed but realized that it had been pulled off its track. Yanking it open to realign it, I noticed the envelope Aunt Emily slipped into the drawer. In bold letters, it was addressed to "Lady Margaret Savoy."

I grabbed the letter, my palms sweaty. The envelope had already been opened, which was not surprising. Yet, I wondered why Aunt Emily would hide it from me. It read:

Dear Margaret,

Please visit 12 Jermyn Street Office 6, for there, Father Time has been kind.

Love,

Dada

Dada? It couldn't be my father. For the fact it was addressed to me, I memorized the words on the letter and returned it to the drawer, closing it firmly. I needed to visit Jermyn Street and discover the truth. If my parents were truly murdered, then

I would be forced to accept that the Poisoner was real as well. At that moment a letter arrived from Miriam, inviting me to dinner in a few nights. It felt like a much-needed escape.

The grandfather clock chimed eleven o'clock. On the top of the steps to the first floor, distinctive knocks rang out through the foyer. I froze, the tips of my fingers tingling and my mouth suddenly dry. Breathe in and out.

I dashed down the stairs, my blue ready-made-dress scrunched in my clammy hands. On the second to last step, I looked up and saw Alexander watching me. His dark indigo-blue promenade suit flattered his golden-brown hair. My feet hit air as I miscalculated the location of the last step and I barely missed careening into Alexander. I straightened up and kept my eyes on my incriminating feet.

Wrapped in a warm embrace, a husky voice tickled my ears. "Well, darling, I didn't realize you'd be this excited to see me."

Aunt Bita planted two wet kisses on my cheeks as her myrrh fragrance mantled me. Beautifully adorned in a grey dress of cotton sateen, embroidered with clusters of lavender and trimmed with Irish point embroidery, Aunt Bita winked at me, looping her arm through mine. The overwhelming urge to sink into the floorboards commandeered my every thought.

"What is the meaning of this?" Aunt Emily's shrill voice bounced off the vaulted ceilings of the foyer. Her austere checked Cheviot dress came to a sudden halt around her ankles.

"Ah. Lady Wellmont." Aunt Bita floated toward my aunt, arms outstretched like a gracious queen.

My aunt stumbled over her words, executing a quick head nod. "Lady Ildwoors," Aunt Emily preened, "what an honor it is to have you in my humble home." She swept a hand over the clutter of useless trinkets ostentatiously crammed into every nook and cranny in a bizarre expression of refinement and respectability.

"Yes, dear. To the matter at hand, I am here to act as chaperone *again* for my nephew, Lord Alexander Rocque," Aunt

Bita cut off my aunt with aplomb, but Aunt Emily, who looked as though she might burst with glee, continued to speak.

"My dearest Rose never told me that Lord Alexander Rocque would be courting her. They danced marvelously together at the Westerly's. Indeed, he should talk to my lord husband. However, he does not arrive until tomorrow. As he is not here, I will grant my permission to such a prestigious character," Aunt Emily simpered, hands fluttering.

"Lady Wellmont. I believe you misunderstand me. We are here for Lady Margaret Savoy, your niece." Aunt Bita closed her hands together as if to end the discussion.

Aunt Emily's mouth flopped. "But, but... No, no. I cannot grant my permission."

Aunt Bita cocked her head, just like Alexander often did. "Why ever not? You did, in fact, just give your permission for your own daughter."

"Well. I-I. Margaret is different." Aunt Emily fixed me with a dark glare, filled with malice.

"Different, say you?" Aunt Bita enunciated in shocked tones. "Have you raised her in poor taste?"

"Well, no, of course not. We raised her with the best of Christian charity," Aunt Emily defended with indignation.

"Then, is it my battle-decorated nephew? Who comes from one of the most powerful old families in our Majesty's kingdom?" Aunt Bita whipped around, her back to my aunt. She gave me a brief smile, her eyes alight with mischief.

"Oh no, my Lady Ildwoors, no. We hold your family in the highest esteem." Aunt Emily clasped her hands together and inched toward Aunt Bita.

Aunt Bita turned around unsettling Aunt Emily, who swayed to a stop. "Then there should be no problem. You can give your permission for this—courtship?" Aunt Bita smiled, like a cat that had caught the mouse.

Alexander put my hand in the crook of his arm, as we waited. Him, filled with confidence, while I had none.

"I see as you say," Aunt Emily gritted out, "my butler will

see you out if you'll excuse me." Aunt Emily walked mechanically from the room, wringing her hands and muttering under her breath. Alexander watched her with suspicion and anger darkening his visage.

"If you're ready, m'dear?" Alexander patted my hand, and we walked out of the house. Aunt Bita held onto his other arm.

"She's livid, Alexander," I whispered, gripping his arm.

"Don't worry. It's taken care of now. She cannot do anything." Alexander patted my hand again. "Please, Margaret, trust me," he beseeched me, amber eyes molten.

I nodded, hoping I wouldn't regret it.

Once the landau pulled away, Aunt Bita slapped Alexander on the shoulder with her fan.

"Aunt Bita!" Alexander rubbed his arm and leaned in toward me.

"You ruined my fun. I wanted her to believe it was her idea." Aunt Bita leaned back, nose in the air.

"It was taking too long." Alexander folded his arms across his chest. I fell back against the seat as the Landau moved forward, the tension stretching across my shoulders forced away.

"My dear boy, you still need to learn patience." Aunt Bita wagged her finger at Alexander, the ostrich feather in her hat bouncing.

"Well, we accomplished the goal, did we not?" Alexander smiled down at me, and I smiled back uncomfortably. Vomit inched up my throat. The Wellmonts would kill me when this was all said and done.

"Diplomacy. Diplomacy. Diplomacy, Alexander." Aunt Bita shook her head. At this point Alexander ignored her, turning to me with a furrowed brow.

"Margaret are you all right?" Alexander pulled my hands into his, forcing me to face him.

"I-I'm. They're going to kill me, Alexander," I blurted out in a whisper, only he could hear. I wrenched my hand from his and covered my mouth. Why did I say that aloud?

"The Poisoner will not get you, Margaret," Alexander

whispered back.

He jumped to the wrong conclusion. I plucked at a loose thread on my gloves, feeling that just as their cleanliness covered my bruises, his gentleness and soft affection could be nothing but subterfuge. I had to believe that, for anything else would mean venturing into the unknown.

The distant implications held by the almost spectral Poisoner hardly compared to the immediate pain Aunt Emily could inflict at any moment. I must deal with them later, or rather ignore them again *later.*

Alexander rubbed circles on my palm with his thumb, and I wrenched it from his grasp, not because it bothered me but rather because it didn't. Something which happened to be more confusing than the former.

At Aunt Bita's house, Alexander hopped down and offered me his hand, but as he did, the carriage lurched forward, and we lost contact. I looked over and saw Aunt Bita speaking with the coachman.

She turned around in her seat and gave a little wave to Alexander. "We'll return soon, darling."

He watched us leave, his arms hanging uselessly at his side, and a dumbfounded look on his face.

Once Aunt Bita's townhouse left our sight, she turned to me. She contemplated me, not only taking in my appearance but also searching, for what I did not know.

Aunt Bita leaned back against the seat and took out her fan. "Tell me about yourself, Margaret?"

I watched the mesmerizing flicks of her ivory fan, carved with a delicate scene of courtiers set amongst trees and flowers. Her eyes followed my gaze. "It's a *zhe shan*, a folding fan from China. In the art of fan making only the Chinese and French remain equal victors."

"You've traveled, quite a lot?" I asked, already knowing the answer.

"The Rocques are quite a well-traveled lot," Aunt Bita fanned herself. "In '82, Alexander was stationed in the harbor of Alexandria during the bombardment. He's been in the Navy since he was thirteen."

"That's much too young," I blurted out. "The family must have missed him terribly." I covered my mouth with my hands, embarrassed by my spew of sentiment.

"His mother, Eleanor, never would have let him go." Aunt Bita shook her head. "He was sent to the Navy just a year after her passing."

"I'm sorry for your loss." A new image of Alexander forced its way into my head and I threw a curtain in front of it.

"Thank you, dear." Aunt Bita grabbed my hand, smiling. "You are quite adept at avoiding, little darling. Perfect for a diplomat's wife, you know."

I blushed and tilted my head in concession. "What is there to learn?"

"I'd like to know how you feel about the situation." Aunt Bita folded her fan and held it on her lap.

No one had ever asked me something like that before and it took me off guard. My sentiments rarely made a difference or were even brought into the conversation.

A lie formed on the tip of my tongue, but the soft look emanating from Aunt Bita's eyes pushed me to speak truthfully, "Confused and honestly overwhelmed."

Overwhelmed by Alexander, overwhelmed by the truth, and overwhelmed by the lies.

Aunt Bita leaned forward and grabbed my hands in hers. "If nothing else, little darling, know you can trust my nephew."

I began to speak, wanting to contest as politely as possible, but Aunt Bita interrupted me.

"You bring out something in Alexander that I haven't seen since his mother passed." She held my gaze for a long time.

I remained motionless, her words filling my mind and sparking a thousand questions. The logical side of me dismissed her words—how could I change him when I barely had any control over my own life. No doubt he saw me as a means to an end, nothing more. I shook my head in an effort to persuade myself that the thought didn't make me sad.

She turned to the coachman. "Smith, please return home."

Aunt Bita and I entered the parlor, this time French in décor, after we surrendered our outerwear to the butler. Alexander stood upon our arrival.

"I hope you had a nice ride." Alexander's eyes narrowed on Aunt Bita as he guided us to our seats.

"Oh, if gentlemen must have their clubs, then ladies must have their secrets." Aunt Bita winked at me as she sat down across from us. She straightened her skirts and elegantly rested her hands on her knees. Silent minutes passed, as she and Alexander entered a battle of sorts, played out in their gazes. Aunt Bita stood and we followed. "I am dying for a nap. If you'll excuse me, darlings."

"Thank you for your help, Aunt Bita."

"You're welcome, Margaret. If you ever need anything don't hesitate to ask." She kissed both of my cheeks.

Standing on her tiptoes, she whispered something into Alexander's ear, before she kissed both of his cheeks as well. She gave us a little wave, her gaze once more going back and forth between us.

Once Aunt Bita left, I directed my attention toward Alexander. "I found a letter this morning addressed to me, in my uncle's study. I don't know if it's of any importance. It was from someone called 'Dada.'"

"Truly?" Alexander asked, his focus wrenched from whatever thoughts had previously clouded his mind. They must have been dark for they created a deep line of worry across his forehead.

"Yes. I memorized its contents, so no one would miss it. Do you have a piece of paper?" I asked.

Alexander nodded and gave me his pocket notebook and stubby pencil. I wrote down the address: *Please visit 12 Jermyn Street Office 6, for there, Father Time has been kind.*

A map of London materialized in my mind. I remembered that Uncle Matthew always sent for items from the area during the last time I was in London, especially from Paxton and Whitfield, a cheese shop. Other than that, the streets were lined with cigar shops, hatters, and tailor shops.

"This address looks familiar. I believe it's your grandfather's office. I saw it on one of his legal documents. Perhaps, it was from him, another letter?"

I frowned considering that the letters had seemed quite different from each other in form and signature, but I had to be wrong. "I suppose he must have sent it before he died. When shall we go?"

Alexander looked up from the piece of paper. "In a few days, I want to make sure it's safe. Also, now that we are... or will be known to be together, there is a consequence. We are easier to follow."

"It could not happen so quickly?" I scrunched my brows together.

"You'd be surprised." Alexander offered a half-smile.

"Disguises?" I asked bubbling with excitement. I had just finished reading Wilkie Collins's *The Moonstone.* I imagined myself as Rachel, the heiress to the missing Indian diamond inherited from my uncle, a corrupt army officer who served in India. Except we weren't trying to find a diamond but trying to, perhaps, save my life.

Alexander interrupted my thoughts, "Yes, someone so common in London no one would notice us."

I looked up from under my bonnet, "Who?"

"Servants, shop girls, waiters, and the like," Alexander leaned back against the settee, his arms spread over the top. "We can explore London without anyone knowing the better."

CHAPTER SIXTEEN

M.

"What's the time?" I asked Alexander.

He pulled out a pearl-encrusted gold pocket-watch. "It's three o'clock now."

"You'll keep your watch hidden?" I closed my hand over it. We'd spent the day wandering the streets of London, Alexander speaking to informants and then relaying the information to me. We asked questions of costermongers, who sold wares near my grandfather's townhouse, to no avail.

Alexander snapped the watch closed. "Yes, of course. This isn't my first excursion out of my ivory tower."

"I'm sorry I didn't mean it like that," I apologized, but I realized that maybe I did mean it like that.

Silence reigned as London homes passed by in a grey whirl, as we went from district to district in our hired Hackney. On the streets, old rag women bought used clothing, and small children clung to their mamas' skirts. Workmen dressed in loose shirts carried tins filled with their lunches, and starched police officers strolled through the alleys. We halted as other carriages and riders crowded around us, blocking the narrowed section of the street until it became a bottleneck.

Out of the window, a scrappy boy, of maybe twelve years, ran through the stands of a marketplace down an alley to the side where the Hackney waited in traffic. He was disproportioned with the long arms, short legs, and a thin torso, standard in most children. Dark soot smudged his face in dark contrast to the fairness of his skin. Equally sooty and ripped clothing, two inches too short on his wrists and ankles, covered his lanky form.

He snuck behind a hat seller's stall. When the Hackney lurched forward, I lost sight of the child. I righted myself, but the boy was gone.

A memory snuck up the back of my neck and crawled into my ear. I grasped my hands together as the memory broke through the alcoves of my mind. I wish I had forgotten.

***

London
Fall of 1871

Grey, only grey, as my vision adjusted to my Aunt's parlor. Shuttered windows filtered in a hazy light and the room smelt of ash. The couch, no longer salmon pink silk, but a deep blue velvet, rose above me. I could barely peek over it, even standing on my tiptoes. I pulled against the puff sleeves of my white dress. Mama always bought me dresses that fit, not ones that left red marks on my upper arms, no matter how I pulled at the tight sleeves. Aunt Emily must have forgotten that I grew this year. I scrunched my nose, remembering the boxes of dresses that arrived for Rose yesterday.

A loud, gruff voice pulled me from my thoughts, and I jumped down behind the couch. My ears took in the brusque sounds, but I could not make out the words. I peeked over the couch. There before me was the biggest man I had ever seen. He looked like an African, and he must have been one, for I had never seen someone with skin so dark. I cowered behind the couch, once more. Uncle Matthew said, "They were savages." Whatever, "savages," meant, he called me that too sometimes. I peeked my head up again and noticed his bucket full of strange tools. Maybe, they're for tribal cannibalism, I thought. I looked at them carefully, expecting to find them dripping with blood. The African yelled at the fireplace, his face marked with rage. Peeking over again, I realized that his skin wasn't black, but layered with soot.

Watching a giant yelling at a chimney caused giggles to climb up my chest, the only bit of entertainment I'd had since Rose got her fingers stuck in the toy she stole from me two weeks ago. My

Dada called the toy, "Chinese handcuffs," and brought them all the way back from a place called China. The toy trapped both of Rose's pointer fingers in its woven grasp, mere minutes after she had commandeered it. In the end, the toy was cut in half and I was punished for my "cruel prank."

A yelp stopped my giggles. I snuck around the couch toward the man, careful to stay out of his sight. Sometimes if I squeezed my eyes tight enough, I turned invisible. I looked up inside the chimney and saw a tiny boy, much smaller than me, covered head to toe in black soot. Clear paths trailed down his face, dripping off in black tears.

The giant yelled at the boy, "I'll light a fire under yor feet if you don't hurry up." The man poked the boy repeatedly with a metal needle. Little droplets of blood fell to the floor, only to be covered by the ashes.

I watched as the giant set a match ablaze and threw it on the kindling. My heart pounded in my chest, and my hands tingled. I looked around the room, desperately searching for someone, anyone that could do something. I took the fire poker next to the fireplace. It fell heavily into my hands, clunking to the floor. The giant turned to look at me, the whites of his eyes growing. I jumped up and swung the poker as hard as I could into the giant's forehead.

He crumpled to the floor, and I stared at him for a moment, before running to the fire. I put it out with quick taps of my foot and pulled the little boy from the chimney. I dragged him by his matchstick arm and ran out of the house. I didn't know where to go or what to do. I ran away from the house, as far as I could. I imagined hellhounds from my father's stories chasing after me, for surely, I had just met Hades. On the corner, stood a police officer and I feared that he would stop me.

"You there." The officer stepped in front of me and bent down to look at me.

***

The Hackney stopped again, and I tapped on the ceiling with Alexander's walking stick. Urgency flooded my veins as the memory slipped away. The driver opened the door. "I would like to stop here."

He gave me a funny look but handed me down. Alexander followed behind me. I needed fresh air. I needed to see the boy.

The driver doffed his hat. "Aye miss, that would be no Barney Rubble. Be quick about it, 'ave a look out for thieves. They don't mind nickin' from a girl. I 'eard last week of a thief takin' a blowen's flag from her nutty arm. Keep your man in sight," he said warily in a thick East End London accent.

I nodded, not exactly sure what the last thing he said meant. Alexander paid the man and followed behind me. In the crowded square, I saw the boy wrapped into a hug by a plump woman who kissed the top of his head.

The sight left the boy from my memory as dead as he'd been six years ago, buried in a pauper's grave. A child chimney sweep forced to work for the Wellmont's, who only paid ten pounds for breaking the law. If the abuse from the master sweep hadn't killed him first, the smoke would have.

A swell of embarrassment stretched through my hands and to the tips of my toes at my belief that this boy was one and the same. He was one of the lucky children living in the East End, especially after the recession. Many of the servants in the household had been affected, and even Uncle Matthew's investments plummeted.

Yet, the horrifying image of my childhood, erased by time until my return to the city, stuck with me. In Somerset, I had watched the residents of the countryside exit the mills looking like wounded soldiers, dismembered, bedraggled, and despondent. I'd all but forgotten my brief encounter with the horrors of the city. As a child, Aunt Emily and Uncle Matthew often threatened to send me to the workhouse if I didn't behave. Only by the grace of God they didn't. I had nightmares for years about being sold into relative slavery or a pauper apprenticeship. I went months without speaking, for fear of inciting their wrath. Perhaps, it had worked.

My vision blurred before me. I must have swayed on my feet for suddenly Alexander stood behind me.

"Margaret?"

"I'm fine." I cleared my throat. "I think I need something to eat."

"We'll go over there."

Across the street, a small café, ensconced in a row of well-worn brownstones with sagging roofs, stood crooked. The red brick building with a navy-blue glass paneled door greeted us with a green metal sign that hung above the door engraved with the word "Trident" in gold paint.

Inside the café, a plump woman swathed in a red cotton calico came to greet us with a broad smile. She had large brown eyes, which crinkled around the edges as if she had spent most of her life smiling. A halo of frizzy brown hair curled around her broad forehead and soft cheeks from beneath a piece of yellowed lace. For some reason, the woman looked oddly familiar. Yet, my memories had already tricked me once that day—London was a big city after all.

"What's your name lamb?" she asked me with a smile and a small furrow between her thin brows. Her voice, a rough, yet soft sound washed over me in dulcet tones of familiarity. The heavy Irish burr hummed as it sank into my ears, as though trying to get at my brain for recognition.

"Margaret." My head swam and I gripped the table.

"Could you please bring us cream tea?" Alexander asked the woman.

"Of course, sir. Lamb, that be all?" The woman patted my back causing me to jump, I nodded smiling self-consciously.

The woman came back with the scones, clotted-cream, strawberry jam, and a teapot along with two chipped cups, which she set on the well-used table. Alexander handed her a nine-pence. The woman looked back at us once more before disappearing. A chill slithered down my spine, less like the scales of a snake and more like the soft brush of a cat's tail against the skin.

The scone sat uncomfortably in the pit of my stomach and I tried to wash it down with the black tea. At least, I didn't faint.

"Margaret, please tell me what's going on?" Alexander leaned in toward me resting his chin on his hand.

I took a calming breath and sipped my tea, hoping my tears wouldn't spill. I could never tell Alexander the truth.

The Wellmonts beat me fiercely that night and I could not leave bed for a week, nor see out of my left eye. They sent me back to Bristol the next day. I felt as if I died with every bump we hit on the road. I ate bread and gruel for that month, but in some ways, it was the happiest month of my life. For the first time, I had helped someone, even if I could never help myself. That hope shattered against hard marble steps like a delicate china vase when I learned of the boy's death.

We didn't search more that day.

***

When I returned home, I found a piece of paper shoved haphazardly under my door. I picked it up and unfolded it.

In an elegant hand it read:

Stop before it's too late.

-The Crimson Crown Society

I crumpled it into my pocket. It had to be Rose. When we were children she'd slide notes under my door from an organization she called, "The Poor Relation Collection Agency." I'd lost a good sum of money, candy, and toys fearing that if I didn't make payments I'd be thrown on the streets. It had to be Rose. I opened the door to my room, but not before looking over my shoulder once, or maybe, twice.

CHAPTER SEVENTEEN

A.

After yesterday, I wondered again if I should involve Margaret. The immense sadness that had escaped from her eyes, made me wish I could take it all away. Pain sadly wasn't like that. It had killed my mother. At one time, it had threatened to kill me.

"You look comfortable," Margaret said, flushing red. The sadness from yesterday only just tinged her brows.

"You know, I am. It's like being in the Navy again. At least when we get far out to sea. We can wear white tunics and brown trousers. The lighter the clothing the faster it dries, and it was always so bloody hot." I forgot Margaret wasn't a sailor. Not that she looked anything like one, she just made me comfortable. "Excuse my language. Otherwise, we wear our undress uniforms. We do, however, wear our epaulets on all occasions. It's not like the clothes in London."

She smiled at me for a second, before shaking her head and looking away. "Where to first?"

"First..." I paused, pulling a pistol from a hidden compartment in the carriage, "I need to teach you to use one of these."

I handed her the pistol, and Margaret took it gingerly as if it were a snake.

"The trigger is thinner than I imagined," she whispered.

"It's not loaded." I took the pistol from her again. "See, the chamber is empty." Margaret looked at the empty slots as I handed it back to her.

The silver barrel gleamed in the light juxtaposed to the grip of the gun, a dark walnut. On one side of the barrel, it read in capital letters, "Holland & Holland 98 New Bond St London."

"It's a Webley Kaufman Double-Action Revolver. For your use, I'll purchase you a Derringer or British Bull Dog revolver. They're smaller and more suited for self-defense."

"I don't think I could ever fire one." She warily handed the revolver back to me, holding it by the tips of her fingers.

"Even so, I'd like you to know how to." I placed the revolver back into its hidden compartment.

"Where are we going?"

"Syon Park in Isleworth, we have use of the grounds, as they are closer to London than any of my family's residences."

"But..." Her nose scrunched.

"I have everything arranged."

Syon House rose before us in three stories of fawn-colored Bath stone. In the distance, past the house, I could just see the glass dome of the Great Conservatory. The sun sparkled off the glass, and I imagined I could see palm trees swaying against the top. Behind the house, the river Thames bisected between the property and the Royal Botanical Gardens.

The carriage turned away from the house, down a dirt lane into the woodlands and stopped in a field. The coachman set down a medium sized chest and then bowed to us, returning to his seat on top of the carriage and drove back up the dirt lane. I picked up the chest and indicated for Margaret to follow me. We walked further into the field until the lane all but disappeared from sight. I placed the chest on the ground, my jacket's sleeves were both a tad short and too tight on my arms.

In green velvet laid a revolver like the one in the carriage, surrounded by some tools for maintenance and a small wooden case labeled "ammunition."

"Margaret, come closer." I waved her over, but she stood as far away as possible. I sighed loudly, "You're perfectly safe."

Margaret reluctantly moved forward until she was looking over my shoulder.

"This is also a Webley revolver," I showed it to her. "I'm going to show you how to load the cartridges." I handed her the small wooden case. "Please, hold this."

Opening the case, I pulled out a golden-colored cartridge. "First, half-cock the revolver, that's the first click. Then, release the gate. Last," I pointed to the empty slots in the cylinder, "these are called chambers. In this revolver there are six chambers, fill each of them, but the first, with a cartridge by sliding it in, as so." I showed her, rotating the cylinder.

Margaret inched away again.

"A bullet won't leave the barrel until you put down the hammer completely." I pushed down a latch on top of the revolver. "To fire the gun, you need to pull the trigger." I looked back at her. She looked delicate with her arms wrapped around her frame. "I'd cover your ears, at least this first time."

She put her hands over her ears, and I nodded and pulled the trigger. The blast reverberated through the clearing, sending some birds flying from the trees. Margaret's face went ashen.

Carefully I walked up to her. "Now, I'd like you to try."

"Must I?" she asked.

"It's for your safety."

Margaret mulled it over, chewing her bottom lip. "All right."

I guided Margaret through loading the single cartridge. "We'll leave the hammer down on the unloaded chamber, as a safety measure." I then stood behind her. "Hold it with your hand as high on the grip as possible, your thumb should be exerting pressure inwards." I adjusted her hands upward.

Nothing but professionalism.

"Your pointer finger will be on the trigger, but for now keep it outside of the trigger guard, and your thumb will point toward the muzzle. The rest of your fingers should clasp the grip." I adjusted her stance. "Stand with your feet shoulder-width apart. Use your left hand to support your right, by securing it around the grip, as well. Extend your arms straight out in front of you, but don't lock your elbows. Bring the revolver up to eye level and check to make sure no one is down range."

She nodded, her hands trembling slightly as she stared down the barrel to the empty field.

"Are you all right?" I asked. Perhaps, I had pushed her too fast.

She nodded in response and breathed heavily.

"Push down the hammer one last time. You will hear the second click." The click sounded, and I continued, "Once you pull the trigger you will feel a recoil, keep a firm grip and stance. You don't want to incur a black eye. Whenever you are ready." I stood back.

She took a deep breath, once more looking down the barrel of the gun. She pulled the trigger. The sound blasted, ringing in my ears. Margaret's body jolted back. She readjusted her stance as the last remnants of the blast disappeared from both the clearing and her body.

"Excellent work. You have more strength than I expected, better than some cadets." A flush of pride infused me.

Her arms remained in their locked position, and she seemed to stare unseeingly down the field.

"Would you like to try again?"

With that, her arms fell heavy to her side, as she vigorously shook her head. "No."

"As you wish." I took the revolver from her and walked back to the chest. With practiced ease, I took out some tools and began to clean the revolver. "If someone is coming at you with one of these, shoot them in the pelvis. They will not be able to pursue you, and it might not kill them. It slows them down faster, in some cases than shooting them directly in the heart. I could recommend aiming at their feet or kneecaps, but for an inexperienced marksman that would be quite difficult. Otherwise, always shoot for the center, which is a large and steadier target."

"Oh." She flushed again.

"If you don't have a weapon and you are fighting a male assailant." I paused and returned the revolver to the chest. "Excuse my crudeness, kick them in their prodigious engine," I bit back a grimace, "if you understand my meaning?"

"You mean their masculine bits?" She nodded, with a barely hidden smile.

"Poking someone's eyes can demobilize them quickly."

Margaret squeezed her eyes shut briefly and nodded. "I understand."

I patted her on the back. Why'd I do that? She's a lady. I stared at my offending appendage.

"Then we're ready to leave. I'll purchase you a derringer, as soon as I can find the time. The best thing you can do in a situation, like the ones I have described, is to run in a zigzag pattern. Find a place to hide or a public space with law officials. My hope was that you'll never have to use anything I've taught you today."

CHAPTER EIGHTEEN

A.

Around noon, on a street corner, I noticed a man watching Margaret and me. He looked familiar. Before I could see his face, he turned and walked away.

We walked through the alleys, the costermongers accosting us to sell their excellent array of goods: from hot eels, sheep's trotters, and pickled whelks to cough-drops, second-hand musical instruments, and live birds. They swarmed the streets with their carts, wearing Kingsman neckerchiefs tied around their necks and scuffling with the police hourly.

I bought us food, thrusting it at Margaret and asking her what she liked. I was afraid she'd be faint again. My father might have let my mother wither away, but I wouldn't allow Margaret to. Keeping our heads down we made it to a park where we sat down on a bench.

"Tell me about your parents," I started in a quiet whisper as I handed her some fried sheep's trotters.

Other pairs strolled around us, most on their afternoon break if they were lucky enough to have one. Children ran through mud puddles pulling little wooden animals with wheels attached to strings behind them, unaccompanied by adults. A gang of boys with flinty eyes prowled the edge of the park, watching pockets.

"They passed when I was six," she began slowly, scrunching her nose. "If they were in love, I wish my mother had stopped him, my father I mean."

"Stopped him from what?"

"Gambling his life away." She twisted her hands together.

"Gambling our lives away."

"I don't believe he gambled." She looked at me with disbelief and I knew I needed to prove myself. Make something right in her world. "I haven't been able to prove it yet, but if your father was killed by, let's called him Paul here."

I looked around, giving an especially ferocious look to one of the pickpocket boys.

"Money was involved, and it wasn't because your father lacked it, but because he had it in spades. I believe you have a missing inheritance and that the Poisoner could still be searching for it."

"No. Surely you've heard *them* snigger at every soiree?" She squinted her eyes at me.

"Yes. But they're wrong. The infamy of your father's downfall would be a perfect ruse to hide an inheritance."

"I would be on the streets, but for my aunt and uncle, as they so kindly remind me," she spat out. "There's no money."

"That would go against Paul's known motives and methods."

"Then, maybe this isn't the..." she paused, "Paul after all. Perhaps, my parents died as the officials said and as my family said," she gritted out, sitting up straight on the bench.

"Your family has already lied to you before and not all of your family believes they died naturally."

Margaret gave my words some thought. "On the chance you are correct, what do we need to do?"

"I'd like to find your father's former solicitor and speak with him. I'll also continue to go through the crate of papers your grandfather gave me. In addition, I need you to, in blatant terms, act as a spy in your house." I pulled out a notebook and jotted down some notes.

She nodded her head in response.

"Is there anything else you can remember about your parents or any connections I could use?" My leg bounced as I looked around at the crowd with tense shoulders.

"I had a nanny, or nursemaid her name was Lou—L, something. I don't remember her much, though. I mean, I don't really know anything. It was so long ago," her voice cracked on the last syllable.

The sadness returned. Would I be able to help her?

"I'll look into that. She could be a suspect."

Margaret glared at me. At least the sadness was gone. "She is nothing more than a sweet old lady. She made me a lamb toy with her own two hands, gave me warm milk tea every night before bed and always sang me lullabies." She folded her arms across my chest. "She's innocent."

"If you say so." I didn't look up from my notes.

"I do say so." Margaret glared at me again. "You cannot possibly be right about everything."

I laughed. "Of course not, m'dear, but neither are you. At least allow me my due diligence."

Her lips thinned.

"I have a meeting planned with your grandfather's solicitors, but I won't be able to speak with them until after the reading of the will. I am hoping it will confirm my suspicions." I needed to prove it to Margaret and then my father.

"And if it doesn't?" she asked.

"Then we'll reconvene on this topic."

***

Again, I found myself in my father's study. A stack of correspondence sat on a silver tray, threatening to lean like the Tower of Pisa. He looked over his golden spectacles at me.

"I hope you have an update?" he asked.

"Of sorts. If the Poisoner is a man of business, then his interest in Lady Margaret must also be related to such things." I waited for my father to respond but he said nothing. "I believe if her parents were murdered that it would be over money or a business alliance gone wrong."

A tick pounded in my father's jaw and I involuntarily took a step back. "Did I not make myself clear before?"

I expelled a breath through my nose. "What if you're wrong? Everything I've pieced together indicates that conclusion. There's no other reason the Poisoner would continue to pursue Lady Margaret unless he hadn't gotten what he wanted the first time."

My father stood, both of his hands planted on the table. "Then you are looking in the wrong direction. I won't tell you again, boy."

A tense moment ticked by and neither of us spoke. My father finished his brandy and I moved to refill it—an old habit that indicated the end of our argument. Yet, I knew I was onto something.

"As you say then. I would like to see the correspondence then between the lady and the Poisoner." I handed him the glass of brandy. "I am sure the C.I.D. has no continued use for it."

"Oh, I am afraid they quite lost the letters. You know the systems of bureaucracy don't quite run like they used to."

My father cracked his knuckles.

He spoke again, "And remember, the girl is our best bait."

CHAPTER NINETEEN

M.

To me, it seemed my grandfather's office remained our last hope for uncovering my past. We walked to the busy square surrounded by tall brick offices and businesses. The scent of burning coal clung to the air as it escaped the chimneys of the shops along the stone road.

"Allow me to look around first to be sure we'll be safe. The C.I.D. cleared the area earlier." Alexander ordered me a pineapple shaped ice at a café and paid the waiter. "I'll be back shortly."

Minutes passed, followed by ten, and then thirty. My ice had long been eaten. I took what must have been the hundredth peek around the square but still didn't see Alexander. How long did he expect me to wait? Patience had never found a place on my list of virtues, I followed Alexander's path.

Walking into a lobby of sorts, I did not see Alexander anywhere. I sat down in a chair—waiting. Behind a desk sat an old man and behind him a set of keys, which seemed to taunt me. I stood and walked toward the man.

"Pardon me, sir. I am Lady Margaret Savoy, and I am looking for office six of this building. Could you help me?" I asked. The man looked up at me squinting before putting on the ugliest gold spectacles in all of London and giving me a cheery smile.

"I was told I would be expecting you," he said.

"You were?" I asked.

"Yes, Mr. Claxton's agent, Mr. Manda, contacted me. One moment," he said missing my stunned expression, as he looked on his ring of keys. "Ah, here it is." He handed me the key. "It's at the end of the hall to the right. I'm surprised you weren't given your own. I could have sworn some of Mr. Claxton's solicitors came in, just yesterday, and took a key."

"Thank you, sir." I backed away and headed down the hall. I fully remembered this office, but not for its good memories of visiting my grandfather here with my nanny or mama. It had been the place where I had seen my father die.

At the end of the hall, I found the door to office six ajar. Why would he give me a key, if the door was already unlocked? The floor creaked inside the room along with a soft rustle of papers. My heart rate quickened. To my right, a broomstick beckoned me—a choice weapon. I snuck into the room and swung the broom blindly and heard an oomph as I made impact.

"Damn and blast." Alexander hunched over, grabbing his midsection.

"Alexander." I ran to him. "I thought you were a thief or a scoundrel or a murderer."

"And, you came at me with a broom?" Alexander looked up at me from his hunched over position, his voice slightly breathless. "What would that have done? If you thought there were any of those types of characters in here, I hope you would have the sense to run in the other direction."

"It worked. Look at you." I crossed my arms.

"Because I don't wish to harm you." Alexander straightened. "You have quite a swing, though." He rubbed his belly. "I taught you to use a derringer because a broom will never do."

"I am sorry, Number Three." I patted his hard stomach, before wrenching my hand away. My mind filled with heated thoughts.

"Don't concern yourself." Alexander shook his head. "I'd rather you come in swinging than come in with no means of defense, no matter how useless a broom would be."

For the first time, I looked around the room. Papers scattered the floor, like lost kites which had crashed to the ground. Every drawer had been opened and rummaged through. Yet, other than that, barely a thing had changed since I was here ten years ago.

It reminded me of my father's office. I could see my father sitting behind the desk piled high with disorganized papers, spectacles on the tip of his nose. My mother, or the nanny, would often bring me to visit him. He always had time for me, opening his arms so I could sit on his lap. He would ask me about my day and allow me to read any book I wished. The memories I had of his kindness and love had been stirred in the past few days. Yet, I still had hardly any faith in the visions, which could be ripped away at a moment's notice.

"Did you do this?" I asked Alexander, to distract myself from the loss that I had never fully accepted.

"No. It was like this when I arrived. Whoever did it was looking for something specific, all the valuables are still here, and the door doesn't show signs of forced entry. I am not sure if they found what they were looking for."

"The man at the front desk said that he had given a key to one of my grandfather's solicitors. Maybe, one of the Poisoner's men got the key first."

"Or, the Poisoner was here himself," Alexander murmured. I shuddered at the thought of being in the same space as the monster. "What were they looking for?" Alexander looked around the room like a lord surveying his land.

"They may have been in a hurry and missed something." I shrugged my shoulders. "We could begin by looking through the papers.

"There must be hundreds," Alexander rubbed the nape of his neck, "but, I see no other way."

A few hours later, we had rummaged through countless carefully illustrated field journals from places as far reaching as China, maps of India, and legal documents shipped from every continent. Alexander found an embarrassing poem by six-year-old me, I entitled "Why Dada is like a Turtle." That was not something I wished for him to see ever again.

We continued to leaf through the drawers a second time, but I had begun to think that they'd found what they wanted. What was it?

"I don't see anything." My shoulders drooped with disappointment, as I walked toward my grandfather's desk where Alexander stooped. My foot caught, and I fell. I smacked into the floor, and a cloud of dust greeted me. The broom rolled innocently behind me.

"The broom has quite a punch, doesn't it?" Alexander said with a smirk as he held out his hand.

"You, Number Three, are no gentleman," I said as I turned my head away still flat on my stomach.

My gaze shifted directly toward the large grandfather clock in the room. I remembered the words in my grandfather's letter. "Father Time has been kind," I whispered aloud.

Beneath the cobwebs underneath the clock, something caught my eye. Something, which had been affixed to the bottom of the clock. Ignoring his hand, I scooted on my stomach and reached for it. My hand revolted as it encountered the grime that coated the floorboards.

Please, no spiders or mice.

My hand inched forward until I felt a smooth surface different from the clock. I pushed on it, and a small flat wooden box fell out. My hand returned covered with dust and cobwebs. Revulsion crawled down my spine. Alexander gave me his hand, and I wiped my dusty one over him as he lifted me up.

"Thank you, Queen of the Dust," Alexander groaned, wiping his own hand on his trousers. "What did you find?"

"This." I showed him the box. "My grandfather told me in his letter that, 'Father Time has been kind.' I believe by that he meant to look at the clock."

Alexander came to look over my shoulder as I opened the box. On the top of the pile, I found a postcard shipped from Bombay, India from the "David Sassoon & Co." Beneath that, I found a small piece of paper yellowed with age. As I looked through the box, I found a worn photograph.

"It's me," I gasped.

"You?" Alexander leaned forward over my shoulder. I was dressed in a white gown and looked to be maybe a year old.

I wore a white crocheted cap, and both of my parents stood around me. It was the only likeness of them I had ever seen. On the back of the card, I found: *zeved habit – August 30*th*, 1864 – Psalm 128.*

"You looked like King Henry the Eighth, quite plump and stern," Alexander chuckled behind me.

"That is not complimentary," I responded, I folded my arms as I looked up at him.

"What I mean is you were a kingly baby. You still have the same adorable nose." Alexander tweaked my nose. "You even looked stubborn then."

I laughed sarcastically. "How can you tell?"

Alexander looked at me with complete innocence. "I can see it in your eyes."

Shaking my head, I showed Alexander the back side of the photograph. "What does this mean?"

"I am not sure." He shook his head. "I'll ask around."

He picked up the yellowed document turning it over. "It's coded." Alexander's eyes lit with excitement. Looking over Alexander's shoulder, which meant standing on my tiptoes, I got my first full glimpse of the document.

((ββ)(δα)(αβ)(αγ))
(εδ) ((γε)(δγ)(αε)(αε)(γβ)(δα)) ((γζ)(αδ))
((αζ)(γζ)(αα)(βα)(γζ)(αα)(γβ)(δβ))
((ββ)(αα)(γζ)(αβ)(γγ)(δγ)(γζ))

The bizarre pairing and organization of Greek numerals, confused both of us the longer we stared, proving our eyes alone could not make sense of the document.

"Do you think this was what they were looking for?"

"It's possible," Alexander replied, his brow furrowed. "Maybe there's a key to the code around here somewhere."

We searched fruitlessly for a key, before giving up. Alexander returned the documents to the box. I kept the photograph in my reticule. At the front desk, we found the old man dozing.

"Sir, we have your key," I whispered, and the man snorted awake.

"Back so soon?" he asked even though it had been several hours.

"Thank you for your kindness. Here is the address you may send the key to. Have a nice evening." I handed him the paper with Miriam's address. The old man nodded, before a look of shock spread across his ruddy face.

"Evening already? Good gracious, the missus will be wondering where I've wandered off to," the old man said as we exited the building.

A thought had been dwelling in the pit of my heart. Something Alexander had brought up at my first London ball—using me to draw out the Poisoner.

I directed the question toward Alexander. "Are you using me as bait?"

For a moment, it seemed like he didn't hear me.

"No," he spat out, too quickly for comfort, and changed the subject. "I'll go to the Office for Property Development to see if there is anything under your father's name that could be your inheritance. I am also in contact with a footman who held past employment with your father. He might know about your nanny or even something about your parents. Her name began with an 'L' correct?"

"Yes, that is correct." Something, or rather someone, shifted in my periphery.

Alexander followed my gaze with wariness painting his face. "Is everything all right?"

I shook my head as if to clear it, my gaze focusing on Alexander as if surprised to find him still there. "Yes. I just felt a chill or something of the sort."

Alexander must not have believed me because he quickly ushered me toward the lights from a restaurant across the street.

"We need to set another time to meet." My gaze roved the square, but I didn't see the man again.

"My schedule can work around yours." Alexander's shoulders tensed as we paused to cross the road.

"I cannot meet tomorrow night. I am promised to a

friend's dinner party," I responded.

"That's perfect I'll go with you," Alexander said, the words taking a moment to enter my ears and slam into my brain.

"What? No. No." I shook my head, calamitous scenarios forming.

He nodded empathetically, smiling. "Margaret, think about it. It's perfect. One, you already were going, two, a place to 'see and be seen,' and three you get to see this devilishly handsome man again in a mere twenty-four hours." He wagged his brows at me, and I couldn't help the smile that crossed my lips.

I worked it out in my mind, conceding to the first two points. "Fine, but you must promise to behave yourself."

"Me? I am always on my best behavior," he responded with a dramatic front.

"Alexander?" I raised my eyebrows, willing my smile into a frown.

"Yes, I promise, Margaret." He put his hand to his heart. "Let's hail a Hackney. I don't want to be in this neighborhood after dark."

CHAPTER TWENTY

A.

Pall Mall, London

On any other day, the intellectual and calm atmosphere of my favorite club, The Athenaeum, would be have been a god-send. However, a source had led me to the infamous neoclassical building rather than a wish for expensive liquor and stimulating conversation. An informant had indicated that the Poisoner or one of his men might make an appearance at the club.

It stood three stories high in ivory white elegance, its vestibule hidden by four sets of paired columns. From the Doric portico above the entrance, the golden statue of the *Pallas Athene* stared down at me. Her intelligent and elegant visage reminded me of Margaret—even there she seemed to haunt me. A flowing tunic draped over her form, a helmet fit her head, with one hand to the side as if in question, and the other holding a spear pointing toward the sky she guarded the club from all who entered. Above her, an intricate frieze surrounded the building. Frozen in time, the marble figures on a dark blue setting depicted decadent scenes of Grecian life.

In the lobby hall, a coffered ceiling arched over the foyer. Six golden, inverted pendant lights hung from the ceiling next to six Corinthian columns, leading toward the grand staircase. To the left of the lobby was a coffee room and to the right, a morning and dining room, along with a writing room. At the top of the staircase was the marble statue of *The Belvedere Apollo.*

Up the grand staircase and into the card room, I looked though the hazy smoke, the low murmuring that buzzed through the room, and the sound of clinking glass, I spotted

Baron Wellmont. He wore an ugly waist-coat over his rotund belly and his side-burns were cut in a fashion ten years too old. He played a game of Faro with two gentlemen.

I sat down next to a window blocked by curtains and did my best to become nothing but a living statue. The Baron, a man of girth rather than height, ran a hand through his receding hairline. His nose, bulbous and bright red gave him away as a man who cared far too much for a drink.

"Damn and blast again, doctor," Baron Wellmont protested.

From around the table, the other men congratulated the doctor, whose face I couldn't see, with light clicks of their glasses. The scene was like many taking place around the room. Yet, something seemed off.

"Nothing, but luck old chap," the man called the doctor responded to Baron Wellmont, his voice did not sound familiar. "How about another game?"

"Perchance, I shouldn't." The Baron hiccuped, even as his eyes remained glued to the cards.

"What's one more game?" Sir William Gordon-Cummings cajoled the Baron with a firm pat on the back. His own feet seemed to twitch nervously.

"I'd wager Bertie would want you to play," Viscount Waverly leaned heavily against the table, as he laughed at his own drunken joke.

Baron Wellmont was silent for a moment as he contemplated the cards. He looked down and back up at his companions, back and forth. With a loud guffaw, he broke the silence and soon the whole table joined him in laughter. "I cannot upset the Heir Apparent, now can I?" the Baron larked and took a large swig of his brandy.

The game continued, and luck was not on the Baron's side. He lost two more turns before he was almost too drunk to stand. The doctor helped the Baron from the card room, and I listened to their conversation as they passed.

"How much do I owe you this time?" the Baron whispered

loudly into the doctor's ear.

The doctor smiled, though it was an uncomfortable smile. "You owe me quite a bit, but I have not called you up on your notes. Do not let it worry you."

A wide grin crossed the Baron's ruddy face, as he gracelessly embraced the doctor. "You're a good friend to have."

They left my sight as they walked down the steps. I stood, coming out of hiding and I was immediately asked to join a table to play a game of Baccarat.

"I don't think I'm much suited for gaming tonight. If you'll excuse me, gentlemen." I nodded my head distractedly to my companions and turned from the game. The stringent smell of sweet alcohol burned my nose.

I took the steps two at a time, but by the time I reached the front of the club, they were gone.

CHAPTER TWENTY-ONE

M.

"Mullons! Mullons, where is my jewelry?" Aunt Emily's screech echoed through the hallway, followed by the sound of a resounding slap.

The morning had barely begun. As I finished sorting a basket of freshly darned socks, I noticed Aunt Emily's jewelry box lying at the foot of my bed. *Damn.* I picked the box up. Aunt Emily shrieked again. The box slipped from my fingers, crashing to the floor. I wiped my damp hands on my skirts and picked up the box again. Taking the steps two-at-a-time to Aunt Emily's room, I held the box tightly to my breast.

"Aunt. Aunt! I have your jewelry box, right here. You told me to clean it, then to bring it to you today." I entered the room to see Miss Mullons holding her cheek and Aunt Emily towering over her. For such a tiny woman, her hand could become as lethal as a whip.

Aunt Emily turned her rage-filled eyes toward me and saw the box in my outstretched hands. She sent Mullons to take it from me.

"You. You, hateful wench. Giving me a fright," Aunt Emily shrieked at me grabbing my ear painfully and pushing me to my knees. A sharp burn spread across my cheek, Aunt Emily's cold hand indenting my face with a decisive smack. "You had the honor of cleaning my jewelry and should be punctual in its return. The next time this occurs your punishment will be more severe. Now, what do you have to say for your actions?"

Aunt Emily stared down at me, my left cheek flamed red. I looked down, so she could not see my watering eyes smarting from the pain. There was no use reminding her I had done nothing wrong.

"It will not happen again. I am sorry."

"Fine. See that it doesn't. You are dismissed." Aunt Emily waved me away as I got to my feet and exited the room. My knees ached from their contact with the wood floor.

I wiped my tears away and headed to my room to press a cold rag to my face. When I reached my room, something flashed beneath my bed. I crawled down to investigate, and lifted a golden, round, pendant locket, two-inches wide, from beneath the bed. In the center of the locket, clock arms covered a clock-like gear, for design rather than functionality.

A woman, dressed in a white nightgown appeared in my mind's eye. Long dark hair fell to her waist. I looked up at her, as though I were smaller than she by several feet. Her face blurred to my sight, and on her neck, the necklace.

I flipped the locket over in my hand. Feeling along the sides, I found a button and it popped open. An engraving on the inside of the locket read, "Time stopped when I first saw you, but with you, it is infinite." Below that, I found a six-pointed star. It looked like the Star of David. Why a symbol from Judaism? On the front side, I found one more engraving: "To E. Love R."

The memory formed fully in my mind. My mother. This locket was hers from my father. How did it get here? I remembered dropping Aunt Emily's jewelry box. Could she have had it? I didn't remember cleaning it, after all. My anger flared at the thought of my aunt possessing one of the few pieces of my history. No one had ever mentioned it before.

Out the window, I could see the sun had dropped significantly, filling the room with different shadows. Setting the locket on my bed, I searched my chest for a dress to wear to Miriam's. The primrose-colored surah, evening gown, passed down to me from Rose after she spilled sherry on it, seemed like the suitable choice.

Seven lace flounces trimmed the round skirt, made dancing-length. On the first flounce, artfully hidden by a loop of primrose-colored satin ribbon in the shape of a rose, the red stain would be undetectable. Sitting down in front of the mirror above my lowboy I arranged my hair, pulling most of it up toward the crown of my head into a large bun. The back strands I arranged into long ringlets.

After swinging on my cloak, I went downstairs, preferring to meet Alexander outside to avoid any unpleasantness. A carriage pulled to the front of the townhouse, and Alexander jumped out. He raised his brows upon noticing me waiting for him and helped me into the carriage. The weather suddenly shifted, as it often did in London, blasting me with a gust of wind. The originally sunny cheerful spring day thwarted by dreary evening clouds and punctuated by a creeping wind-chill reduced any cheerful mood my escape had created.

Cold entrenched my blood. I rubbed my arms vigorously, pulling my cloak more tightly around my torso. The wind, blocked by the thick wood frame of the carriage, howled against the windows.

"Alexander, I-I, f-found something," I whispered through chattering teeth.

"Here give me your cloak, and take my Chesterfield," Alexander said offering me his long coat. I slipped my cloak from my shoulders and took the coat from his outstretched hand.

Alexander examined my threadbare cloak, his brow furrowed. "This is useless, you'll catch a sudden chill. I'll remedy this immediately."

"It's fine," I responded snatching back my cloak, feeling its rough, worn velvet slide across my fingers as its familiar scent tickled my nose—lavender and horse.

"But, it's threadbare." Alexander's frown deepened.

I shivered. "My lord, you will not remedy the situation. We are business partners and nothing more." The words, even though they were true, felt wrong to say. Business partners.

"They treat you little better than a servant." He waved his arms in exasperation. "I've seen your hands, and no lady should have hands like yours. It's not right. I promised myself, and I would like to promise you, that I will never let them do that to you again."

I sighed at him. In a way, he was so innocent.

"Oh, please don't. Do not feel sorry for me. Don't pity me. Don't tell me that my hands, my hair, my emotions, my anything should be different because I'm a 'lady.' That's a piss-poor argument. I have never been a lady but don't feel sorry for me, because some of the nicest people I've met are not ladies. If I really were a servant, you would not look twice at how they treat me. Arguing that it is not right because I am a lady, makes my humanity of less value than a title. That is not me, nor is it right."

"I-I," Alexander, for the first time, stumbled for words. "My apologies."

"It's fine, Number Three." I had become too comfortable around Alexander. He didn't need to know this part of me.

I sighed and leaned back into his coat, finally heating up from his left-over body heat. His scent enveloped me, soft and subtle, not overdone like many men on the ballroom dance floor.

Alexander leaned forward, breaking the silence, "What did you find?"

I pulled the locket from my reticule. Alexander held out his palm and I dropped the necklace into his hand, watching the cord snake into his palm.

"Where did you find it?" Alexander turned it over in his hand.

"Perhaps in a hidden compartment in my aunt's jewelry box, it fell out this afternoon by accident." I held my hand out, and Alexander returned it. I popped open the locket and gave it back to Alexander. "It was my mother's. Do you see the engraving?"

"Yes. It's strange your aunt wouldn't give this to you." Alexander rubbed his chin, weighing the locket in his hand.

"Cruel you mean and thus not strange," I shook my head.

"I don't believe the locket has been opened in a long time." I watched Alexander's long fingers intertwine with the cord of the locket. Half-heartedly he returned it to me. "Do you think it has any significance?" I asked.

"I will make some inquiries." Alexander ran his hand through his hair. "In the end, it might be nothing more than a gesture of affection."

"Terribly romantic, but terribly useless," I sighed, not thinking of my parents but of Alexander.

CHAPTER TWENTY-TWO

A.

A butler opened the door. He seemed to know Margaret and fondly beckoned her inside. He looked at me expectantly, and I handed him my calling card. He nodded and allowed me to follow Margaret. I dressed in my best, a ten-inch midnight top hat, pristine white waistcoat, starched white wing collar, and formal black suit. All of which seemed to suffocate me, but I hoped would impress Margaret, though I didn't *think* about it at the time.

"Lady Margaret, my lord." The Butler took our outerwear. "The ladies of the house are entertaining in the parlor. If you'll follow me?" The Butler led us down the hallway.

"Thank you, Richards." Margaret smiled at the man.

On the table in the foyer, I noticed an impressive stack of calling cards. On the top, reserved for the most esteemed of callers, the Earl of Ainsworth had left a card with the corner folded over, indicating he had brought it himself. Interesting, considering Ainsworth's family abhorred anyone with new money, especially if they were Jews.

Margaret looked around the room with wide eyes, and I wondered if she'd ever been there before. Pictures of familial tranquility covered the walls of the hallway to the left of the staircase from almost floor to ceiling.

Margaret leaned into me, whispering, "Miss Jacobs once told me there are over 900 paintings throughout the house."

She blushed, looking down. "Most are innocent in nature, but she said that in her parents' room there is a painting of a nude woman. She said it was by Dante Gabriel Rossetti," she dropped off, once more looking around the room, blushing.

A diverse group of people filled the room with conversation. I looked about, cataloging the people in attendance, several bankers, scientists, scholars, and merchants. I trailed behind Margaret as we weaved through the crowd. She stopped abruptly, her gaze locked on something in the glass case. I bent around her to see a narrow silver box, about six inches high and engraved with Hebrew letters.

"Margaret, I wasn't sure if you would come." A petite blonde woman embraced Margaret in a hug. A bright light infused Margaret's face as she moved to respond.

The blonde woman spoke again, exuding energy, "Whatever has your attention so captured?" Her sky-blue dress fluttered around her ankles as she came to a full stop.

"This," Margaret pointed to the box behind the glass. "What is it?"

"Oh, that's a Tzedakah Box. Mama received it from the Ladies' Conjoint Visiting Committee." The woman leaned in next to Margaret, their mannerisms similar. "Her pet project, you know, she finally got Papa and the men on the Jewish Board of Guardians to approve of the idea."

"What is it used for?" Margaret asked, her eyes lit up.

A little *moue* of confusion formed on the blonde woman's lips. "This one is mostly decorative, but they represent the moral obligation to give to charity. Why do you ask?"

"For a moment, it looked familiar." Margaret tilted her head, her brows furrowed.

"Oh, you must have seen one when we went to the Synagogue in Birmingham." The blonde woman smiled.

"Of course, that must be it." Margaret smiled back forcefully, but her gaze wandered to the box.

The woman turned to me, her eyes rounding as she bit her lip. Margaret looked at me, as well, as if surprised I was there.

"Miriam, I hope you don't mind, especially on short notice, but I brought a guest. Allow me to introduce Lord Alexander Rocque. Lord Alexander Rocque, this is Miss Jacobs, my dearest friend."

I doffed my hat to Miss Jacobs. "A pleasure to meet you, Miss Jacobs." I found myself relieved to see Margaret had an ally, if not I'd worry about her when I finally left. *You'll worry no matter what, you fool.*

"Indeed. I am pleased to make your acquaintance, my lord." Miriam executed a quick curtsey, her gaze on Margaret the whole time. "If you'll excuse us, my lord. I must talk to my esteemed friend, for a moment, alone."

"As you wish, my ladies." I left them, even though my curiosity beckoned me to stay. One of my acquaintances called me from across the room. My gaze remained with Margaret.

CHAPTER TWENTY-THREE

M.

Miriam pulled me out of the room and into the hallway. "Margaret, I have never seen you look at a man the way you looked at that one."

"I don't look at Alexander any differently than any other man of my acquaintance." I folded my arms over my chest. I paused when I realized I used Alexander's Christian name.

"Alexander, is it?" Miriam smiled, head tilted, and eyebrows raised. I'd entrapped myself.

"Yes," I replied through gritted teeth. "May he stay?"

"If you tell me what he means to you." Miriam tapped her foot, a grave expression on her face.

"I don't know yet." I bit my lip in partial truth. A veil of shyness tightened around my chest. "He's courting me, officially, and the Wellmonts are not pleased."

"Margaret. Am I not your dearest friend? I know when you're lying to me."

I grumbled, bouncing on my feet. "Fine." I whispered into her ear so that no one else could hear, "For the sake of my safety, please tell anyone who asks that Lord Alexander is courting me. He is a gentleman, and I am not in danger from him, but from outside forces he is doing his utmost to protect me from."

"What does that mean? Will you be all right? Why are you in danger?" Miriam's eyes scoured the room, fixing upon Alexander.

A footman knocked into us before I could respond. Miriam and I gave each other a look, our eyes narrowed at his retreating back.

"I believe that was our footman, John Kiles. I'll have Mr. Richards speak with him," Miriam clucked impatiently.

"It was probably an accident."

"Nevertheless," Miriam shook her head, "he did not apologize. Now tell me everything."

"It has to do with my parents, but that is all I can tell you." I hedged, guilt consuming me.

"I've been in London for three weeks, Margaret. I hadn't heard from you once until you accepted my invitation." Miriam's wounded eyes cut through me. Miriam and I visited each other every week in Bristol since we were seven years old. Three weeks was a long time.

"I..."

"Has this man kidnapped you or forced you in any way?" Miriam grabbed my shoulders stretching on her tiptoes to look directly into my eyes.

"What? No. Lord Alexander is a man of good character. I promise. This is not a gothic novel." I half-laughed, wondering if perchance gothic heroines didn't know they were in gothic novels. "I am sorry for not visiting sooner."

Miriam scanned my face, and I could tell she did not fully believe me. "If that is all you can tell me so be it. But, I'll reserve my judgement on liking him." Miriam hugged me. "I'm happy you're here."

Somebody cleared his throat. "Lady Margaret?" I looked over my shoulder and met Alexander's eyes.

Miriam looked up at him, her eyes narrowed with suspicion before she smoothed her facial expression. "It's your lucky night Lord Alexander, Mr. Gibbins had to leave early. We have a seat open for you at the table."

Alexander raised his brows. "How generous, thank you."

From the parlor, Mr. Richards announced dinner. Mere seconds later the hallway filled with the rest of Miriam's guests.

"Oh, Margaret, darling!" Mrs. Jacobs' singsong voice, tinged with a German accent, saturated the hallway. Blonde-grey hair in an elegant coif, Miriam's mother embodied the epitome of beauty. She sashayed over to me giving me a kiss on each cheek. "It has been so long, dear. The season has been ever so lovely to us." I watched as Miriam's face went ashen.

Miriam stopped her mother from speaking further, a strained smile upon her lips. "Mother, let me introduce you to Lord Alexander Rocque, Margaret's guest, who will be joining us."

Mrs. Jacobs held out her elegant hand, and Alexander kissed it. "A pleasure to have you attend our little party, my lord."

"Thank you for making accommodations on such short notice." Alexander straightened.

Mrs. Jacobs nodded her head humbly as she looped her arm through mine, guiding me to the dining room, "I do hope you'll escort my daughter, my lord." I looked back over my shoulder and saw Alexander and Miriam sizing each other up.

At the table, the other guests stood near their chairs. Miriam came in behind me and scanned the table. "Lord Alexander Rocque? Pardon me for not knowing, but what is your rank?"

"I prefer to be ranked by my earned position, I am a First Lieutenant in the Royal Navy," Alexander responded dryly.

Miriam looked over at me. "Let me rearrange the table."

Alexander put up a hand to stop her. "It is no matter, Miss Jacobs. I will sit where you put me."

"I insist, my lord."

Miriam moved her guests around so that Alexander was at his proper place next to her mother. I, on the other hand, sat on Miriam's right hand at the opposite end of the table. She had separated us on purpose rather than by rank.

With our first course in front of us, I leaned toward Miriam and whispered, "I know what you did."

She smiled impishly in return. "I want you all to myself. I don't need dimples distracting you."

The tension flowed from my shoulders. At least she was

not angry with me. With a sigh of relief, I put Miriam on the sticky wicket. “Why is the Earl of Ainsworth leaving his calling card for you?” I waggled my brows suggestively. Miriam’s eyes lit up, as I had never seen them do before. I thoroughly distracted her. Whatever, questions she had about my own odd behavior evaporated like water on a balmy day.

Miriam blushed prettily and went on to tell me of the wonderfulness of Marcley Chambers, Earl of Ainsworth, and how he was the most perfect gentleman in all of London. “Mama and Papa want me to marry a mensch—a good Jewish man. But if a Rothschild can marry a Christian, why can’t I?” She glared across the table at her unaware mother, before laughing.

After dinner, we sat on the settee side-by-side, drinking tea from delicate white china cups detailed with golden spirals. I filled myself with treacle tart and clotted cream. Being with my dearest friend felt like returning home. I promised myself that when the investigation ended, I would spend more time with Miriam before she married the Earl of Ainsworth or even more likely use him to explore the world. Her parents rarely could do much to stop her, once her mind was made up. I hoped he was worthy of her innocent kindness. Many times, in our childhood I had to protect Miriam from those who wished to use her generous disposition for their own gain.

A knot of unsaid words formed in my stomach and I found the urge to bring the new knowledge of my past to our conversation, but something held me back. All the while, I watched Alexander circle the room out of the corner of my eye. He always could naturally integrate himself into any situation that arose. I wish I had that skillset.

After dessert, Miriam made me promise her I wouldn’t let more than a week go by before seeing her next. In the carriage with Alexander, a semblance of my past reality fit back into place. I didn’t realize how much I missed Miriam, or how comforting her familiar life would be, especially when mine had been completely up-ended.

“I’m glad someone else is protective of you,” Alexander

broke the silence.

"Yes, she is." I paused, "Who else is protective of me?"

"I am," Alexander looked straight into my eyes, "which is why I want to ask you to stay close to home for the next few days."

"Why?" I asked, immediately suspicious.

"I'll be away," Alexander responded.

"Where will you be?" Every thought I'd had of danger, dumped like a slop bucket onto the street, hit me with sudden dread.

"I've found your father's solicitor in Camden Town."

"Isn't Camden Town dangerous?" I asked, my breath escaping me.

"No, only unfashionable," Alexander laughed. "I shouldn't be gone more than three days, and I'll be back by four days at most. Promise me, you'll stay close to home?"

"Yes, I promise."

CHAPTER TWENTY-FOUR

A.

Camden Town, London

Passing the Regent's Canal, whose banks were lined with factories and warehouses, the crowded mixed suburb reminded me of more impulsive moments in my youth. On the rare occasion that I came home from the Navy, I would go to bawdy shows at the Old Bedford Music hall with my mates. We had all been a little bit in love with the star of Nelly Power. The hairs on the back of my neck twitched and I turned around to face the crowd. Yet, I didn't even see the expected pickpocket just the never-ending stream of working bodies. Three-story yellow brick houses lined the wide roads—they had become even more soot-stained and run down since I had last visited.

Shaking my shoulders, I carried on. It had taken me several weeks to learn the executor of Viscount Stanhild's will was alive. His fortunes must have plummeted for him to now be residing in a working-class neighborhood. I doubted that any member of the peerage would choose an executer without the highest qualifications. I stopped in front of a plain brick building with a sign that read "Law Office of Robert Winfield."

Up the stairs to the third floor, I knocked on a peeling door. An old man with snow white hair, sagging jowls, and wary brown eyes opened it. With only his head peeking out from the room, he looked down the dark hallway.

"Who are you?" he asked his voice barely above a hissed

whisper.

"Lord Alexander Rocque, I contacted you a week ago. You're Mr. Winfield, correct?"

He looked me up and down, but his gaze didn't stay on me for long. It moved back down the hallway and stayed in that direction. His dry lips stretched over his teeth in something of a grimace.

"Is everything all right?"

Mr. Winfield nodded. "Come in, my lord."

Opening the door, Mr. Winfield allowed my entrance into the cramped room, scattered with papers, which smelt of leather polish and cheap whiskey. Mr. Winfield removed a stack of papers from a cracked leather chair with a sagging seat cushion.

"Please have a seat."

I sat down as Mr. Winfield moved aside the curtain covering the one window to look out on the street before he sat down.

"Mr. Winfield..."

"Lord Alexander..."

I waved, indicating that Mr. Winfield should continue. He composed himself, but for his shaking hands, and poured himself a snifter of whiskey. He offered me some, but I shook my head it was far too early to partake in libations.

"You've endangered me by coming here, my lord, but I am sure you know that. The Duke of Auden has little care for those he steps upon." Mr. Winfield wiped his chin with his stained shirt sleeve.

"How do you know my father?" I asked. My father had too many connections to this case. Each connection put down another nail, but I didn't know what it was building.

"Who doesn't know your father in this city?" Mr. Winfield snorted, setting down his glass with too much force. "He sent you here?"

"He didn't. I am investigating on behalf of Lady Margaret Savoy. Her late father was your client."

Mr. Winfield stilled. "The little girl?" He ran his hand through his stringy white hair.

"Young woman, now." My cheeks felt hot.

"The Duke didn't send you?" Mr. Winfield asked again, his voice shaking.

"No. Why does it matter?" I leaned forward, the creaking chair echoing my movements.

"He..." But before Mr. Winfield said anything further, he took me in with narrowed eyes. "Why is the young lady in need of your assistance?"

I didn't trust the man. His flinty eyes, attraction to booze, and his tremors did not instill me with any sort of confidence. However, I needed information.

"We believe her parents were murdered."

Shock did not mantel the man's shoulders. He rocked back in his seat and stared at the light amber liquid swirling in his glass. "Yes."

Every scrap of information I had been able to collect over the last month led me to the same conclusion, but I wondered why the solicitor so readily affirmed it. "Do you know who did it?"

The solicitor dragged his teeth along his lips, setting down his glass. "I think you would know, my lord—who commissioned their deaths that is."

"The Poisoner?" Something wasn't quite right, but I couldn't put my finger on it.

Mr. Winfield's eyes moved toward the door. "Something like that."

I could tell he wasn't telling me everything and I wondered how far I could push him to speak.

"Why would he be commissioned to kill them?" I leaned forward again as Mr. Winfield leaned back. His breath came out labored and he once again ran his hand through his hair.

"The inheritance. Her father spoke of a code," Mr. Winfield mumbled. He stood and began pacing the floor.

I remembered the coded document Margaret and I had found in her grandfather's office. Was it was something worth killing over—why? Now, I wished I hadn't handed it over to my father so easily. For a moment it had seemed like pride or something of the sort had flashed across his eyes.

***

"If you find the key, you can return to the Navy or any sort of life you'd like," my father said as he caressed the coded document found in Mr. Claxton's office. "I'll even give you the information you want about the Frenchman."

"Could the Poisoner have the key already?" I asked. "What does it mean?"

My father looked up for the first time with dark eyes. "It's not important what the code means, only that the Poisoner doesn't have it. It's mine. It was always mine."

His last words rang through my mind.

"May I remove Lady Margaret from the investigation?"

My father folded the code into his pocket, and for a moment it didn't appear as though he had heard me.

"No. No, we need her to bring out the Poisoner." He absent-mindedly played with the silver rings on his fingers. "You need to stop investigating her parents' deaths. I hear the whispers. They were natural nothing more or less."

"But..." Putting Margaret in danger was the last thing I wanted. I would have to be more careful in my investigation of her parents' deaths so that my father's associates couldn't track my movements. Why didn't he want me to investigate? The evidence should have persuaded him. What was I missing?

"Alexander." My father fixed me with his signature steely gaze. "It's the way of things, you'll understand someday. You need to leave, I—."

As I stood a man entered the room. He looked to be in his forties or fifties, with a rotund figure, a balding head and what hair he had spotted with grey. His impressive mustache met his sideburns on either side of his face. Wisps of black hair grew from his ears.

"Mr. Chater." My father nodded, coming to a stand and giving me a sharp look.

"Please call me Catchick." With his hands behind his back, he purveyed the maps along the walls. "I hope you've heard of my wish

to enter the Legislative Council in F.D. Sassoon's place."

As I shut the door, I remembered the postcard we had also found in Margaret's grandfather's office with the name—Sassoon. I dismissed it from my mind, a postcard from decades ago was unlikely to help me protect Margaret.

"Of course. I've also heard of your prowess with the Hong Kong Cricket Club," my father laughed.

***

My mind returned to the present conversation and left my father behind. Mr. Winfield looked at me with dark eyes, nursing his whiskey. He coughed loudly.

"Your mind seems occupied, my lord."

"My apologies, Mr. Winfield. Please continue. In our knowledge, Lady Margaret has no money of her own. It's well-known in society that her father gambled away his wealth." Though I believed none of what I said, I wanted Mr. Winfield's reaction.

"Gambled?" Mr. Winfield snorted. "The man was an academic, very astute with his money. I worked for his family for two generations, as did my father before me. Only *his* father gambled, Lord Richard saved the family estate."

"Then where is Lady Margaret's inheritance?" My back-molars ground together in frustration.

"She receives an annual sum, but the rest of the money is... I don't know. Lord Richard didn't trust anyone toward the end, probably for good reason."

"An annual sum?" I asked. It wasn't what Margaret or the gossips of the dance floor had told me.

"Yes, to her guardians for her care. It's quite a generous package."

My foot tapped as I put everything together. Margaret's aunt and uncle were stealing at least a piece of her inheritance and had lied about her financial security. But where was the rest of the inheritance and why was it hidden? More importantly, why was the Poisoner willing to kill for it?

Something crashed from the room next to us. Mr. Winfield's pacing stilled, and his fingers hovered at his lips.

"You need to leave, my lord." His voice dropped several octaves as his eyes darted around the room. "I'll contact Lady Margaret myself and give her information."

"How do I know you're telling the truth?"

"I owe it to her family," Mr. Winfield gritted out. "I won't tell you anything more. Leave, my lord."

The old man pushed me from the room and watched me until I made it down the stairs. At a pub on the corner, I grabbed a hot meal of pie and mash. I ignored the hum of voices around me and looked around the crowd wrapped in smoke. My mouth watered for the London jellied eel in parsley liquor sauce, yet it sat uncomfortably in the pit of my stomach. Not even the comforting taste of the mash dispelled my thoughts that something wasn't right, and worse, it had to do with my father. I'd be visiting Mr. Winfield again tomorrow, whether he liked it or not.

***

The next day I returned to Camden Town, hopeful that I'd secure the last nail in place. First, the stench of waste from the alley assaulted my senses. Second, the unnatural silence made the hairs on the back of my neck stand on end. Only pieces of litter that rolled along with the wind filled the empty streets, which had been crowded only yesterday. Down the street, on either side, people gathered and moved about their daily lives. On the opposite end of the street, a well-dressed man with blond hair, noticeable because of his lack of a hat, entered a carriage. The brownstone towered before me, and even in the windows, no movement could be detected.

I made my way toward Mr. Winfield's brownstone and up the cracked steps, my gaze flickering across the site for any sign of motion. My meeting with Mr. Winfield the day before had brought up more questions than answers. With any luck, the second visit would bring the answers I needed. The answers I needed to keep Margaret safe even from my own father, and perhaps myself.

The door stood ajar with a splintered door frame. I pulled out my pistol and gently pushed the door open further. As I made my move to enter, gruff voices and heavy tread stopped me. I backed down the steps and moved to the side of the alley, hidden from whoever exited the building.

"The chuffin' boss will be mad the solicitor didn't 'ave more information. He were worth less than the rats that swarm in this hell-fire-hole. Ten fingers and 'e barely squealed." One of the men walked down the steps, a smatter of blood marking his collar.

"He weren't much fun. But, there's plenty ter offer in this town," another man followed behind laughing. Both were dressed in roughshod clothing and worn leather boots. Yet, gleaming rings shone on their fingers, and one even possessed a gold tooth.

Damnit. Once they were out of my sight and down the street, I cautiously entered the brownstone. I cleared the first floor, the second, and then ran up to the third floor, taking two steps at a time. The silence and the smell of blood told me I was too late.

I took in the scene, the solicitor dead. Tied to a chair, bloodied and bruised. His apartment torn to shreds and the papers left floating through the air. Too late, I heard the creak of the floor. A fist swung at my face. Several times my knuckles found the other man's flesh. We watched each other panting. The other man, dressed as a day laborer, gave me a smirk. Something hit the back of my head extending pain through my spine.

The ground came up to meet me and as I blacked out I heard, "No we mustn't kill him, mates. The boss wants him alive for a little longer yet. The girl trusts him."

CHAPTER TWENTY-FIVE

M.

Uncle Matthew arrived a week later than expected and when he found out that Alexander was courting me, he thought to beat me. It would have been worse if Aunt Emily hadn't told him of Lady Ildwoors visit. I was not sure if she did it to protect me or to protect herself. I guessed the latter. In any case, it made me grateful I had the letter, for the many times I had seen the tick in Uncle Matthew's jaw and the clenching of his fist. His dark gaze followed my every move.

The energy of the townhouse, as ordinary as ever, prowled with an evil insistence along the familiar papered-walls, slinking beneath cherry wood floors, and wafting from the kitchen. It was the constant feeling of waking in the middle of the night to see a dark shape in the room looming, only to have the shape turn into a chair with the light. Everything that was once normal to me, or should have been normal, held a sinister intent. Had I always been tempting fate?

Everyone bided their time—my family, the Poisoner, and even Alexander.

I hadn't received another threatening note, which strengthened my first thoughts that it was Rose. She believed she had won so there would be no point in another letter. I hadn't seen Alexander for several days, and the family didn't know I was still seeing him.

Locked in my room for talking back to Uncle Matthew, I

decided to organize the contents of my reticule. I dumped my reticule out onto my bed, and I immediately noticed a piece of folded paper. The usual contents of my reticule would have been a small rose perfume bottle, which used to be my mother's, a tin of mints, a kerchief, and my coin purse if it didn't fit in my skirts. I opened the paper, and it read:

M.S.

I have information about R.S. that you need to know. Meet me at the row home 1334 next to the Trinity Café at your convenience.

Sincerely,

An Old Friend

The handwriting was not familiar, and I could not think of any old friends I had in London who wouldn't reveal their identity. Less likely was an old friend who could tell me anything about my father, Richard Savoy. Alexander's fourth day was arriving, meaning he would be back in town. I returned all the items to my reticule, including the note. I needed to go to Alexander's residence and exchange information. I could not wait a day more with all that I'd discovered, at least that's what I told myself.

***

Down Piccadilly along Green Park, women carried baskets ladened with fruit, merchants pushed carts filled with goods, and coffee-stall keepers peddled their products, as they made the daily journey from Fulham to Covent Garden. I stopped for a moment acquiring a cup of coffee and a two thin for a penny before plodding along once more, the early morning sun poking through the grey sky.

A short thirty-minute trek later, I arrived at Alexander's bachelor residence. Constables patrolled the street, stopping periodically to bang on the lower windows, awakening servants and waiting for the "All right!" before passing along. I wrapped my cloak tightly around myself and pulled up the hood, so no one would recognize me, not that many would. A lady should never knock on the door of a bachelor's residence. In any case, Rose did say I wasn't a lady.

A hastily dressed butler opened the door. He looked me once over, before saying, “No solicitations, especially of your kind.”

He moved to shut the door. I put out my arm to stop him. “My name is Lady Margaret Savoy. Lord Alexander Rocque will see me.”

The butler’s eyes widened, but he nodded opening the door. “I am only letting you in because his Lordship told me of your name. If you have pulled the cap over me...”

The minute both of my feet were in the foyer, he shut the door almost catching my cloak. “Thank you. Where is Lord Alexander Rocque?” I handed the butler my cloak, in my haste practically throwing it at him.

“He’s in the parlor,” the butler began, as I went the way he indicated. “My lady, wait. You cannot go in there.”

I opened the door to the parlor and saw the Butler's warning laid out before me. At once, my eyes widened as every piece of etiquette training told me to shut them. On the divan, lay Alexander, fast asleep, one arm falling off the side toward an empty tumbler. His hair fell around his face in soft wisps that fanned across his cheeks. A blanket covered him from the waist down, but from the waist up I could only stare at his exposed chest.

I’d never seen the like and realized I shouldn’t have seen it in the first place.

I backed away and put all my effort into the tips of my toes avoiding every creak in the unfamiliar floor. I moved to step back, but my heel fell back off the edge of the Persian rug. A hunting rug of course. I crashed to the floor. I froze. A groan and the rustling of fabric reached my ears. I searched wildly around the room for a hiding place, avoiding the divan as if my life depended on it. I felt like a flailing goose. Seeing nothing, I wrapped my knees in my arms and set my head upon them. Not my brightest idea.

Footsteps. The creaking of the floor. A soft hand on my shoulder. “Margaret, are you all right?”

I made the mistake of looking up and received a full view of man. Alexander wore a white button-up shirt, though he hadn't buttoned it yet, and trousers, thank the Lord. I stared at him, trying to formulate the proper response. Even Mrs. Florence Hartley, author of *The Ladies' Book of Etiquette, and Manual of Politeness* could not have helped me then. She never could really.

Alexander crouched down to my level, which did not help. "Margaret? What happened?"

The butler answered, "She came and knocked on the door this morning. I tried to keep her from coming in here, my lord, but..."

Alexander cut the Butler off, "Yes, thank you Hartridge. Please shut the door behind you." The door shut.

"Margaret?" Alexander crouched down to my level again, his hand on my forehead.

I shook my head, and squeaked, "Yes?"

Alexander made the executive decision and picked me up and set me on the still warm divan. He sat across from me in a wingback chair.

"Margaret, did they hurt you?" Alexander's hand clenched his knee.

"No. Dash my wig. This was a mistake." I picked up a pillow from the divan and hid my face in it, but even that smelt of him.

"Margaret, then what is it?" Alexander moved next to me on the divan.

My gaze wandered to a line of hair going... *No Margaret, no.* "I will not be able to tell you anything, until you, at least, button up your shirt." I peeked from over the pillow, before hiding again. "This is highly improper."

Alexander snatched the pillow from me. "Is that why you've been hiding?"

He dangled the pillow in front of me. "Yes. Give that back!" I reached for the pillow and pulled it from his grasp.

"Well, Margaret, I believe you deserve this for coming to

a bachelor's residence unannounced." The smile was evident in his voice.

"It was a stupid idea. Please, please, put on a shirt, Number Three," I pleaded through my pillow. Nothing reached my ears but the rustling of fabric.

"You can look now." Alexander laughed.

I peeked hesitantly from behind the pillow and saw that he was indeed suitably covered. I lowered the pillow while keeping it firmly clutched to my chest.

"M'dear, did you miss me so much that you could not have waited for a more reasonable hour?" Alexander leaned back in the chair, pushing back his hair. Dark circles gathered under his eyes, and a white cloth, speckled with red, covered his knuckles. He refilled his tumbler with amber liquid and drank it in one gulp.

CHAPTER TWENTY-SIX

M.

I swallowed. "What happened, Alexander?" I scooted down the divan, closer to him, and our knees touched.

"You know, I probably shouldn't tell you this, you're a lady and all." He refilled his tumbler, yet again. "The solicitor, he was dead--murdered. I found him tied to a chair, beaten to death. They broke every one of his fingers and then trashed the place. I had spoken with him the day before, and there he was--dead. I met with one of the ruffians and had to fight him off."

He gulped down the liquor again looking like he wanted to say more, instead, he went to refill his tumbler. I put out a hand to stop him, but he ignored me.

"It made me think how I was there, and you were here, and if anything happened, I would be too far away." He grabbed my fingers and brought them to his lips. "The thought of someone harming your delicate hands..." He kissed my fingertips.

"Alexander, you're drunk."

"I am, aren't I?" He sloppily tried to kiss me but missed my lips. The scent of whiskey reached my nose.

"Alexander. You're really drunk." I pushed at him, and he fell away from me but wrapped his arms around me.

"I'm sorry. I shouldn't have done that."

"I am not afraid of you, Number Three."

He drew me closer to him, whispering nothings into my ear. With his arms around me, he nodded off, his grip never slackening. I lay my head against his shoulder and closed my eyes. I hoped he would never hurt me.

***

"M'dear?" A soft voice reached for me in my dreams.

"Mmmhmm." I yawned, snuggling into the warmth.

"Margaret?" There it was again--the voice. I opened one eye and saw Alexander looking down at me.

I sat up on the divan, squinting around the room. "What time is it?"

"It's ten o'clock," Alexander answered. "Margaret, I was loathsome. Can you forgive me?" Alexander sat down next to me, sitting as far away as possible and creating proper distance.

"Yes, though I'd prefer if you kiss me when you're sober." I sat up, straightening my skirts, my cheeks heating. Alexander's also flared.

My palms sweated as I reconsidered our interaction, an overwhelming sense of embarrassment swamping me. Yet, a small piece of me wished to leap back to that moment where the rules of society matrons weren't ringing through my head.

"Thank you." Alexander stood. "Allow me to get dressed more appropriately, and I will return. I'll send some tea for you."

I nodded, distractedly as I pulled the pieces of myself back together. I feared he had kept something of me that I would never be ready to give. A housemaid came in with the tea service and then left me. A while later, Alexander returned fully dressed, hair wet and lips pale.

"You look cold." I poured him a cup of tea.

He quirked a smile at me and took the cup. "You never answered why you've graced me with your presence."

I grabbed my reticule and pulled it open. I slid out the card and handed it to Alexander. Silence reigned for a moment, Alexander's brows deeply furrowed, and his shoulders tense.

He set the card down on the table and looked at me, his gaze discernibly worried. "Mr. Winfield, your father's solicitor, told me you should be receiving an annual sum for your care from your father's estate. The remaining part of your inheritance was hidden by your father before his death. Perhaps that is the information this 'old friend' has?"

"But, I don't have any money of my own," I whispered. A chill shook my shoulders as I truly considered the solicitor's death and I wondered what end the Poisoner had in mind for me.

"Either the money has disappeared into thin air or your aunt and uncle have been stealing from you as long as you've lived with them," Alexander responded matter of factually.

I came to my feet. "No, that cannot be true. They have their own money. What use do they have for mine?" my voice cracked. Alexander made a reach for my hands, but I pulled away.

"It could have been Mr. Winfield," Alexander mollified me, but it was an empty thought. It was my aunt and uncle. I'd seen them skim profit for themselves in every financial interaction as if it were the most normal behavior. I simply assumed they did the same to me through my "free" labor. My throat constricted painfully. I wiped my hand by my eyes at the injustice of it all.

"I wish I never had to go back there," I whispered, rubbing at my eyes, once more. All those times they had made me feel guilty about wanting the tiniest thing from a bar of soap to a spool of thread. They were using my parents' money for themselves, while I lived as if I were worse than the dirt beneath their feet.

Alexander passed me an embroidered handkerchief with the initials E.E. I took it from him, as my eyes irritatingly teared up, no matter how much I dabbed at them. The only person who had seen me cry was Miriam, and that was after Rose burned my dollhouse when I was eleven. My mother had given it to me for my sixth Christmas, my last gift from my parents. Rose decided she wanted it. When I didn't give it to her, she set fire to it.

I returned the handkerchief to Alexander, but a warm look infused his face, and he closed my hand over it, "Keep it."

I nodded my thanks.

After I took a few breaths and rejected in my tears, I said, "Do you, do you, think that my family could be involved with the Poisoner too?"

Alexander pounded his fist into the wood table, causing me to jump. He took a deep breath, his nostrils flaring. "It is as I suspected." Alexander stood up and stalked back and forth across the floor.

"How are they involved? Why?" My hands trembled as I waded through countless memories in search of clues.

"I don't know, but we need to find out. Soon." Alexander looked to me, before pacing again. "I have reason to believe your uncle may be involved with Poisoner through gambling."

"What could Poisoner gain from gambling with my uncle? There are richer men. Doesn't the Poisoner have money?"

"Both are true. You must remember not everything is for a monetary gain. Power can be seized in many ways," Alexander paused, his eyes alighting with an idea he didn't impart to me.

"Blackmail?" I asked.

"Perhaps," Alexander nodded. "In any case, you need to be wary. Trust no one."

Not even you? I thought to myself, before dismissing the idea. I could trust Alexander. I had to. "They could also be victims of the Poisoner," I whispered, not ready to believe anything else.

Alexander watched me with guarded eyes, "Perhaps," he said again. He gave me no indication of what he truly believed.

"Why do you think the note asked to meet at the Trident Café?" I asked, changing the topic and following him with my gaze.

"We must have been followed," Alexander growled.

I clutched my skirt, rolling the fabric between my fingers.

"Do you know who the old friend might be?" Alexander asked.

"No, especially not one who would know about my father," I responded evenly, watching him cross the floor.

"Something is in motion, and I don't know what it is. We need to find out what this 'old friend' knows. Nevertheless, after what happened to Mr. Winfield, we need to tread carefully. I won't let anything happen to you."

"When? The writer of the note said at 'my convenience,' but I don't know when I received the letter or who slipped it to me. I was only in public as myself at Miss Jacobs' dinner party."

"If they really have information, or whatever they have, then they will wait." Alexander shoved his hand through his hair. "Give me until tomorrow to prepare our backup. I will not send us in blind."

I nodded, wrapping my arms around myself, sick to my stomach at the thought of returning to my house. Alexander closed in on me putting both hands on my cheeks, "Margaret, you're going to have to return, and not let them know anything is wrong."

At that moment, I wished Alexander could save me, but like every time in my life, I'd have to save myself.

CHAPTER TWENTY-SEVEN

M.

"I watched the house most of yesterday, and I only saw an old woman come and go." Alexander tapped his foot against the floor of the carriage.

I pulled my cloak resolutely around my shoulders, watching the townhouse disappear as we turned the corner. "We may visit then?"

"Yes," Alexander said, further words paused on his lips. "I only wish we had more time to be sure."

I avoided his eyes the whole ride. When I first left him, my mind hadn't fully absorbed the complications I had created for myself. I should never have gone to Alexander's residence alone. Alexander didn't want to marry me, he didn't even love me, and I had allowed him to take wife liberties.

The liberties only a girl of loose morals would give.

A mix of shame and compassion filled me as I faced my own culpability and the extensive list of admirable women who'd fallen before me. I wondered if the matrons, the judges, the Queen, and even God were right. Yet, even their verdict of my sins, whether real or reserved for the last judgement, didn't ring through my head like it usually did.

That scared me the most. The idea that I had completely given myself over to another person. A person who had the ability to ruin me and toss me out like I had little more value than the contents of a slop bucket. If things got out of hand, no one would believe my word. I had completely given myself over with no expectation, or hope, that he might return my affections.

I needed to protect myself and that meant pushing away Alexander.

Alexander watched me with hooded eyes, arms folded across his broad chest. "We must proceed with caution. Remember that, Margaret. Be aware of everything and if something seems wrong, even if you're not sure, tell me. I'll bring my pistol, but that will only get us so far if this turns out to be a ruse."

"I will." I bit the insides of my cheeks, nausea settling in the pit of my stomach.

Ruse--a word I was all too familiar with now. I quickly glanced toward Alexander, his dark gaze searched mine as though trying to extract information from me. They all wanted something from me. What did I want?

Alexander broke the silence as we neared our destination, "I've been thinking, maybe, you should stay in the carriage." He peeked out of the window at the small terraced house, located near the Trident Café. We pulled in on the opposite side of the street from the address, in case we needed a speedy escape.

"Absolutely not, Number Three. The note was for me. With your large stature and that fearsome expression upon your face, you will likely frighten away whoever wishes to speak with *me*."

I looked at him straight in the eye for the first time, an anger growing inside of me. He held my gaze, before looking away. I left the carriage without his assistance.

Alexander jumped down and immediately pushed me behind his tall frame, shielding me with his body. I breathed in his scent, and with his eyes forward it gave me a moment to soak him in. At any moment, this all would end. I wrenched my gaze away, shuttering any thoughts of a future--I wouldn't allow myself to be hurt.

We crossed the street, pushing our way through the crush of pedestrians, and keeping out of the way of the horses. The building was made of cheap red brick with cracked grey mortar.

Slightly warped with age, the wooden door stood as the gateway between questions and answers. After a moment of hesitation, I lifted my hand to knock on the door. Alexander did the same, we both stared at each other.

With deafening inelegance, we knocked on the door at the same time. The door creaked open, and a face popped out--she looked like the same woman who served us at the Trident Café. I wish I'd paid more attention.

"Is this the right place?"

"Ah, milady, come in, come in. Glad I am ye got me note. I did not expect your young man to be with ye. Maybe it was best if he waits outside," the woman said.

This time, however, her Irish brogue didn't tickle my memory as it did before.

"I will not be leaving." Alexander's mouth formed a straight line.

Her facial expression darkened momentarily before it broke into an excessively enthusiastic smile. "As ye wish."

She ushered us into a dark, cluttered hallway and then a sunny kitchen with a small table. She set us down at the small table and offered us tea, which we both politely accepted. I had been particularly grateful for the common courtesy on that chilly day. The woman set the teacups in front of us, before seating her plump, wholesome figure across from us. I took a sip of my tea, as did Alexander.

"Ye no remember me, do ye, dearie?" she questioned, as I shook my head. Alexander's knee brushed mine under the table, but I ignored it.

Alexander's tension exuded from his frame, yet as he looked around the room, his face showed only mild curiosity.

I looked again into her brown eyes. I took in her frizzy brown hair hidden under a white mobcap, peeking out in short bangs, her wide mouth, her plump cheeks covered in freckles. Again, I listened to her heavy brogue, my neck tensing at the sound.

My legs dangled off a woman's cushioned lap, as we sat in a rocking chair. She gently brushed my hair with a soft-bristle, silver brush. Smothered in a white nightgown, I listened as she softly sang some sort of cradlesong, "Hush ye, my bairnie. Bonny wee lammie. Sleep. Come and close the een heavy and wearie. Close are the wearie een rested ye are takin'. Sound be your sleepin' and bright be your wakin'."

But, it was not the woman who sat before me.

She looked quite like whoever they wanted me to remember. At my realization, slight differences appeared beyond her voice, the color of her hair was too light, the crinkles around her eyes were not quite deep enough, and her figure was more curvaceous than plump. I squeezed Alexander's knee under the table. He looked down into his cup of tea but otherwise, gave no other indication.

"I am sorry, ma'am, but I do not remember you." I shook my head in honesty. I knew who she wanted me to think she was--my nanny Louisa Kiles.

"I am your old nanny, Mrs. Kiles." She smiled at me with empty eyes, confirming my suspicions.

I never called my nanny, Mrs. Kiles. It was always Louisa. Working it through my head, I tried to find the best reaction to this bit of news--false news.

Alexander moved out ahead of me. "Why have you waited so long to contact Lady Margaret?" The fake Mrs. Kiles pursed her lips but smiled when she looked at me.

"Oh aye, lassie, even though ye were taken from me after your parents' deaths, God bless their souls, and your grand da's health issues," Louisa said while crossing herself, "I never did truly give ye up lamb. About a year past, me nephew was hired at your guardian's estate, as a footman, good John Kiles, a strong red-haired laddie. I asked me, boy, to check on ye to see if ye were treated well and kindly. I apologize, lamb, for havin' someone look in on ye, but I had to know. However, things were not as I expected, or what he-they, I mean your parents, hoped for ye. I had to find a way to contact ye, but as luck would have it, ye came into my café, pretty as a spring flower, ye were. I took me chance, and I slipped that little note into your bag." She spoke hastily, her eyes alighting at each new sentence that escaped her mouth as if proud of her creation.

I squeezed Alexander's knee again. Whoever she was, she did not know anything about me. If she did, she would know I knew every footman at the estate by name, and we had no John Kiles. Two, she didn't slip the note into my bag when I was at the Trident Café, as it could not have been there until after Miriam's party, meaning it must have been John...

My thoughts disappeared, and the room shook.

I blinked, but instead of helping, Mrs. Kiles doubled before me. I wanted to tell Alexander of my confusion but turned to see him slumped over in his chair.

The fake Mrs. Kiles stood her face emotionless.

"Margaret? Margaret?" She came up to me, holding my face painfully between her fingers, forcing me to look up at her.

Her face, grotesque in my vision, faded in and out.

"Margaret you're going to tell me what you know. Where is it, Margaret? Where is the money?" Her accent changed, sounding more East End by the minute.

I shook my head to clear it, but she held me still. Her touch, hot and clammy, branded my cheeks and her nails dug into my flesh.

"Don't shake your head at me. You'd much rather answer me, than him."

"Nu-nugh..." My tongue laid heavy on the bottom of my mouth.

"Shite." She released my face. My head fell to my chest. "I must have given you the heavier dose, and the giant, your dose. Shite." She went to the door she was sitting in front of and gave it three swift knocks.

At that moment, Alexander leaped from his chair and lunged across the table at her. He knocked her to the ground, hitting her on the head with the butt of his gun.

"Bloody hell." Alexander stood and rushed to me. He lightly slapped my face, bringing me to some awareness. "Margaret?" I squeezed my eyes shut, as buzzing filled my ears.

"Al-eeeh..." My tongue stopped functioning, this time stuck to the side of my mouth.

Alexander swung me over his shoulder. He secured me, and my arms dangled as the room spun around me.

The door crashed open.

Two men dressed as day laborers walked in, guns pointed at Alexander and me.

The world flipped.

Everything turned upside-down. I moved to grab my head, but I missed, instead, punching myself in the throat.

BANG. The first shot fired. Alexander's frame rocked back, but he stood his ground. In the same moment, another shot fired. BANG. Alexander dropped me to the floor behind the overturned table. My face slammed against the wood floor. It didn't hurt. I didn't feel anything. A bullet whizzed through the tabletop, leaving a splintered hole, inches above my prone figure. Another door crashed open. Two men dressed in black came to stand behind us.

"Lord Alexander Rocque." One of the men nodded. One last BANG. Silence.

My vision went black.

CHAPTER TWENTY-EIGHT

A.

She sat up abruptly, vomiting into a metal bucket, as I reached to rub her back. She couldn't have eaten much that morning, as mainly dry heaves wracked her body. I wiped the bile from around her mouth. She waved the bucket away and I took it to the kitchen.

"I apologize, my lady." The doctor, a long wiry man, with steel grey hair and wire-rimmed spectacles, watched her.

"What happened?" her voice rasped out.

"You were poisoned with opium, or in this case, laudanum, I believe." The doctor wiped her brow with a cold cloth. "I administered an emetic. You'll also have a rather large bruise on the side of your face, but you didn't fracture it."

I brought the doctor a cup of coffee, while he unnecessarily thanked me. He saved her.

"How are you feeling, Margaret?" I asked her.

"Like the River Thames, through Five Points, decided to leave my body," she groaned, resting her hand on her forehead.

She would be fine.

"In any case, my lady, I would have you drink this whole cup of coffee. It's known to do quite some good in cases such as these." The doctor handed her the cup. The coffee was pitch black, and Margaret made a face. "Yes, it is black coffee, no sugar or crème, for the strongest effect."

I watched her take small sips of the bitter brew. "How did I get opium poisoning?" she asked.

"It was in the tea we were served by Mrs. Kiles." I could not quite face her. I should have warned her not to eat or drink anything.

"No. No." Margaret shook her head, rubbing her temples. "That's not Mrs. Kiles, it's someone pretending to be."

That's why there was a body--a woman rather, who looked a bit too much like Mrs. Kiles. She must be the real Mrs. Kiles. My blood thrummed through my veins. I couldn't keep Margaret safe.

"Wait, you had the tea, too. I saw you. You were slumped over." Margaret took a sip of the coffee and grimaced.

"I pretended to drink it. Once I realized the effects it had on you, I imitated your symptoms, to see what the imposter's end game was. At that point, there wasn't any time to tell you not to drink it. If they wanted you dead, they would have tried already." My hand clenched at my side. "But, I should have told you not to drink anything anyway. I am sorry."

She watched me with sad eyes. "It is of no consequence. You did your best."

The doctor stood. "Now, my lord, may I look at your arm?"

Momentarily, I had forgotten my throbbing arm and my white shirtsleeve drenched in blood.

"What happened?" Margaret pulled herself up further, but I gently pushed her back down to rest.

"Margaret, I'm fine it's a graze, nothing more." I sat down for the doctor.

"You were shot," she protested, almost spilling her coffee.

"Yes." I could not help but laugh a little, as I took her coffee and moved it to the table. "I've had worse. It is you I am worried about."

"Either way, my lord, I would like to take a look." The doctor opened his black leather medical bag pulling out some scissors. "May I, my lord?" The doctor indicated toward my ruined sleeve, and I nodded.

Margaret weakly pushed herself up. She didn't flinch as

the doctor began to clean my wound with water. The sharp burn of alcohol hit my nose only after, it seared through my arm. I clenched my fist and let out a long hiss. Margaret's eyes widened with concern, and I did my best to smooth my expression.

"It looks as if you'll need a few stitches, my lord," the doctor said, and I nodded my consent. He stitched up the three-inch gash on my upper arm and then wrapped my wound with clean linen that spotted with blood.

The doctor returned his attention to Margaret. "Now young lady, you've had quite too much excitement, which is quite dangerous for a lady's delicate constitution. I want you on bed rest for the next two days. We don't want to have to call in a hysteria doctor. And don't forget to drink the coffee." The doctor put on his black bowler hat and nodded to me. "If that will be all, my lord?"

"Yes, thank you," I gave the doctor his payment, "and there will be no mention of this?"

The doctor nodded and pocketed the money.

"I am told to go on bedrest, and you aren't? You're the one who was shot." Margaret glared at the doctor's retreating figure, her arms crossed over her chest.

"Well, you know how weak ladies' constitutions are." I shrugged my shoulders in jest. A sharp pain extended from my wounded shoulder, and I rotated it to ease the pain.

Her gaze narrowed in on my wound once more with a calculating gleam in her eyes, before looking at me. "What happened to the fake Mrs. Kiles?"

"We still have her. She's tied up in the other room. The two men have since been removed," I cleared my throat, as it constricted with the unpleasant image of Mrs. Kiles' dead body. "We also found the other, or rather the real, Mrs. Kiles."

"Yes?" she responded, taking a hesitant sip of her coffee, scrunching her nose in disgust.

I removed the coffee from her hands once more, as her head tilted alarmingly to the side. The opium still impaired her. I sat next to her on the couch and took her hands in mine. "Margaret, she's passed on."

"Oh." She visibly swallowed, her brows scrunched together. "How?" She stared blankly past my head.

"She passed a few hours before we arrived, I don't know how, yet."

I stood, nervous energy filling me once more. Rarely did my emotions consume me. Not during the bombardment of Alexandria and not when I went through training at the Royal Naval Academy.

"Before we start, I want to ask if you'd like to be in the room while we interrogate the imposter?"

Her eyebrows rose, a soft smile lighting her face. "You'd allow that?"

Her smile brought a warm tightness to my chest, and I cleared my throat to dispel it. "Well, it is about you, after all. Even if I'd rather you not be subjugated to it." I held out my hand to her, wondering if she'd be able to stand, "Is that a yes?"

"Yes," she squeaked, clutching what I imagined was a sore throat. She took my hand, her blanket falling to the floor.

She swayed slightly coming to her feet, and I steadied her, wondering if bringing her to the interrogation was safe. I bent down and picked up her blanket, draping it over her shoulders.

"Thank you," she whispered, shuffling. "Who are these 'we,' you keep referring to?"

"My father's men." I strolled with her as she continued to sway. "I don't know if you were out before they arrived or not."

"I think I remember."

We entered the room adjacent to the kitchen. Closed curtains covered the windows. Everything, but a table, was pushed to the sides of the room. The imposter sat at one end of the table, tied to the chair and gagged. She exuded defiance. Across the table sat one of my father's men dressed in inconspicuous black. The other man stood behind her.

"My lord." The seated man stood and executed a quick bow to me, as did the man behind the woman. "We are ready to begin."

"Then let's begin." Neither man moved their eyes on Margaret. I glared at them. "Let's begin," I gritted out. Both men nodded, though barely. My father's influence ran deep.

I pulled a chair out for Margaret in one of the corners of the room. She sat down wrapping the blanket tightly around her shoulders. I stalked toward the imposter.

"Now, mistress, we will remove your gag." I sat in the chair across from the woman. "I believe my associates have shown you the consequences of calling out for help."

I leaned back in the chair, my legs casually folded, and placed my hands calmly in my lap. The woman nodded, and the man behind her untied the gag and removed the bonds from her hands.

"Water." I flicked toward one of the men. The man brought the woman a glass of water. She eyed it with suspicion. I quirked a brow in amusement, before looking at Margaret and remembering her form slumped in the chair.

"We haven't poisoned it, unlike your treatment of my companion and myself. I'd drink it if I were you. We have many questions."

The woman took a hesitant sip, before placing the cup on the table. She cleared her throat. "I won't tell you anything." She looked away.

"Well, mistress, you are both in a place of bargaining and a place without any power. It is your choice." I watched her, not moving from my casual posture. Minutes ticked by, neither of us moved.

When the silence seemed unbearable, the woman blurted out, "He'll kill me."

I leaned forward. "He'll kill you if we let you go. We can protect you if you give us information."

"You cannot protect me. You think you can protect your girl. Well, you can't. Not even you, the high and mighty Lord." The woman leaned back with a cruel, yet mournful smile. Her words hit me close to the chest with a grinding awareness.

My father's men shuffled impatiently at my relaxed approach, but I was ever aware of Margaret's presence. She slumped in the chair, her head bobbing as she tried to stay awake. It might be best she fell asleep because then I could get the woman to impart her information in a timelier manner.

I turned back to the woman but left my gaze with Margaret. "I believe you underestimate my connections. If we let you go right now, what's to stop the Poisoner from believing you already spilled his secrets?"

The woman swallowed, her brow furrowed, and her eyes calculating.

Margaret slumped in her seat, asleep. I stood. "I'll give you time to think."

I walked over to Margaret and lifted her up, carrying her back to the couch in the other room. I set her down, covering her with the blanket. She turned, snuggling into it, her eyes closed and her lips slightly parted. Beautiful, I realized for what must have been the hundredth time.

When I returned to the room, one of my father's men approached me. "My lord, this is from his grace."

I took the envelope from his outstretched hand, tension filling my shoulders. With a steadying breath, I broke the red wax seal.

Produce evidence. This is your last chance. Exitus acta probat.

"The result justifies the deeds." I clenched my hands at my side and shrank into duty.

CHAPTER TWENTY-NINE

A.

I returned to the room. The woman remained closed-lipped, following me with her eyes. I slowly walked around her, "Well, you must not know anything." I came up from behind her, slamming my open palms against the table on either side of her body. "You're worthless, that's why the Poisoner used you. You're expendable," I came around and yelled into the woman's face. "Nothing, but a dried-up old hag." That got her, and her mouth tightened, even as she shook in fright.

My father always said, "Attacking the self-image of a proud and overconfident prisoner will break them."

Still, the woman didn't speak, which didn't surprise me. I had hoped it wouldn't come to that, but she still believed the Poisoner would be worse to cross.

I nodded toward one of my father's men. He pulled out a black hood and stalked toward the unaware woman. He roughly shoved the hood over her head, bringing her to a stand as she pushed against his arms.

He handed her to me, and I put her into a painful submission hold, whispering into her ear, "I'm going to release you to the Poisoner, tied up and trussed like a lamb to slaughter. There will be no possibility of escape. If he doesn't want you, you'll remain there at the mercy of the streets."

I tightened my hold, thinking of the pain she brought to Margaret. The woman gasped.

"You're only as useful as the information you can impart to me."

I needed to keep a level head, even as rage threatened to overwhelm me. This was not the Frenchman who murdered my mother. This was not the Navy nor many countless bloody encounters.

"I am not the law, and I won't give you a fair trial." I slammed her into the table. Her head bounced against the wooden surface.

"Please, please, stop," she sobbed, "I'll tell you everything."

I released her as if she were a poisonous snake and one of the men pushed her into the chair. He untied the black hood and removed it from her head. She immediately rubbed at her neck, her hair fell in a mess around her face, and she panted heavily.

"Now, tell me everything you know." I sat across from her, my shoulder throbbing.

"Yes, milord." The woman bowed her head, touching her neck briefly where I could see faint red marks. She took a sip of water from the cup, looking anxiously around the room.

"Let's begin, mistress, with your real name." I flicked my hand toward one of the men, who pulled out a notepad and pencil.

"My name is Annie Marchland. I'm an actress." She took another sip of water, wiping her brow with a hand. She didn't meet my eyes.

"Work has been slow?" I pretended to brush lint from my sleeve, again playing the game of cat and mouse.

The woman's face flamed and thundered. "Nobody wants an old lady actress. All they want is a fresh dove, who will lick their boots." She coughed violently.

"How were you recruited?" I asked.

"Two men asked me to follow Mrs. Kiles for a couple of weeks, learning her mannerisms and schedule. I look quite a bit like her, you know. Anyway, I was then to tell them if she interacted with the girl." She pointed toward the room where Margaret slept, and I wanted to wrench her arm away. "They gave me ten pounds. They said they'd give me another forty, more than I make in a year if I pretended to be her when the girl came by."

"Who are 'they'?"

"They said they worked for a man who was interested in the girl. They said he was a man who would kill me if I crossed him. They never mentioned a name. They didn't need to. It was the Poisoner. Everyone in these parts knows about him." Mrs. Marchland worried her hands, before pushing back her greasy hair. "I told them that the woman met the girl. They told me to come here several days ago and that the girl would be here soon. I was to impersonate Mrs. Kiles and then put the girl to sleep with laudanum if it seemed like she didn't know anything. They said they would pick her up. You weren't supposed to be here, milord."

"What do they believe she knows?" I leaned forward.

"Who I was and why I called her. She didn't seem to know anything. They must have been wrong. She's nothing special. I can even see that." The woman once again looked at me with a smirk. I swallowed my emotions.

I remembered Mrs. Marchland said something about the footman John Kiles, while she was in character. "Who is John Kiles?"

"The old woman's nephew," Mrs. Marchland sighed.

"What is his significance?"

"He gave the girl the note, I don't know what else."

I stalled, thinking. Margaret must have received the note when we were at Miss Jacobs' residence or her own residence. Meaning one of the Poisoner's men was closer than I could have guessed.

"Do you know why Mrs. Kiles would have summoned my companion?" I leaned back again, deciding to visit this John Kiles or rather beat him to a pulp.

The woman took her keen eyes from me and shook her head. "They forced me to watch while they interrogated the real Mrs. Kiles. She didn't tell them anything, but that only the lady would be the one able to find it. She said she could not tell because she made 'a promise on her own mother's grave never to tell anyone, but the lady.' I'm good at remembering lines," she stuck her nose in the air. "When they threatened to kill her, she said nothing. When they left her for a bit, she told me that 'if I were going to see her lamb give her, her love.' The old woman was delusional at that point. They came back, killed her and stuffed her in the trunk. When she was dead, they ransacked the place, but they left with nothing. Took me days to clean it all up." She had no sympathy for the deceased Mrs. Kiles.

"Why should I believe you?"

"As you said, milord, I have nothing to lose." She gave me a black smile.

"My last question. What were they going to do with my companion, once they got her?"

"They never told me that, and I didn't ask." The woman crossed her arms across her chest. "I told you everything I know. Even more, than they know. I didn't tell them what Mrs. Kiles told me."

I stood abruptly. "That will be all, Mrs. Marchland." I nodded to one of the men.

The man tied Mrs. Marchland's hand together again but untied her feet from the chair. He pulled her up roughly by her arm. Mrs. Marchland looked over her shoulder as the man escorted her out of the room.

"Take her away," I told the men.

"But, where are you taking me?" Mrs. Marchland wailed, pushing against the men.

"Jail, Mrs. Marchland." I turned away as she grabbed at the door frames as the men pulled her from the room.

CHAPTER THIRTY

M.

"How are you feeling?" Alexander came before me, crouching down, and brushing the hair from my eyes.

I yawned, looking around and finding myself once more on the couch. I missed most of the interrogation, but Mrs. Marchland's last words, "She told me that if I were going to see her lamb give her, her love," echoed hollowly in my heart.

"How much did you hear?" Alexander asked with deceptive calm.

"Only the last of it," I swallowed, choking on a sob, "how they killed her."

"Margaret," Alexander began. He handed me a handkerchief embroidered with the initials, MKR.

Wiping my eyes, I moved to hand it back to Alexander. He shook his hand, closing mine over the handkerchief.

Losing my balance, I fell into him. Alexander brought us to stand, his arms fully around me. My fingers scrunched around the back of his shirt, and I buried my face into his chest. He smelled warm if there was such a scent. His soft linen played against my wet cheek.

I squeezed my eyes shut, tightening my grip on Alexander's shirt. "Please, hold me."

"As you wish."

I breathed in his words, loosening my grip on his shirt and allowing myself to sink into him.

I let go first.

Alexander released me, tilting my head up. His amber eyes traced my face, a worry line between his brows. After a long moment, he must have decided I was all right because he released my chin.

"Perhaps, what Mrs. Kiles wanted to give you is still in the house," Alexander broke the silence.

"Should we look now?" I pulled the blanket from the crooks of my arms and folded it. Anything to not think about Louisa, the Poisoner, or the Wellmonts.

"Are you able?"

"I have to be." I nodded.

"Did any of what you heard Mrs. Marchland say bring anything to mind?" Alexander took the blanket and placed it on the table.

"No, but maybe something in this house will." I rubbed my foot against a scuff on the wood floor.

My mind all at once filled with thoughts and memories of the real Mrs. Kiles. The thoughts I wanted to scream out to the world, remained stuck in my throat like a piece of stale bread.

"My father's men are guarding the house but stay close in case." Alexander stepped away from me, and a vast ocean filled the space he left behind. I wanted to reach out, but I had been the one to create the ocean within moments of being close. "I'll begin looking over here," Alexander indicated to the parlor we were previously.

"I'll look in the bedrooms." I floated away from Alexander, my mind filled with a bleak awareness.

Bright and airy, wallpapered with a yellow flower pattern, the first bedroom gave me little clues. A patchwork quilt covered the lofty bed that filled the room. The room smelled like pastry dough and cinnamon. I choked on the cloying scented memories and slammed the door shut.

In the hallway, I noticed a tall narrowed hutch, shadowed in the corner. Glass panels lined the top front door. I peered into the hutch. At first, little knick-knacks: wax flowers, stuffed birds, trinket boxes, and China pulled my attention. Then, I noticed something out of place. Deep within the recesses of the hutch was a hunched over, stuffed animal, that would be about ten inches when upright.

Pulling out the toy, I followed the path of fallen knick-knacks, as if the lamb had been pushed hastily into the back corner. I remembered Mrs. Marchland's words or rather Mrs. Kiles. She said to "Give my lamb, my love." Mrs. Kiles or Louisa used to call me lamb when I was a child. Maybe, her words held some double entendre. My hands shook slightly as I weighed the lamb toy. Squeezing its belly, I found that hard edges protruded from its soft plush.

I held the toy to my chest and rushed into the parlor. "Alexander. Alexander, I think I found something."

Alexander peeked his head into the room from the kitchen, before his whole body came into view.

I held up the toy lamb proudly, only to receive a look of confusion from Alexander. I sighed setting the lamb on the table. "Do you have a knife?"

Alexander reached into his pocket, pulled out a pocketknife, and handed it to me. He came to stand behind my shoulder. With the knife, I cut a line straight down the lamb's front. From within the fine wood shavings, a swath of red velvet poked through. I felt as though I had grievously injured the lamb, and I promised myself I would sew it back up.

Past rough wood shavings, I pulled out a red velvet drawstring bag, about six inches in length and four in width. Aged and weathered, the velvet smelt of a Dowager of the Almanac's perfume. It was surprisingly weighty, and on the first inspection there seemed to be a few layers of content.

Before I could pass the bag to Alexander for his inspection, one of the men in black entered the room. The man leaned toward Alexander and whispered something in his ear. Alexander tensed immediately. From the front door, heavy tread sounded.

Alexander grabbed my hand. I held the velvet bag and lamb in my other. "Margaret, we need to go, now."

The front door splintered as something crashed into it. The hinges on the door heaved as the door bowed. I looked at Alexander, memorizing his face.

He pushed me in front of him. Alexander and the men in black walked on either side of me as we escaped from the back door of the house. In the back, two black carriages waited for us. Once we were outside, the first carriage left. After a few minutes had passed, Alexander helped me into the second and then we were off.

Alexander yanked the curtains closed. I leaned back into the squabs. "Where are we going?"

***

A.

"My father's, for now." I removed one of the seat cushions and pulled out a pistol, before shutting the hidden compartment once more.

"Do we have to?" she asked, white-knuckle gripping the seat.

"Yes, but we won't stay for long." I avoided her gaze.

I rubbed my chest, so it might stop racing. So that I might regain control. Margaret stared out of the window, her lips just parted and the amber light creating a golden glow over her face. I wrenched my gaze away and clenched my hands at my sides. This was foolishness. This was nothing but a mission.

She means nothi—, but I could not even say it. Even though I needed to.

Bring the evidence to my father and finish this, I repeated as a mantra in my head. Finish this, before I made a fool of myself. Margaret wouldn't be another one of my casualties.

The carriage slowed and then came to a full stop. The door of the carriage swung open, and a footman waited with his hand out. Margaret took his hand and stepped down from the carriage. I followed behind her, my hand reaching to grab the ribbon that trailed from her dress, but I held it back. My feet were heavy. Everything told me to turn around, but I had long forgotten to listen.

She put her small hand in the crook of my arm and smiled hesitantly at me. In her other hand, she held the lamb and velvet bag. The footman led us up the steps. The tall double door swung open, without a creak. The grim butler bowed to us. All of the sudden, I felt like a small boy.

CHAPTER THIRTY-ONE

M.

"Where's my father?" Alexander asked the butler, releasing his hat, but not his coat.

The Butler, a tall, gaunt man, cleared his throat. "His grace is in the Northern parlor, my lord. If you wish, I will take you there."

His grace? My heart began to pound in my chest. A Duke. What if it was *the* Duke. But that would mean... I looked at Alexander. He shook his head, and the butler bowed, leaving us alone in the cavernous foyer. I once again reached for Alexander's arm, but he brushed past me.

I let my arm fall.

He walked behind the stairs in the direction of a long hallway, and he didn't even check to see if I followed. I lifted my skirts and hurried after him. I could feel the ocean again, and I was once more set adrift alone in the strange house. Alexander's form was tall and firm, his long gait unrestrained from hurry. We walked in silence until we reached the end of the hallway. Alexander stopped before a door on the left, pausing, noticeably still, his hand frozen as he reached for the doorknob. For the first time since entering the house, he looked at me. My heart beat unevenly in my chest, as he kept his indiscernible expression locked on me.

Confusion bubbled to the forefront of my mind, and I resisted the urge to wrap my arms around myself. What happened? What did I do? Sick nausea, perhaps the remains of the opium, played in the pit of my stomach. Disenchantment seemed to hang heavy in the air around us. Sucking in my cheeks, I opened my mouth to speak.

"Margaret, I need the bag." He didn't even wait for my response, instead taking it from my shaking fingers.

"Alexander?" I reached for the bag as much as I reached for him. My fingers trailed along his sleeve, and he slipped like sand through my fingers. He took a step away from me and then another. My heart thumped with each of his footfalls.

"Margaret sit down and stay here." Alexander indicated to a needlepoint chair to the side of the door and pushed my hands to my side. When I shook my head in a silent plea, he physically pushed me down on the chair.

Alexander watched me with guarded eyes. All I could do was stare at him, the hard back of the chair pressing into my erect spine. A numbness settled over me, something all too familiar. My mind wandered to its familiar compartments, as my heart whispered "Pay attention. Take him and never let go."

Alexander turned from me, a finality in the rigid set of his shoulders, and opened the door. I chewed on my cheeks, and my nails dug into my palms. I brought the lamb to my chest, heedless of the wood chips that spilled against my bodice. Alexander seemed sure as he stepped through the door. I was less sure of anything, but the fact that I should've learned by now--I could only trust myself.

With scarcely a toe in the door, the Duke's booming voice broke through the quiet. "I've heard there have been some developments?"

I could see the room reflected in a mirror across the hallway. The Duke sat on an intricately carved parlor chair. An identical chair sat next to him at an angle, inward toward a dark blue velvet sofa made of a mahogany finish like the chairs. To the side of the Duke was a sideboard with decanters and glasses on silver trays.

Alexander remained standing in the doorway, and I held

onto the hope that he'd come back to me.

Please come back.

"What did you find?" the Duke asked, pouring himself a snifter of brandy. He did not offer Alexander anything.

"I gained information from Mrs. Marchland, an underling of the Poisoner, and this." Alexander held the velvet bag up.

Pain constricted in my chest, and I took several short breaths through my flared nostrils. Any thoughts that Alexander wanted to protect me from his father, vanished in a plume of Opium smoke, which I'd been breathing in all along. I'd been asleep.

Alexander looked back at me in the mirror, directly into my eyes, and pulled the door shut. Panic clawed up my throat. The click of the door bounced around my mind with a resounding finality. I looked down at my palms, covered with small red, painful crescents. I unclenched my hands, though a part of me called for self-punishment. How could I be this stupid?

Nausea swirled in the pit of my stomach and the feeling seemed to run along my jaw. I turned my body in the chair, and my feet ran parallel to the door. I stared at it--the door a symbol for every barrier in my life. Every time someone had taken my freedom and my right to choose away from me, it had been behind a closed door. I rubbed my hands along my knees, the soft, familiar fabric of my dress bolstering my courage. I grabbed the doorknob, cold and slick in my hands. Inch-by-inch I turned it ever so slowly. With nary a sound, I pushed the door open a minute crack, and put down the poor lamb.

Through the crack in the door, Alexander handed the velvet bag to his father--the one my grandfather had warned me about.

No.

I jumped to my feet. No more. My life would not be decided without me. I braced my palms against the door. Voices of malcontent rang in my ears. *You're not good enough. He never cared about you. How could you be so stupid?* Taking a steadying breath, I pushed against the door and crossed to the other side--heedless of the consequences.

Alexander and the Duke paused, their gazes fixed on me in disapproval. I let the silence fill the room, before breaking it with a clear, calm voice, "Return that at once. It was meant for me."

My stomach stormed like a tempestuous sea, but the helm fell into my hands. The Pharaohs of Alexandria entered my mind's eye, guiding me forward. With as much certainty that I knew I was a human, that whatever was in the bag was meant for me and me alone. Alexander and the Duke had no right to it.

I looked at Alexander, beseeching him one last time with my eyes, but he looked away.

The Duke smirked at me, pulling at the drawstrings of the bag with the glee of a Coptic priest at the burning of the Library of Alexandria. Blood pumped through my veins, and I covered the space between the Duke and myself, pulling the bag from his grasp.

With the bag in my hand, the shock of what I'd done overtook me. I backed away and crouched into a little ball on the floor, the velvet bag between my folded legs and torso. Reflexively, I covered my head and neck with my hands, waiting for the blows that would inevitably come. Indeed, this was a position I had often taken with Uncle Matthew and Aunt Emily. It felt instinctual. My breath fell hot and heavy against my face. Only the worn fabric of my dress, shadowed by my head, was visible. I gritted my teeth, bracing myself.

"Margaret, let him have the bag."

I looked up from my crouched fetal position. Alexander's eyes were cold, his expression blank. With my head up, the bag became visible. As Alexander snatched it, I was pulled to my feet. One of the Duke's henchman pulled me away and held my arms painfully behind my back.

I mouthed, "No" to Alexander as the horror unfolded before me. Alexander brought the bag to his father.

My heart squeezed tightly, sending a searing ache through my chest. I'd been led like a lamb to slaughter. Time seemed to freeze as I watched Alexander, the Alexander I always feared existed. Even when I opened the door, I hadn't fully accepted the fact that he'd been holding a blade to my neck all along. The past few weeks burned to a painful crisp, left nothing but ashes at my feet. I gulped in short breaths, my vision blurred.

How could I be so foolish?

The Duke opened the drawstring bag. He pulled out a piece of paper from the bag and scanned it quickly before a look of disgust marred his face. He tossed the paper to the ground and it floated toward the fire.

My breath caught as the paper fell safely to the side. I could not even bring myself to be astounded by the Duke's callousness. His every mannerism and now Alexander's were echoes of what I'd experienced my whole life. I couldn't help but take the blame, stabbing it into my own chest.

Next, he pulled out a slim book about the size of the bag itself. He opened it, and his face pulled into the same expression as it did for the paper. The book and velvet bag fell to the floor with a resounding thud. I flinched at the sharp sound in the otherwise silent room. Exhaustion mantled my shoulders, heavy and bleak. The words I had always wanted Alexander to say--anyone really, even myself, sunk like a lost anchor. Maybe, I always knew the answer.

"Absolutely nothing of use." The Duke stood, gulping down the brandy.

The pressure on my arms disappeared, and I rushed to the site of desecration--careless of the Duke's parasitic presence. I dropped to my hands and knees, hastily shoving the papers into the slim book and scrunching the velvet bag in my clammy hands. I crawled to the paper near the fire. The last words of the paper, super fine to my fingers tips and transparent in places from age, gave me pause:

With our everlasting love, eternally yours plus a day,

Your parents,

Papa and Mama, Richard and Esther

Another wave of pain washed over me. It took hold of my body, threatening to mold me back into what I once was. Love, the only thing I'd ever wanted had betrayed me just like everything else. I trembled as hot tears burned behind my eyelids. All I wanted was to remove every piece of that inadequacy from my heart--close my eyes and become a new person, who never needed to be patched together. I folded the paper into the bag. I did not want to further defile it or its intentions, by reading it in that place.

"You, foolish girl." The Duke looked at me with disdain. "The world does not revolve around you."

I imagined I saw Alexander's face fall, but tears clouded my vision. I pushed to my feet, allowing a blankness to wash over my face. With a sigh I entered the compartments of my mind, they cocooned me in a bleak indifference and I focused only on the idea of returning to my own territory. I stood and faced the Duke, holding my chin up high, only four feet from his oppressive presence. I didn't even deign Alexander with as much as a glance.

"I would like to leave now," I spoke clearly, proud that my voice didn't tremble, though my feet wished to sink beneath the floor's undertow.

"I'll take you home," Alexander's voice came from my side.

I swallowed back the lump in my throat, as the traitor spoke. I turned to look directly at him, shooting knives with my gaze, even as my gaze traced his every feature. I squared my shoulders and set my jaw. I told myself I didn't even see him, but I took in every piece of him, every good memory and now every bad.

"No." It passed softly from my lips, but to me, it felt like a roar of survival.

I wanted him to know how badly he hurt me, to feel the same pain. If he felt that pain, I would know we shared something still. The "no," reminded me and protected me from the fact he didn't. Alexander did not deserve my emotions or the energy behind them. I had every right to say "No." I should have learned that years ago.

Though I wished to run from the room, it was too dangerous with the Poisoner on the loose to walk home. With growing resolve, I faced the Duke once more and stared him down.

The Duke flicked a hand to his henchman. I planted my feet into the ground, but relaxed slightly at the Duke's words, "Take her home."

Alexander made his first move toward me as the Duke said, "Let her go, she is of no importance."

He let me go.

CHAPTER THIRTY-TWO

M.

Upon entering the townhouse that evening, Rose's gaze found me from the parlor, and she stood up. I quickly retreated from the foyer, but Rose followed behind me.

She slammed me into the wall gripping my forearm painfully, whispering in my ear. "You are the cause of all my problems." Her eyes shifted to a darker blue. "You've wreaked havoc on my life from the moment you were discarded on our doorstep. I will ruin you." Rose shoved me against the wall one more time before sashaying away.

My arm burned, and she left white finger marks. I rubbed my arm and shook it to get the blood flowing. Tears prickled at my eyes as I trudged up the stairs. Everything felt bruised.

Once in my room, I changed into my nightgown. The second my head was covered by my gown, a small moment of hysteria that someone was watching overcame me. I wrenched it over my head and looked around--nothing. I shut the door to my room and put a chair under the doorknob for extra measure. Taking my pillow from the bed, I sat with my back against the wall and my knees scrunched into my body. I screamed into it with any sentiment I had left in my constricted and wrung out chest. My mouth tasted faintly of vomit and I brushed my teeth furiously with dentifrice. Slipping into bed and bringing my blanket up to my neck, I stared at the door until my eyes watered, and my neck stiffened.

Huddling under the covers, I wanted to think of Alexander in a rational manner, instead of as a lovesick, emotional dolt. I reminded myself that men didn't do favors for women without ulterior motives, especially poor women, who wished to become spinsters and live alone forever. For the first time, my affection for him formed in my mind, not yet in words, but there nonetheless. I wanted to ask my heart how it could still betray me. Hadn't we learned by now?

The line from *Old Maid in the Garrett* came to mind, "There's nothing in this wide world would make me half so cheery as a wee, fat man who would call me his own deary." I reminded myself I was not yet five and forty, even if I did live in an attic. The poem ended with, "If I could not have a man, then I'll have to get a parrot." A parrot might suit better, as they could do little to break your heart.

With renewed, albeit, forced focus, I opened the red velvet bag. My fingers hovered above the contents, the velvet soft in my other hand. A sense of falling overwhelmed me, as if within the depths of the velvet bag appeared a maelstrom and instant destruction. I pulled out a folded paper, closed my eyes and couldn't dare to open them. Moments passed, and my breath rushed along my lips as if in awe to find myself still breathing. My hands shook as I opened the paper and laid it against my knees, setting the velvet bag on the floor next to me. The paper read:

My dearest Margaret, my little Athena:

If you are reading this, it means something has befallen me. Your mother passed on just days ago, but her words follow my hand as I write to you. Perhaps, this is also my last will and testament. We have bequeathed to you all our earthly goods (other than those entailed to the estate, which will go to a distant cousin). We wish to give you choice in love, life, and freedom. Take care of your inheritance for it can consume even those with the best intentions. Look to the Crimson Crown Society, but don't trust them completely.

In the words of Plato's, The Symposium*: "Humans were originally created with four arms, four legs and a head with two faces.*

Fearing their power, Zeus split them into two separate beings, condemning them to spend their lives in search of their other halves, and when one of them meets the other half, the actual half of himself, whether he be a lover of youth or a lover of another sort, the pair were lost in an amazement of love and friendship and intimacy and one would not be out of the other's sight, as I may say, even for a moment...Love is born into every human being; it calls back the halves of our original nature together; it tries to make one out of two."

Upon your birth, we found complete love. We hope, someday, if it is your wish, that you'll find it for yourself. Your grandfather will care for you, listen and learn from him--he can be trusted in all things.

I am swiftly running out of daylight with so much left to say. This letter has been left in the care of Louisa Kiles to give to you when the time is right. Your grandfather also has a copy of this letter, should anything happen. We wish we could have spent the rest of our waking days with you. Never doubt that we are always with you, watching your progress.

With our everlasting love...eternally yours plus a day,

Papa and Mama, Richard & Esther

The words on the letter blurred as hot tears, unfamiliar to my cheeks, fell from my eyes. Thousands of different pain-filled memories washed my face with each teardrop. They fell for my misconceptions of my parents, for their deaths, and for what should have been. I wept for the loss of Alexander and my own innocence. I wept for the doll Rose brutally destroyed so many years ago, and I cried at the fact that the old gardener, Rodger, would someday die.

I gripped my stomach, rocking from side to side to keep silent. With each breath, my ribs grew heavier as if they were about to puncture through my skin. Memory after memory, forced its way through, each well-placed spear sharper than the next. Numb and cold, I couldn't feel my toes or fingers.

***

I cracked my eyes open, a white light expunging my vision. I blinked but could not push away the idealistic feeling that

I was seeing the moon for the first time. A warm calm embraced me, like the breeze of a tropical ocean after a storm. It whispered around the wisps of hair that curled around my face, tiptoed beneath my skin warming my blood, and tickled the tips of my toes. I stood with pins and needles in my feet and washed my face with cold water from the water basin, once again remembering the bruise on my face. With ginger fingertips, I traced along my cheek.

On the bed, like a beating heart, the velvet bag called to me once more and unlike before, I felt ready to answer. Opening the bag, I reclaimed the slim book entitled in faded letters *The Jewish Manual, Or, Practical Information in Jewish & Modern Cookery: With a Collection of Valuable Recipes & Hints Relating to the Toilette* by Lady Judith Cohen Montefiore. Reading the title itself threatened to put me to sleep. The linen surface, a cool grey-green, hid water stains and snagged against my hands. Why would my parents give me a Jewish book? On the inside of the front cover I found an inscription:

"Blessed are You Who causes the groom to rejoice with his bride."

Love,

Ima

Leafing through the pages, I found little annotations throughout, remarking on cooking techniques, sometimes in agreement and other times with utter condemnation. I flipped to the section on "Preserves and Bottling," and a small paper fell out. I carefully unfolded the paper, and it read:

	α	β	γ	δ	ε	ζ
α	A	B	X	Δ	E	Φ
β	Γ	H	I	J	K	Λ
γ	M	N	O	Π	Θ	P
δ	Σ	T	Y	V	Ω	X
ε	Ψ	Z	0	1	2	3
ζ	4	5	6	7	8	9

I squinted at the paper trying to discern its meaning. I flattened it onto my desk and pulled out a blank sheet of paper. With my eyedropper fountain pen to paper, I tried to work out a pattern from the sheet. Greek letters and numerical digits made up the page, which made sense as my father studied ancient Greek warfare and literature, while at Cambridge. As to what it meant, I hadn't a clue.

Alexander might have more insight than I did. But, then I remembered I couldn't speak to him. A pang of sadness washed through me. My fingernails indented into my palms, allowing me to escape and return to the paper before me.

My father had often told me tales of the Greeks, both of their semi-historical battles fought in *The Iliad* and of the age of gods and men found in Ovid's *Metamorphoses*. As a child, I'd spent my time memorizing myths my father told me word for word, and proudly telling them to anyone who'd stop and listen. They seemed wild, other-worldly, and all-powerful in my eyes. However, none of that knowledge helped me, it only comforted me.

Laying my head against my pillow, my eyelids shut on their own accord as my pillow became more comfortable. Questions bounced around my laudanum impaired head...

How did my parents die? Where is my inheritance? What is the Crimson Crown Society? What are my relatives hiding? What do I want?...

***

I awoke gasping for breath. My fingers clutched the bed covers, only relaxing their hold with each breath that returned to my body. Running my hands through my hair, and yanking through the knots, I found that the pain returned me to reality. Pushing away from the safety of my bed, I surveyed my room. A plan formed in my mind.

From under my bed, I pulled out my rose-colored carpet bag, scuffed and frayed in places from age. The cherry wood stain on the handle rubbed away from use, filled me with calm familiarity as my hand glided over its smooth surface. The stiff metal clasp gave me trouble as I pried it open. Filling my bag with a simple green dress, a nightgown, fresh socks, and undergarments, I scouted my room. From under my mattress, I pulled out my pouch of saved money and with my small wooden dressing case placed both atop the neatly folded clothes in my carpet bag.

I dressed in one of my few tailored dresses: a madder rose serge, with dark red velvet trim. I put my arms through my half-fitting cloak and buttoned it up the front. If I looked put together, I would be put together.

A knock sounded on my door, Samantha entered.

"You brought the powder?" I asked.

Samantha nodded. "Will you be all right, Margaret?" She dusted the powder across my bruised cheek.

"Yes." I hugged her for the first time in months. She stilled in surprise. "Thank you."

I left Samantha, grabbing the velvet bag and putting it into my reticule. I slid on my calfskin gloves. I found a piece of stationery and wrote a quick note:

I have accepted Miss Jacob's invitation to stay at her London residence for a few nights.

–Margaret

I left the note on my aunt's desk, finding it rather novel to allow myself to do what I wanted. Practically skipping down the stairs, I swung my bonnet at my side by its strings with an element of forced cheer.

"Margaret, what are you doing walking in that fashion? It is completely unkempt. I will not have it my house, no matter how ill-bred you are," Aunt Emily's shrill voice came from behind me.

I turned around on the landing. Aunt Emily leaned down peering at me from the balcony above the foyer. If I could face a Duke, I could face my drunkard of an aunt. I clicked my heels together staring up at her. "I am going out, Aunt. My walking will not be in your presence."

I turned on my heels hopping to every other step until I reached the front door. I turned to see my aunt had followed me. "Go to your room, you will not speak to your betters this way."

I opened the front door, and I stepped outside.

CHAPTER THIRTY-THREE

A.

The breeze whispered through my hair. A part of me wished it were a gale blasting me from the docks and into the sea. Maybe the pounding wind would knock some sense into me. I liked to think that's what my father thought when he put me in the Royal Navy.

The smell of the sea, decaying fish, salt, and bird droppings, shouldn't have been a pleasant mix, but it was always more familiar to me than the place of my birth. All around me the coarse cries of sailors, the creaking of tethers as shipments were loaded, heavy tread against thick wood, and seagulls' sharp cries that filled the air were more soothing to me than the most renowned symphony.

If my father hadn't forced me back to London, back to land, I wondered if I would have ever left. A sort of freedom could be found at sea, unlike anything on land. A floating island free of the land's mores and laws. Ranking existed, of course, but at sea, you could earn your standing. On land, it seemed, the more I tried, the farther I fell. What happened to the seventeen-year-old who decided to forge his own path? I thought the years away would prove to my father that I was capable. At least, prove to myself that I was capable. Instead, I found that I was still that small boy, groveling for father's approval. None of my accolades, my metals, my adventures, or my successes meant anything to him. Did they even mean anything to me?

Every time I stepped foot in that house, I became something different, timid even. I stuffed my hands into my pockets and moved closer to the water, careful to avoid those at work. I could not return to the Navy unless my father allowed it, and the thought filled me with a bitter rage. Often, that thought alone made me wish I weren't the son of a duke. Made me wish, I could do as I pleased and let my accomplishments, not my name, be my signifier. I'd always known my father wanted me to follow his example. I wanted that too, but no longer did I want to please him. I didn't know if they could be mutually exclusive.

When I brought him the evidence I had gathered, he barely turned his gaze to it before dismissing it. There had to be something there, something of significance in the red velvet bag. After all, it was worthy of murder. I squeezed my eyes shut, gritting my teeth and trying to ignore the solemn grey eyes that stared at me with condemnation. They pained me more than my father's ever could.

CHAPTER THIRTY-FOUR

M.

With the heavy weight of my carpetbag, I set off to Miriam's house. The familiar Mr. Richards opened the door and told me that Miriam was in the garden. He took my carpet bag from me and showed me the way.

Through the townhouse and out the French doors that led from a patio to the garden, Miriam's petite form kneeled before a yellow-pink rose bush. A Celadon-green draped her form and a straw hat covered her face, which hid my approach. Her leather-gloved hands handled the roses with reverence and she kneeled on a leather pad so as not to dirty her dress. Beside her, a metal bucket held an assembly of gardening tools, both delicate and sturdy. Many of which I could not name.

"Miriam?" I asked softly as not to startle her and put myself in her sights.

"Margaret!" Miriam jumped to her feet, pulling me down to her in a fierce hug, and accidentally smudging my face with soil.

"Oh, goodness me, look what I've done," she said leaning back as she wiped the dirt from my face, only to have it increase in diameter with her dirty leather gardening gloves.

I grasped her hand and pulled it down. "Let's get you cleaned up."

Miriam put up her hands in mock surrender and nodded to me with a shy smile.

"It has been much too long since we saw each other last. How was the country?" I asked.

"As one might expect. At least it was only for the weekend or I may have gone mad without you there." Miriam shrugged her shoulders. "The gossips were at large without the excitement of the city. What do I owe your unexpected visit?" Miriam asked. "Not that I'd ever mind, of course."

I avoided her question. "Where are your parents?"

Miriam's eyes narrowed, but she answered anyway, "Mama is helping Babette set up her nursery for a few days, and Papa brought Thomas to Brighton to learn about shipping. I am alone, other than Great Aunt Aphra, who spends most of her time in her room, which has become quite toxic. It smells of nothing but prunes and rancid sherry."

We both made faces, before falling into a fit of giggles. I sobered first and asked, "May I stay here for a few nights? I need your help."

Miriam stilled. "Of course, you may stay as long as you'd like."

I bit my lip with guilt, the hot sun beating down on my cheeks. "Thank you."

Miriam remained quiet for a few moments, before asking with a soft and understanding voice, "What's happened?"

I nodded, before clearing my throat. "It's a long story. It may be best if we sit."

Miriam nodded, a little worry line creasing between her lightly arched brows. "Allow me to freshen up, and we can talk about it in the parlor."

I nodded and moved toward a small white outbuilding. Miriam took off her apron, gloves, and put her tools away, before leaving me in the parlor. Catching my visage in one of the mirrors, I used my handkerchief, or rather Alexander's, to wipe the dirt off my face. Why I kept it, I still couldn't say.

In no time at all, Miriam returned, dressed in a light blue day-dress that matched her eyes. Other than her slightly skewed modest lace fichu, she managed to dress, per usual, better than I could in the same amount of time. Miriam sat down next to me on the red brocade settee and took my hands in hers. A servant brought in the tea service and left.

Miriam looked at me meaningfully and I swallowed uncomfortably. "When did you return?"

"Late last evening," Miriam responded. Her expression, once curious, shifted and darkened. With slow deliberation, she asked, "Margaret what's that on your?"

I felt my cheek, wincing as my fingers alighted upon my bruise. I must have wiped the powder away with the dirt. "It's inconsequential. I fell is all."

"Did he hit you?" Fire burned behind Miriam's eyes. "Margaret, tell me now."

"No." I pushed her hands away. "He's never laid a hand upon me in that way. I fell or was rather dropped."

"Dropped?" Miriam's voice broke as it vaulted upwards in pitch.

"Oh, I am truly botching this all. I was involved in a shootout of sorts. Lord Alexander did his utmost to protect me," I expelled in one breath. Saying his name aloud, brought a painful tension to my chest.

"A shootout?" Somehow Miriam's voice managed to ascend several more octaves.

"Have you read my letter?" I asked, sliding my foot back and forth across the floor. I had sent her a letter, hand-delivered by Samantha, only a few days prior. In it, I told her everything, I had come to learn about my parents, the Poisoner, and my missing inheritance. If it even still existed.

"I haven't had the time. I was going to do so after I tended the roses." Miriam narrowed her eyes. "Margaret, don't change the topic."

"Would you read the letter, please?" I said.

She gave me a look of frustration but stood up and walked to a ladies' cylinder roll writing desk. With a key, she unlocked the desk and opened the cover. Miriam leafed through the correspondence, before picking out a card. Giving me one last enquiring look, she began to read.

Tension built in my shoulders as I waited for her condemnation to rain down on me--and ever so did I deserve it. Instead, Miriam wrapped me in her arms and I burst into tears. Miriam rubbed my back, with no words.

I hiccuped, my nose running. Miriam handed me a handkerchief, and I wiped my eyes, blowing my nose loudly. "Miriam I've been so confused. I thought..." my voice broke as I wrung the handkerchief between my hands.

"I wish you had come to me sooner." Miriam was quiet for a moment. "Margaret, I am worried for you."

"I'm afraid, Miriam. I feel like I am on a runaway train and there's no stopping until I either run out of fuel or slam into the end of the line."

"We'll figure it out before it comes to that." Miriam patted my back. Silence reigned for a few minutes, only broken by my sniffles. "Lord Alexander will continue to help you after all."

"No, he won't." I shook my head, squeezing my eyes shut. "I can't trust him anymore."

"Why?" Miriam asked, rubbing circles on my back.

"I don't wish to speak on it," I whispered my voice cracking. "He'll solve the case, but it won't be for my benefit or protection. I was wrong about him."

"Oh." Miriam hugged me.

***

A time later, after the tea had gone ice-cold and the biscuits had been consumed, a small smile played on Miriam's lips. "Not to make light of the situation, but a part of me is glad I am finally able to help you."

"What do you mean?" I sniffed, rubbing at my nose.

"You've always been so, what's the word? Self-sufficient. You've dealt with my numerous, meaningless dramas, but you've rarely given me the chance to deal with yours."

"I didn't want to bother you," I whispered.

"Margaret Admina Savoy, you zounderkite!" Miriam slapped the seat, before pulling me into a hug. "Do you not know the definition of 'friend?'"

She squeezed me tightly until I couldn't bear the hug, not from dislike, but rather like a cat who could only take so much. "Love you." I kissed her cheek and she released me.

"Always a prickly cactus," she mock pinched my cheek. "Now that we cleared that up, how may I *help* you?"

"Only you could be happy that we're both fools," I grumbled, before breaking into a full-bodied laugh.

"Equality is never a terrible thing," Miriam smiled. "Now let me help you."

I laughed, dabbing at my eyes and pulling out the velvet bag from my skirt pocket. "I received these from my parents and I found this photograph in my grandfather's office."

From the bag, I drew out the book, my baby photograph, and my mother's pendant. With a pang of irritation, I remembered that Alexander had the coded document in his possession. Miriam took the items from my outstretched hands looking them over. I watched her carefully as she looked over the items, watching her worry her lip and her eyes narrow.

Finally, she looked up, placing the items in front of her on the table. "Are you Jewish?"

"What?" I asked as little pieces started falling into place all around me. "No. Why...why do you ask?"

"I always thought your middle name was odd," Miriam's hand came to rest on mine, "but it makes sense now." I shook my head in confusion and she continued. "Admina is a Hebrew name.'"

"But, why would I have a Hebrew name?" I asked.

"It could be only that your parents liked the name, but with the book and locket," Miriam took a deep breath, "it could mean you have Jewish heritage."

"Why would no one have ever told me?" I whispered as I let the idea ruminate in my mind. It clanged around the cavernous space of my mind, filling in holes that had, for a time, seemed like natural occurrences.

"It could be that they left the faith or that they were in hiding. It's not always safe being Jewish and hasn't been for almost two thousand years." Miriam shrugged her shoulders, watching me with a new, careful, gaze. "Papa's family left Germany for our own protection. Let me show you something." She opened the book and showed me the inscription. "My mother received this very book from her mother upon her marriage. The inscription is the last of the *Sheva Berakhot* or the Seven Blessings, which are abundant blessings for a bride and groom."

I read the inscription, "What's an Ima?"

"Mother in Hebrew. So, if you received this from your parents it was likely a gift from your grandmother to your mother," Miriam responded. "Your mother could have been Jewish, as the Star of David is etched in her pendant."

"Am I half-Jewish?" I asked.

Miriam shook her head. "I can't be certain, and it will depend on your mother's heritage."

I nodded without much contentment. "And what does this mean?" I showed her the inscription on the back of the photograph: *zeved habit – August 30th, 1864 – Psalm 128.*

"In the *Torah*, Psalms 127 and 128 represent the Lord's plan for those who wish to build a plentiful household. Psalm 128 represents child rearing." Miriam looked over the inscription once more. "*Zeved habit*. I am not sure what it means. If my brother or father were here, they'd be better able to tell you."

"Is there anyone else we can ask?" A buzzing filled my center, and though the words may turn out to be unimportant, a piece of me wished to squeeze out every bit of knowledge for myself.

"My father has been fascinated of late by the *Kabbalah*--Jewish mysticism. If you are in urgent need of information we can go to Watkins Books. It's a spiritualist bookshop, with all manner of intriguing secrets. It's located near the train station and Trafalgar Square."

CHAPTER THIRTY-FIVE

M.

26 Charing Cross Road

A delicate breeze filtered through the air, and I must have been used to the aroma of London because for once I didn't smell coal or the Thames. Well, at least not as strongly. A few people milled about the streets, most to get into the carriages that waited for them. The others were servants and tradesmen. I clutched my reticule tightly to my chest, remembering that any one of them could be working with the Poisoner. Miriam grabbed my hand and pulled me into the waiting carriage.

We stopped at Charing Cross, and Miriam gave instructions to the driver to wait for us. In front of Charing Cross Railway, the replacement of the original Eleanor Cross, erected in '65, stood in seventy feet of Gothic opulence. Miriam pulled me along behind her as we trudged on past the station, forcing me to ignore all the sights my mind and heart yearned to explore.

Watkins Books, a tall brick unit in a row of similar brick shops, had two large windows with protective fencing, on either side of its large black door. Above the door, hung a black sign with a white frame, its gold lettering spelled out "Watkins Books."

"Watkins is a favorite of those inclined toward Freemasonry, seances, and the occult. Connecting with the departed has become increasingly popular amongst ladies with too much money and time on their hands." Miriam blushed, her hand hovering on the doorknob. "At least that's what Papa says."

She pushed against the door, and a little bell chimed our entrance. I sent up a prayer to God to protect us. Would He help if I truly had Jewish heritage? Who was my God? Yet, the familiar and comforting smell of musty books came to my nose like a dear friend and cast me from my doubtful thoughts. Old-fashioned lamps hung from the ceiling, casting golden rays of light through the dust motes. Sapphire silk swathes of fabric lay draped over boxes in the building's two front windows, like altars in a church. Selections of books, an antique globe, and some sort of bronze occultist instruments sat on top of the silk boxes. The display represented the promise of intrigue within the confines of the bookstore.

Books stuffed the cases from floor to ceiling in an organized muddle that someone must have understood. Some of the items on the shelves were not even books but scrolls and wooden tablets. Labeled categories ran up and down the shelves: alchemy, astrology, augury, black magic, clairvoyance, demonology, esotericism, fortune telling, and many more I couldn't even pronounce. I could have spent hours on one shelf if I hadn't remembered my task.

I slid through the narrowed gaps between the bookshelves to the side of the shop a man sat behind a counter. Tall, with a full head of salt and pepper hair, and a full-length beard, he reminded me of Merlin. He wore a startling sapphire blue waistcoat with vivid emerald stripes and a light grey wool pantsuit. Black ink-stained his hands, and his hair stuck up on one side. I soon saw why, as he twirled his hair between his fingers as he read *Cosmopolite Ou Nouvelle Lumiere Chymique* by Alexander Seton, 1723. The book had the man fastened to its pages, nose-to-binding.

I didn't want to interrupt his reading, and I waited a few moments. Miriam, who must have had enough of my dawdling, pushed me forward. The man behind the counter looked up for a moment before sticking his nose back in his book.

He looked up again.

Using a crimson silk ribbon to mark his place, he slid the book onto the counter as though it was physically attached to him and he could not bear to let it go. He followed it, his gaze filled with longing, before wrenching his attention, with much disappointment, toward me.

"May I help you, Miss? My name is Mr. Watkins. I am the owner of this establishment." Mr. Watkins folded his hands into an inverted-v, his half-rim spectacles on the edge of his nose, as he leaned toward me over the counter.

"I'm Lady Margaret Savoy," I responded, his deep voice as mesmerizing as his appearance. I pulled the photograph from my reticule. "I was wondering if you could tell me what this inscription means?"

He took the photograph from my outstretched hand and looked it over. "Aramaic, interesting. It means the 'the precious gift of a daughter.' It's a Sephardic ceremony welcoming a newborn baby girl."

"Sephardic?" I asked as Miriam came to stand behind me.

"Ah, Miss Jacobs," Mr. Watkins smiled. "Your father's order of Tarot cards has arrived. Would you like to take it with you?" Leaning under the counter he pulled out a brown wooden box, put it in a brown paper bag and slid it to Miriam.

"Oh, yes, of course." Miriam took the package as if it held some ungodly creation, and perhaps it did.

"I'll put the cards on Mr. Jacobs' bill."

"Thank you, sir." Miriam nodded.

Mr. Watkins turned his blue gaze to me. "Sephardic Jews, were those expulsed from Spain in 1492 who then moved throughout Europe, the Middle East, North Africa, and even India."

"My family is Ashkenazi since we are from Germany." Miriam nodded to Mr. Watkins. "That's why I didn't understand the inscription, we don't celebrate naming girls like we do boys."

"Thank you, sir. Would you mind if I had you look over something else as well?" I asked.

Mr. Watkins nodded his consent and I pulled out the paper

I had found in *The Jewish Manual.*

He carefully took the delicate paper and inspected it over his spectacles. His bushy eyebrows rose in speculation. He slid further forward on his stool, elbows on the counter as he turned the paper over in his hands.

"One moment, I need my magnifying glass." Mr. Watkins looked underneath the counter, before completely disappearing beneath it. He grumbled before he popped up narrowly missing smashing his head into the top of the counter. Setting the paper down, he looked over it with a large golden-framed magnifying glass. He squinted at it adjusting his angle.

"I can say with certainty that this is a Polybius square." Mr. Watkins frowned. "I haven't seen one like this for many years." He looked up at me, "What's your name again?"

"Lady Margaret Savoy."

"Was your father Lord Richard Savoy?" Mr. Watkins leaned forward the paper all but forgotten.

"Yes," I said with suspicion, immediately worried.

Mr. Watkins next words eased my fears. "He almost bought out my whole collection of rare Greek works," he chuckled. "A great scholar your father."

Tears tickled at my eyes. "He gave me the paper."

"The Polybius Square, yes, I am not surprised. He was always fascinated by cryptology."

"What is it used for?" Miriam asked.

"It's a key of sorts," Mr. Watkins pulled out a piece of paper. "In English, it would look something like this..." He drew on the paper and slid it toward us.

On the page, we saw:

	1	**2**	**3**	**4**	**5**
1	A	B	C	D	E
2	F	G	H	I/ J	K
3	L	M	N	O	P

4	Q	R	S	T	U
5	V	W	X	Y	Z

Mr. Watkins pulled the paper back toward him and wrote on the page again. "For example, to create a code I could write, (4,4), (1,1), (4,2), (3,4), (4,4), which wouldn't look like much without the key or knowledge in cryptology. However, with the key, you'd know it spelled out Tarot."

The note that I found under the grandfather clock must be a coded message using the key from my father. Excitement rolled through me until I realized I would have to find a way to get the code from Alexander. My heart leaped just the smallest bit and I had to remind myself I didn't want to see him again.

I had to mentally still myself, so I didn't run out of the store. "Thank you, Mr. Watkins," I said.

"I'll let my father know about his cards," Miriam said as I pulled her out of the store.

"Good luck," Mr. Watkins called after us, "as above, so below."

A chill crawled down my spine, as I swung open the door. Mr. Watkins words reverberated through my mind. I looked around the crowded streets, tension climbing to my shoulders as I braced myself for the image of someone following me. Instead, I found nothing out of the ordinary. Even so, my heart didn't calm, and I leaned heavily against Miriam.

CHAPTER THIRTY-SIX

A.

"Baron Houghton has generously given us some selections from his pornography collection. They'll be your only way into the back rooms of Bertolini's." My father slid the obscene photos into an envelope, much too pristine for its carriage.

"The poet?" I asked as I gingerly took the procured photographs. It was not that I hadn't seen my fair share of pornography at docks around the world, but the type that befitted the Cannibal Club passed even the social dictates of masculine sexuality.

"Yes, Richard Monckton Milnes. He's become better known in recent years for his work in the advancement of women." My father scoffed. "He joined Parliament as a Conservative and has had the *indecency* of becoming ever more liberal as his mind has left him." The Duke took a swig of brandy as if to wash away the "foul" stench of liberalism.

"Won't the members of the club wonder why I'm bringing the," I paused, "photos instead of the Baron?"

"No, he's been of poor health and has been holed up in Vichy, France for the past year." My father took another drink. "We have reason to believe the Poisoner might be a member of the club."

I nodded without surprise. The Cannibal Club, for those who knew of it, was best known for its members' caustic hatred of obscenity laws, their belief in the theory of polygeny, or rather the inherent supremacy of Europeans, and their unapologetic sexual hedonism. Every man in Britain knew about the exploits of the founder, Sir Richard Burton, some followed him with hatred and others with adoration.

A few years ago, a rumor circulated that he'd told a young vicar, when asked if he'd ever killed a man, "Sir, I'm proud to say that I have committed every sin in the Decalogue." In the Navy, I'd met my fair share of men like Burton, their hubris ruled their every action and they gave little thought to the man next to them unless they had something to gain. His publication of the *Kama Sutra* in '83 had created an uproar in every gentleman's club in Europe. Another man might have been excited to enter the infamous halls of the Cannibal Club, but I'd seen enough of the Empire's dirty work abroad that I had no wish to see it at home.

"I'll await your report." My father dismissed me with a flick of his hand.

***

Fleet St., London
Bertolini's Restaurant

Crowds swelled past me through the narrow opening between the buildings, on what could barely be called a road. It had widened since the addition of Farringdon-circus, but not enough for me to enjoy the street any more than I had before. Past the billowing black smoke of a train as it crossed the bridge, I could see the dome of St. Paul's Cathedral and the spire of St. Martin on Ludgate Hill. Cast-iron lamps lined the street casting a muggy glow across the crowd. I cleared my throat and pushed my way through to the Franco-Italian restaurant--Bertolini's.

Clinking glasses and murmured conversation met me at the door with a waiter. "Take me to the back rooms," I told the man, holding back my manners to fit the character.

"Are they expecting you, sir?" the waiter asked.

I nodded, the wheat blond mustache affixed to my face tickling my nose. I pulled against the bottom of my jacket, the added cushion around my midsection causing the fabric to bunch.

"Your name, sir?" He pulled out a list from behind a painting of a Grecian woman reclining on a lounge as women fanned her with palm leaves.

"Charles Milnes, I am Lord Houghton's distant cousin," I responded. "I may not be on the list, but he sent me with items of *particular* interest to the club."

The waiter set the list down. "I see. I will ask Sir Burton. If you'll wait here, sir."

Anxious minutes passed, while the waiter went to the back room. It felt absurd to be relying on the worth of pornography to gain entrance to a "gentleman's club" let alone continue an investigation. I felt like a schoolboy caught masturbating by a matron of the Society for the Suppression of Vice.

"Follow me, sir." The waiter ushered me down a dark and twisting hallway. We stopped in front of a rather ordinary door, but for the image of a white skull painted above the doorknob. The waiter knocked six times, paused, knocked six times again, paused and knocked a further six times. The door opened, and the waiter left, leaving me to enter on my own.

Cigar smoke clouded the air and the smell of brown liquor emanated from the space. A tall man with an impressive black mustache shot with grey stood up at the head of the table. An impressive scar covered the left side of his face and with a boisterous voice, he asked, "You're Houghton's lackey?"

I walked forward eyeing my companions, who totaled to seven men. Algernon Swineburne, one of the few I knew, stood leaning against the wall and smoking a pipe. He stood at only five feet, four inches, but none would dare beat him for fear that he'd like it.

"Cousin, but what's the difference?" I laughed loudly, filling the space with my presence. Burton liked the move and sat down again.

"Give the photographs to Swineburne, he's the most debauched of us all." Burton pointed Swineburne in my direction. "He'll tell us if it's worth more than those French postcards."

Swineburne came to me, his weasel-like mouth fixing into a grimace as he took the envelope from my outstretched hand. He slipped spectacles on the tip of his nose, and slowly pulled the photographs from the envelope. Turning away from me, he hunched over the photographs for a few moments, shielding them from everyone but himself.

He straightened, licked his dry lips, and turned to the crowd of men. “Houghton’s been holding out on us.” He smiled.

The envelope quickly exchanged hands until it reached Burton. “Sit, lackey,” he told me.

I chose a seat in the middle of the table to better observe all the members of the club. The men were mostly gentlemen in their sixties, but for a few who may have been in their forties. Their clothing showed them to be well-to-do and many had scientific journals laid out before them.

Burton stood, clearing his throat. He held a wooden gavel, and upon closer inspection, that which I wish I had never partaken in, the head of an African gnawing on a bone. He slammed it into the table and the members quieted. “Who’d like to give the Catechism?” Burton asked, squinting around the room.

A tall man stood, he looked over the crowd with icy blue eyes like Swineburne’s, and a straight mouth. “I will, sir.” His blond hair reflected the warm gaslight, but little echoed in his gaze.

“As you wish, Doctor.” Burton gestured for all the men to stand.

“Preserve us from our enemies; Thou who art Lord of suns and skies; Whose meat and drink is flesh in pies, And blood in bowls! Of thy sweet mercy, damn their eyes; And damn their souls!”

The words would have set even a worldly man’s mustache on end and I cannot say it didn’t do that to my own, albeit, fake one. Darkness filled the men’s souls and they fed off each other with a frenzied appetite.

“Amen,” laughed one man when the doctor finished his recitation. Murmured amens filled the room and I forced myself to answer in like.

Burton stood as the last amen disappeared, clearing his throat. “While I have your attention, gentlemen, we have another application for membership to consider."

"Who has applied?" asked Swineburne.

"They haven't applied quite yet." Burton shifted slightly on his feet, but his steely eyes never left the gathered crowd. "I'd like to open the invitation to Robert Jardine."

"Of Jardine Matheson & Co?" asked the Doctor, leaning back in his chair and covering a yawn.

Jardine Matheson & Co stood as one of the most prevailing British trading agencies in the Far East. It had the largest cotton-spinning production in Shanghai and its own tea mixture. All projections showed its growth would not stop anytime soon. It hadn't since its inception in '32 nor through the outbreak of the Opium Wars.

"Yes. A nephew on the Buchanan line." Burton sat down, lighting a cigar. "We need another member who knows the East like us, eh, Doctor?"

Swineburne sighed, setting his feet on the table. "At this rate, Burton, our membership will be overrun by East India Company members. Why can't they go to their own club?"

"He was not a member of the Company." Burton pushed Swineburne's feet off the table.

"Jardine's Uncle was labeled a privateer by the Company for quite some time." The Doctor swirled the amber liquid in his crystal glass.

"You remember then?" The Doctor nodded to Burton's question. "A proponent of free trade, gentlemen." Burton looked at the assembled men. "Something any modern man can stand behind."

"Both companies are one and the same." Swineburne laughed. "The difference being, while Jardine took to the changing tides with Adam Smith, the over-bloated East India company sank with its greed."

Murmured agreement circulated the room, including from the Doctor.

"We can discuss his membership when he's actually applied." Swineburne patted Burton on the back. "For a moment,

Burton, allow us academics to have a majority rule."

Burton puffed on his cigar, searching the room. "I can see I am outnumbered, but only for a short bit more, Swineburne." He laughed heartily, before spreading papers across the table. "Today, as always, we will first begin with Mrs. Grundy," Burton began. Grumbles of disgust bounced around the room.

"What have the prudes got for us now?" a man asked his ruddy skin flushing. "More advancement for the weaker sex?"

"I will not get into another argument with you on the merits of birth control today, Mr. Campbell." An older man in the corner straightened. Mr. Charles Bradlaugh, well known for his staunch atheism and freethinking, leaned over the table. He'd made many enemies and friends over the years.

"Gentlemen, gentlemen," Burton interrupted. "We know Mrs. Gundy to be an errant whore, and don't give a goddamn for her."

A few of the men around the table nodded in agreement. Burton continued, "A hypocrite if you will, hell-bent on ruining our pleasure and scientific study."

For the next hour, the men fell into a heated conversation about the advancement of women, some men ardent supporters and others filled with odious hate for the idea. They spoke on matters of obscene publications like *The Pearl* and their wish for a more Liberal London.

The doctor, Dr. James Francis, an ethnologist, and physician, quietly interrupted the conversation. "We must speak on the Jewish question."

The room quieted, and Burton spoke, "They exist between Europeans, true Europeans, and Africans."

"Not German Europeans, we've all read *The Battle of Dorking*," said Mr. Campbell with a feverous intensity. The crowd nodded their heads.

"Yes, they're controlling the money to what ends we don't know. Look at the Rothschild family," grumbled one man. "Even that Shylock, Marx, has remarked upon it."

***

I found a Hackney cab some hours later, sick to my stomach from the company or the copious amounts of alcohol. I could only assume both had knocked my morals to swim in the pit of my stomach. More than anything, men like the Poisoner surrounded me on all sides, he seemed as elusive as ever. If he existed within the London elite, he'd be difficult to separate from the crowd. I didn't know if I would be able to save Margaret, I doubted she wanted me to.

CHAPTER THIRTY-SEVEN

M.

I woke up with sandy eyes and matted hair. I looked to my right in the large canopy bed and saw Miriam's limp form hanging partially off the bed. I untangled myself from the sheets and crawled over to her. Slipping off the side of the bed, I pushed her torso back onto the bed.

"Ugh," Miriam moaned as she rolled over into the bed. She opened one eye squinting at me with heavy eyelids. She looked around the room, covered in hats, shawls, gloves, and any number of accessories strew across the floor. "What time is it?"

"It's about half-past nine, I believe," my voice came out scratchy and rough.

Miriam moaned again covering her eyes with her arm. "How late were we up last night?"

"Too late," I responded. Her room looked like a hurricane barreled through it.

"We probably shouldn't have eaten that whole box of--what are they called again?" Miriam yawned, clenching her stomach.

"Seafoam taffy?"

"No, I don't think that's it. Atlantic City taffy? No, that's where it comes from." Miriam sat up.

"Ocean wave taffy?"

"Definitely not. Why do the Americans have to have such peculiar names for things?" Miriam swung her legs out of the bed and slipped into her slippers. She shuffled to a little rope hanging on the other side of the bed.

As Miriam pulled the rope, inspiration struck me. "Wait. I remember. Saltwater taffy."

Miriam turned to me, a smile growing on her face. "Yes, that's it." She walked over to the discarded box. Pieces of the taffy still stuck to the wax paper in muted pastels. "Papa will most likely be mad we ate it all in one sitting. He found it quite by accident last year when he was visiting Atlantic City. One of the stalls selling taffy had their entire stock soaked by a flood of seawater."

"It's too good to be an accident," I sighed, sitting on the bed. "Do they sell it here yet?"

"I think they only sell it in America as of yet, and maybe even solely Atlantic City," Miriam replied, putting on her wrapper.

"I'll have to go to America then, and get some salt water taffy." We laughed together.

A knock sounded on the door and Miriam moved to open it. From the doorway, I heard: "How may I serve you, miss?" A woman dressed in an upstairs maid's uniform executed a curtsy.

"We would like two breakfast plates, and make sure that a carriage waits in front at eleven o'clock," Miriam said to the woman.

The woman curtsied again. "As you wish, Miss Jacobs."

Miriam closed the door behind the woman and sat on a chair. I bounced a little on the bed. "Are we having breakfast in bed? How afternoonified."

Miriam laughed, leaning gracefully back in the chair, in complete opposite form to her sleeping state. "What are you going to do about Lord Alexander?" she asked with false disinterest.

I had told her little about him. "Never see him again. And if I am so unlucky, run in the opposite direction."

"Margaret..." Miriam whispered.

"No." I shook my head. "Don't spin fairy tales."

"Dearest," Miriam sat up straight, "I would not be so callous as that. But you've always told me it's better to leave without pain attached."

"Who said I was in pain?" I asked with false assurance.

Miriam rolled her eyes at me. "Someday what you're hiding from, will catch you when you least expect. I, for one, cannot wait."

I shuddered, afraid it already had.

"I think I have an idea how we might be able to find out if you have Jewish heritage," Miriam spoke after a long and strained silence.

"How?" I asked with a mouthful of scone.

"Where did your grandfather live?"

"Baker Street in Marylebone," I responded, swallowing the dry scone without chewing, only to be rewarded with a fit of coughing.

Miriam handed me some tea. "There are several synagogues in the area. My family and I attend the Central Synagogue, but since your family might be Sephardic, I believe we should first look at the West London Synagogue because they cater to both Sephardic and Ashkenazi traditions."

"Will they have records then?" I asked.

"Perhaps, or a cemetery."

Cemetery. The word sank to the pit of my stomach like a lead weight. Words etched into a stone--finite evidence to my past, my heritage, and my future.

After breakfast, promptly at eleven, Miriam's family carriage stopped at the bottom of the stairs to the townhouse. Miriam wore a stylish wide-brim white hat, covered with large pink flowers and pink ribbons, which matched her dress. On her hands, she wore white lace gloves. I sported my green traveling costume from the day before. A footman came to help each of us into the carriage, but Miriam stopped on the landing.

"Blast it all," she muttered under her breath. "I forgot Mama wanted me to visit the poor in Stepney for the Ladies' Conjoint Visiting Committee. Will you be all right on your own? We can go another day?"

"No, I'll be fine," I said with false confidence. "I need the information."

She'd never have let me go off on my own if she knew the extent to which the Poisoner hunted me. I, knowing the full of it, should have stayed within the safe confines of brick walls.

CHAPTER THIRTY-EIGHT

A.

Margaret, I looked up, once more, from the papers filling my desk. The clues, the unanswerable questions, and witness accounts. None of them held my attention, like Margaret's eyes when she walked out of my father's study. Grey and fathomless, they held me captive like a ship in a turbulent sea. Hurt. I wrenched my thoughts away from her, and away from the choices, I'd made. I could not do anything to change them now.

All I could do now was move forward. Move forward on this blasted case, which bested me at each turn. A little voice in my head whispered that this case bested my father too. I pushed it aside for the facts in front of me. One, the Poisoner had returned to London after several years abroad, wreaking havoc on the continent. Two, he has worked as a money launderer and procurer of acquisitions, by blackmailing aristocrats, thievery, drug dens, brothels, and controlling the streets, if any of my sources were to be believed. Three, in some way, though against my father's beliefs, Margaret was at the center.

In her case, the Poisoner likely murdered her parents. The only motive, at this point, money. However, money could not be the only motive. Otherwise, the Poisoner would not hunt Margaret and he was hunting her, that fact was indisputable. First, at the ball in Somerset. Second, at the ball in London. Third, through an imposter. Five people dead already, her parents, her grandfather, the solicitor, and the nanny.

I paused in my thoughts, at the absurdity of my father's disbelief that Margaret did not play a vital role in the Poisoner's next move. I could not allow the fourth incident. I shuffled my papers together and put them in the locked drawer. I swung my coat off the back of the chair--I had to see Margaret. See that she was safe, even if only at a distance, and maybe then I'd be able to focus. At least, that's what I told myself.

The townhouse of Baron and Baroness Wellmont glared down at me with condemnation. I wondered if Margaret watched me from one of the many windows or if she read a book in the private hideaway I imagined her creating. Again, I shuffled with indecision. The steps up to the door stood before me like the Queen's guard. I flexed my hands around the silk wrapping the stems of a dozen yellow roses.

What the hell.

I stomped up the front steps, repeating everything that I was going to say in a loop in my mind. As I was about to knock on the door, it swung open to emit Lady Wellmont and Miss Rose.

Both of their eyes widened as they took me in. Miss Rose's lashes fluttered as she looked to her mother, a smirk coming to her face.

"My lord." Lady Wellmont nodded her head, her eyes narrowed with suspicion.

"My lady, Miss Rose." I doffed my hat to them, as I stepped down the stairs to let them pass. "I am here to call on Lady Margaret."

"She is not in." Lady Wellmont's face pinched.

My brow must have visibly furrowed for Miss Rose pounced, "You're wasting your time, my lord." She squealed as her mother pinched her arm.

I ignored her statement. "Where may I find the lady or when will she return?"

"That is unknown." Lady Wellmont's nose lifted into the air. "If you'll excuse us, my lord. We are off to meet with some *very* important personages, who do not like to be kept waiting."

With that, they turned from me and entered their waiting

carriage. I watched them leave, the bouquet of roses useless at my side. The carriage turned the corner and disappeared. Could Margaret be in danger?

"Milord?" A small hand touched my shoulder, and for a moment, I imagined it was Margaret.

I turned around. A woman with brown hair, dressed in housemaid's garb looked up at me expectantly.

"Yes, miss?" I asked.

"Lady Margaret is at the Jacobs' residence," the woman whispered, looking back at the house nervously.

"What is your name?" I asked, relief flowing through me that she was safe.

"Samantha James, milord." She curtsied, again looking back at the house.

"Thank you, Miss James." I bowed to her at the waist.

"You're welcome, milord." Miss James curtsied again. She ran up the steps to the house and closed the door behind her.

I put the bouquet beneath the lapel of my coat and returned to my horse, pointing him toward the Jacobs residence.

John Kiles.

The name hit me, and I remembered, with startling clarity, the words of Mrs. Marchland. He had served me at the dinner. The spy in collusion with the Poisoner, under the same roof as Margret. With that, my relief disappeared into a vat of swarming guilt and fear. I spurned my horse forward.

At the Jacobs' residence, I knocked on the door, waiting impatiently for it to open. The wizened butler, Mr. Richards as I remembered it, opened the door. With an impassive face, he looked me up and down.

"The household is not accepting visitors, my lord," the man intoned.

"Please, give this to the lady of the house." I pulled out my calling card and handed it to Mr. Richards. "I'll wait on the steps."

Mr. Richards nodded his head and closed the door. My foot tapped as I looked around the street, uncaring that I looked the fool for waiting on the steps. After what seemed like an hour later, but was doubtless mere minutes, Mr. Richards opened the door to allow my entrance. He took my hat. I kept my flowers.

"If you'll follow me, my lord." Mr. Richards began his slow walk down the hall. I chafed at his speed, wishing nothing more than to run into the room and see that Margaret was safe with my own eyes.

I entered the parlor, searching for Margaret. For a few moments, I stared around the room in disbelief, trying to conjure Margaret from velvet drapes, from behind the couch or even from the painting. Instead, Miss Jacobs stood her gaze hard as ice and a frown marring her pretty face.

"What are you doing here?" she asked.

As I asked, "Where is she?"

We both paused, looking at one another like caged lions at the Colosseum. I bit my tongue, watching Miss Jacobs as she regained her composure. She sat down and rearranged her skirts but did not offer me a seat. I moved forward anyway but did not sit down. She watched me with the same voracity as I watched her. Still, she said nothing.

Losing my patience, I spoke, "Is she safe?"

Miss Jacobs bit her lip, hesitating, before looking at me with clear eyes. "Yes, I believe so."

Her words didn't give instill confidence, but I didn't push her for more in that regard. Margaret must not want to see me, I decided. "Do you have a footman by the name of John Kiles?"

Miss Jacobs' eyes widened, and her hands fell into her lap. She looked at me, her brow furrowed with suspicion. "Yes. Why do you ask, my lord?"

"I would like to speak with him if I could?" Anger thrummed through my veins as I thought of the coward.

"Why, my lord?" Miss Jacobs didn't make a move to call him.

"How much has Mar--Lady Margaret told you?" I asked.

Miss Jacobs' eyes, for the first time, fixated upon the bouquet of roses in my hand. "I believe I know everything, my lord." Again, she glared at me, but her gaze wandered to the bouquet once more.

I swallowed. "I believe Mr. Kiles is involved with the man who is hunting Lady Margaret."

"What?" Miss Jacobs stood, wringing her hands. "How could you think that? My family would never do anything to harm Margaret. Unlike you," she accused me, her pointer finger poking at my chest as she came to a stand.

Her words stung, and I could not refute them. I removed her hand from my chest. "I am not accusing you of anything. He left a note with Lady Margaret that put her in danger."

Miss Jacobs paused as if remembering something. "He, most rudely, bumped into us at my party a few weeks past. I didn't think anything of it," she whispered.

"Please, could you call him?" I asked again.

"I'll call him, but I'd like to be a part of the conversation," she tapped her foot, glaring at me. "You must be wrong."

I said nothing, not wanting to involve her and not truly knowing whom to trust. Nevertheless, there was no other way. I nodded my consent.

Miss Jacobs went to the door and opened it a crack to whisper to someone on the other side. She shut the door and sat down. She waved her hand in front of her toward the couch. "You might as well take a seat, my lord."

I sat, placing my roses on the side table. Within moments the door opened and a sheepish young man, barely sixteen, opened the door. His hair was shockingly red, and a smattering of freckles dotted his face. Maybe, he truly was Mrs. Kiles' nephew.

"Miss Jacobs," the young man bowed, "what may I do for you?"

"Kiles, this man," she indicated toward me, "Lord Alexander Rocque has requested your presence. He has charged you with some serious offenses."

I stood ready to use force on the young man if necessary. He looked at me and looked to the door. His face crumpled, and he began to tremble.

"They would have killed her." He burst into tears, looking wildly around the room. "I just wanted a job. I never wanted any of this mess."

I sat the young man down on a chair. "Explain, or I will ship you to Pentonville."

He hiccuped. "I used to work in the stables with my da. A year ago, I was hired to work in the big house. Not much later, this man came to me, offering me money to spy on Lady Margaret. I didn't want to, so I refused." Kiles swallowed. "I thought that was the end of it."

"It wasn't?" I prompted.

"No." He shook his head. "The man came back, but this time, they said if I didn't do as they said, they'd hurt my family. They had my little sister thrown into the well on her way home from school. She could have died if someone hadn't found her."

"So, you began spying on Lady Margaret?" I prodded again. "How long ago?"

"About a year," Kiles' knees bounced as he, once more, looked around the room. "I never did nothing bad. All they wanted to know was where she was and who she was with when she were with the family."

"How did you communicate?" I asked.

"Unaddressed letters, but it was them," Kiles shivered. "The letters changed when I got to London."

"How so?" Miss Jacobs jumped in, her cheeks flushed and her gaze hot.

"They began to threaten me that they'd kill my aunt, who lives in London if I didn't keep snitching. They gave me the letter to slip to the lady. I was supposed to keep my eye out for you too, my lord. You made them real mad." Kiles chewed on his fingernails.

"Where's your aunt now?" I asked, the pieces coming together. This young man was nothing more than another victim in the Poisoner's twisted game.

Kiles scrunched up his face. "Her home in London, I suppose."

"Kiles." Though I felt sympathy for the young man, I spoke bluntly, "Your aunt was murdered by the people who you were working for."

He stood, knocking over a chair. "No, that cannot be true. I did everything they told me. They even asked me today, and I did it. What are they gonna do to my family? I have to go to them."

"What did you tell them today, Kiles?" Miss Jacobs yelled at him, her voice trembling.

"That the lady went to the West London Synagogue," he fell, his head cradled in his hands. "What have I done?"

My mind swam with confusion as I looked between Miss Jacobs, who had tears streaming down her face and the distraught Kiles. "Where's Margaret?"

"She went to the Synagogue about an hour ago." Miss Jacobs wiped at her eyes, "Kiles saw her leave. If something happens to her," her breath caught. "I shouldn't have let her go."

I blinked, my heart pumping slowly in my chest and my jaw throbbing with gritted teeth. "Please tell me she took someone with her?"

Miss Jacobs shook her head. I looked outside and saw storm clouds gathering. My mind made quick calculations, and I realized anything could have happened to her.

"Do you have a piece of paper?" I asked, and Miss Jacobs guided me to the desk.

I jotted down some quick information. "Miss Jacobs, please contact Captain Trent in the New Detectives Division of the London Police, with my name. Tell him what has happened here and that I may need back up at the Synagogue. Can you do this?"

"Yes, I'll send for him immediately," she nodded. "Please, find Margaret."

"I won't be able to live with myself if I don't." I looked to Mr. Kiles, "Wait for the arrival of Captain Trent. If you run, we will not be able to protect your remaining family. You now work for me Kiles, you must not, under any circumstance, allow the men you work for to know. You must go about your business like usual."

"I will, my lord. I'll do whatever I can to make things right." Kiles wiped at his nose with his sleeve.

"Miss Jacobs are you amenable to this?" I asked.

"Yes, for Margaret, anything," Miss Jacobs said.

I ran out of the townhouse and jumped onto my horse, urging him toward Marylebone.

CHAPTER THIRTY-NINE

M.

A chill lingered with me as I moved through the gravestones. The Poisoner could be around any corner. A man powerful enough to be hunted by the Duke. Alexander. What was I to do with him? I should tell him what I had learned, but I was disinclined. However, I also realized I needed to think practically. My life held more importance to me than the pangs in my heart. Oh, how it shook in my chest--a loose thing, hanging by threads.

The man in the synagogue told me I would find my grandparents' graves in the small cemetery in the back. It would prove that I did have Jewish heritage, but I didn't know what to do with the information. My only understanding came from Miriam, as well as, the hatred that poured from the newspapers daily. Even more so, like everything in my life, I didn't see where I fit in. If society found out about my heritage I would become even more of a pariah, yet I couldn't see the Jewish community accepting me either. I didn't know the customs, the small consistencies of life, or the history. A warm tear trickled down my cheek, I swiped at it with my hand. The taste of salt filled my mouth. Would I be defined by *la belle juive*, Rebecca, from *Ivanhoe,* or the crooked Fagin from *Oliver Twist*?

I stopped and looked down at the gravestone engraved at the top with the name *Claxton.* In the cemetery, some stones were upright, some buried in the ground, while my grandparents', like those that surrounded them, were horizontal. Above my grandparents' names, I found an engraving in Hebrew and then English: *May their souls be bound in the bond of everlasting life.* Below that, my grandparents' names: *Heman Claxton & Reem Sopher.* I fell to my knees, the dewy grass sinking into the folds of my skirt. Tracing over the names in the smooth stone, again and again, my fingertips searched for the faint swell of connection.

A wet cloth pressed against my nose and mouth at the same moment the crunch of gravel hit my ears. It smelt rather sweet, like almonds.

***

I woke to the swaying of a carriage, and nausea climbing up my throat. My palms began to sweat. The pawn moved onto the next square. My mouth was dry. I looked up to find Dr. Francis watching me, his eyes impassive and his mouth a straight line. Next to him, sat my Uncle licking his lips. A sheen of perspiration dotted his brow. My head swam, and I gripped my seat, trying to focus on what they said.

"She's awake," my uncle whispered to Dr. Francis as he dabbed at his brow.

"I can see that, you fool," Dr. Francis responded in even tones. "Tell her what she needs to know." His eyes held mine, until I looked away, a tingle of familiarity running through my mind. His thin mouth curved in a sneer, but then transformed into a gallant smile, quickly, and with such ease, that I question if I ever saw the sneer at all.

"Margaret?" my uncle's brusque voice permeated my anxiety, as I swayed again.

"Yes, uncle?" I mumbled my tongue sticking to the roof of my mouth. I couldn't remember what I had been doing before I got into the carriage. Did I get into the carriage? The thought confused me, and a buzzing filled my mind.

I considered Dr. Francis. Eyes that were familiar. Eyes that had been stalking me since I arrived in London, if not before.

"We have some excellent news. Dr. Francis is quite taken with you, now, and when he first met you. He has asked for your hand in marriage, and I have accepted his offer for you," Uncle Matthew said gripping my hand in his, not as a doting father would at telling his daughter her fiancé had been accepted, but as a master of an unruly horse. The kindnesses I had seen from Dr. Francis felt false now.

Vomit inched to the top of my throat. My mind awakened as if it had been splashed with a bucket of icy water. "Pardon me?" I looked at him again.

"I thank you for your acceptance of marriage, Lady Margaret. I shall endeavor to be an excellent husband," Dr. Francis said smiling at me like the Cheshire cat in *Alice's Adventures in Wonderland.*

"What, no," I yelped, shooting to my feet and hitting my head against the top of the carriage. "No."

"Margaret," my uncle roared at me. "I have accepted, and as your legal guardian, you have an obligation to follow my wishes."

"No," I screamed back, gripping my pounding head. My tongue seemed unable to formulate another sound but abject pain. I swayed in my seat, thinking of Alexander.

Uncle Matthew backhanded me. A sharp sting infiltrated my cheekbone as his gold signet ring cut my face. The ringing in my head intensified. Blood trickled down my cheek. My head fell back against the squabs, the image of my uncle and Dr. Francis blurring in my vision.

"I wish to get married tomorrow. I have already procured a special license and chosen an officiant who won't take, 'no,' for an answer," Dr. Francis told my uncle. The manacle tightened as if I sucked in air through a small hole.

"Gads, man, twenty-eight guineas on the chit, you must have some high connections," Uncle Matthew whistled appreciatively. Their voices seemed further away than before as if I heard them through cotton.

"You had best remember that Wellmont," Dr. Francis answered

My head drifted toward my chest. I tried to lift it, but it felt like an anchor, tossed into the sea. Only one way—down.

***

Two men dangled me above the black pit of a well, laughing as I screamed. I looked down, but instead of darkness, a gaping mouth with gleaming white teeth charged me. The men holding my arms dropped me, and I fell into the mouth. I tumbled through the dark abyss as laughter bounced me around the invisible walls. I slammed into the ground, the sickening smell of almonds filling the space. Dizzy as I stood, the image tilted. The sound of a gun blasted through my ears. I looked up and saw Alexander, standing and watching me, his eyes empty and his mouth slack, a bullet hole through his forehead. He collapsed.

CHAPTER FORTY

M.

West London Synagogue

The wind whistled past me as I searched for Margaret, and my horse danced beneath me. Straining for a glimpse of her dark hair, grey eyes, anything, a swell of anxiety filled me. She's fine. I was unable to believe anything else. A throat cleared behind me and spun around, my pistol at my fingertips.

A man in black nodded to me from another horse. "His grace has sent me to retrieve you."

"How'd you know I was here?" I asked, my guard only heightened.

"His grace sent me to this location."

My father was having me followed--the conclusion didn't surprise me. The fact that I never saw anyone gave me a pause of caution. Yet, my father had men more skilled than myself in the art of surveillance, I swallowed my pride and took the hit.

"Tell him, I'll see him tonight." I glared at the man. "I don't need a governess."

The man didn't take my bait. "He said immediately, milord. There's been a development in the case."

I looked over the cemetery once more, the grey stones in a sea of green seemed like the last place one could be in danger. The Poisoner never made moves in public and the busy street corner was no exception. My father might have information that would help me keep Margaret safe. Turning my horse away, I indicated for the man to lead the way.

***

"Dawdling is for boys," my father grumbled as I entered

his study. He shook out a newspaper and flattened it against the desk. He looked up but gave me no indication that I should sit down.

I ignored his barb and sat down anyway. "You picked up Mr. Kiles?" I asked.

"Yes, of course." My father's gaze shifted away from me and he cracked his knuckles. My ears perked at the sound as I waited for lies to pour from his lips. "He was rather inoperable, you turned him too early."

Opening my mouth to speak, my father cut me off by lifting his hand. "I don't have time to argue, especially when I am right."

"Then don't," I responded. "Why have you called me here?"

My father stood and from his shelf pulled out a folder. He sat back down and pulled out the papers. He left the papers on the desk and poured himself a drink--swirling the amber contents in the crystal glass. He stood watching me for several minutes.

"If this is your punishment, you're wasting both of our time." I leaned back in my chair and plunked my shoes on his desk.

My method worked, and my father returned to the desk, irritation furrowing his brow as he pushed my feet off his expensive desk. He sat down and picked up a piece of paper, "Intelligence has indicated that the Poisoner is in Cromer. This might be our only chance to capture him. You need to leave immediately."

Relief flowed through me, and I had to keep a smile from my lips. If the Poisoner wasn't in London, Margaret had to be safe. "And Lady Margaret Savoy?"

My father looked me in the eyes. "She's being watched and is to attend Marchioness Salisbury's party tonight. I'll be in attendance myself."

***

Cromer, Norfolk

I remembered my childhood summers in Cromer, the pure

air, and the soft waters. The sailing and crabbing expeditions with my father, and our stays in the Hotel de Paris. Along the sides of the road, sprouted brilliant red poppies that swayed in the breeze, making it clear why the stretch of coastline was known as "Poppyland."

After snagging a meal at one of the many stands that dotted the beach, I made my way to a pub closer to the docks than the tourist culture. Smoke hung in the air, clinking glasses, and rancorous voices filled the space. I noticed a man with a full beard, skin made brown by the sun's hot gaze and a navy-blue flat cap. He nursed a half-empty glass of some bitter brew. I made my way through the rowdy crowd, just missing a drunkard who knocked over a barmaid. I sat down across from the man, and he looked up.

"Lord Alexander Rocque?" the man asked his voice slurred slightly.

"Yes." I took off my hat and placed it on the table. "Are you Captain Warner?"

"Yes, sir, that I am." Captain Warner took a swig of his drink, the foam sticking to his beard. "You look quite a bit like your father, son."

"So, I've been told," I gritted out, wondering why my father sent me to a drunkard. "I've been told you witnessed the man we've been looking for."

"Oh, aye." Captain Warner hiccuped. "I did, with my very own eyes. I had just left the pub, it was late, probably around three o'clock in the morning. I was walking to my ship, the *Marina*, named for my mother, God bless her dearly departed soul." Captain Warner hiccuped again.

"I am sorry for your loss, Captain." I longed to return to Margaret.

"I was coming out of the pub, and the ship, the *Veronique,* were docking. As you know..." The Captain took another swing.

"I don't know." I shook my head.

He leaned into me, whispering loudly while looking around the pub. "Our rival ship. Don't tell your father, but I think she brings in the *tea* faster than I do. The opium has stopped trading well in the Orient. They must be selling something different. I've never seen the like," the Captain burped loudly.

"Opium?" I asked.

"Aye." The captain beckoned a barmaid for a refill. "The *man* you search for is our biggest competitor. I would have thought you knew?"

My mind whirled trying to piece together the facts from fiction. "You saw this man near the docks? What did he look like?"

"Right-O, milord." The Captain slapped me across the back. "I saw him, I'm sure of it. He were barking orders to the crew. The man's the one who owns the *Veronique* after all. Captain Oser wouldn't let no other boss him around like that. He were a blond man, tall and slim. Around the age of fifty."

"When was this?" I asked. Mr. The Captain's description seemed familiar.

"Oh, about a week or two ago, milord," the Captain scrunched his bushy brows together, "which was why I were mighty confused you came all the way up here to talk with me. I already sent a message to his grace, the night after the incident, once my head had cleared some." The Captain laughed.

All my thoughts came to a sudden halt. With the Captain's words, I realized that my father sent me on a fool's errand. The Poisoner would not stay in a town like Cromer for two weeks, meaning he was not here. My heart pounded. Margaret.

"Thank you, Captain," I stood, "I must be going."

"Aye, milord. Fair winds and following seas." The Captain rose to his feet, swaying slightly as he shook my hand. Swinging his cup in the air and taking a large gulp, he sang, "Red sky at night, sailors' delight. Red sky at morning, sailors take warning," to my parting.

I left the pub in the early evening at a sprint to catch the train, the Captain's words chasing me. Why would my father send me down the wrong path? Even at the end of my four-hour journey, I could not allow myself to believe that my father had done anything to harm Margaret. Not yet anyway.

***

As a child, my father's study was as sacred as a throne room. As an adult, it was something to aspire to, at least, a month ago it held that power over me. Sitting in his chair was something that I always wanted for myself, not as the next Duke of Auden, that was always my brother's destiny, but as a master of intrigue. I liked the danger, power, and the ability to travel all over the world. It gave my father and I a point of agreement. It brought us together after my mother's death. It was my way to track her killer. Fix my sins in both of their eyes.

Now things had changed. Once that space called to me, now there was nothing but the sound of silence. When that silence filled me, a new voice called out. A voice and life that I never knew I wanted. A life I still feared.

My father was a hard man to love, yet somehow my mother found a way to do so. She was gentle and beautiful. She featured often in my memories with soft brown eyes and dark russet-golden hair, always pinned properly in place. Even then, she always seemed free and untamed. Sometimes she would bring us out into the garden and tell us stories about the fairies, who slept in beds of moss and rode bumblebees through the flowers. She would tuck a rose in her hair, and we would pretend she was the Fairy Queen. I remembered my brothers and I dancing around, using our foils in a sort of Morris dance.

She would have liked Margaret for her bravery. At least I hoped she would have. The sudden image of her vacant eyes startled me, and I looked away, only to see my mother's ghostly figure. Her eyes were downcast, and she shook her head at me, before turning away. I called after her, but all I heard was my own voice echoing back.

CHAPTER FORTY-ONE

A.

Back in London, I sent my hired Hackney directly to Lady Salisbury's address, who greeted me upon my entrance and tried to introduce me to her daughter. The need to find Margaret had grown into a ferocious beast over the passing hours. Misgivings filled the pit of my stomach. I looked through the crowded ballroom trying to catch a glimpse of Margaret's face. Her dark curly hair. Her long nose. Her grey eyes.

Anything.

A tension in the back of my neck paused me for a moment, my mind unsettled as if someone watched me. I weaved in and out of the crowd. Where was she?

Light flooded the ballroom soft and warm. Yet, none of the warmth soaked into my veins. A piano and a sextet played the *Roger de Coverley* on a small stage to the side of the room. Not a single light shined upon the face I wanted to see most.

From the corner of my eye, Margaret's cousin, Miss Rose beckoned me. Though I wished to have nothing to do with her, she was my connection to Margaret. The beast wouldn't leave until I found her unharmed.

I gave Miss Rose a barely passable bow. I had no respect for the girl. "Have you seen your cousin, Lady Margaret?"

Miss Rose twirled a strand of her hair looking up at me, her eyes hidden by long lashes. "I have, my lord. If you'll follow me I can take you to her." She turned and swayed her hips as she flounced toward a hallway.

What could Margaret be doing in there? Was she hurt? I pushed away my misgivings and followed the girl.

She opened the door to one of the rooms down the long corridor. I walked in looking around, only to see a large bed and some furniture.

I turned to face Miss Rose. "What is the meaning of this?" She walked toward me. I backed up. Someone's hands came around my neck, and I found my mouth covered by a wet cloth. I reached for my gun and then everything went black.

***

Margaret brushed past me, her soft dress like a summer's breeze against my skin. She twirled around, laughing, her eyes wide and bright, as she said something I could not quite grasp. She fell both gracefully and freely against my father's chair in his study. She beckoned me, and behind her, a warm fire glowed in the fireplace, which was rarely lit. Again, she spoke, whispers and hums in my ears, both indiscernible and altogether familiar.

The room faded around me to a sullen grey. A frigid wind blasted me, and I couldn't see Margaret. The ceiling grew taller above my head, the desk a behemoth of cold calculation. I was at once a small child, stuck in the gravitas of my father's steely world. Spymaster was not the title I wanted for myself anymore.

Images blurred by me. Margaret running toward me, before the ground swallowed her up, her fingers sliding through my grasp. Hazy images of warmth and family sucked into a black abyss. My mind shrunk from the scene as I fled.

My vision shifted once more, and I was in my mother's parlor. It was a bright and cheery yellow, with plush furniture and landscape paintings of the ocean. Picturesque views of Devon, the place of my mother's childhood, and the location of most of our holidays eddied around me. I could hear the waves against the shores as if they came from the paintings. In one painting, my mother, her arms outstretched, as a young boy, maybe me, ran into her arms. To the side, stood a man or the grey shadow of a man. My father? Or maybe my mother's killer? Were they one in the same?

I didn't want to play the game anymore. My mother's life would not be Margaret's death. I wanted to keep her safe. Once again Margaret appeared, her hand soft against my face as she smiled up at me. A summer meadow, glowing warmly with golden rays of the sun as insects buzzed lazily through the flowers and over a clear brook surrounded us.

My father's face threatened to push through the hallucination in which I was lost. Margaret's face filled my vision, soft lips moving toward mine. The hazy summer daydream enveloped me once more.

CHAPTER FORTY-TWO

A.

I cracked my eyes open. First, an agonizing pain sliced through the back of my head, along with a headache that stretched across my forehead.

"Damn." I squinted my eyes open.

My bed was in the center of the room, rather than pushed to the side. At the foot of the bed, stood an unfamiliar green cushioned chair draped with a woman's dress. I looked down at the coverlet--a deep forest green. I didn't own a deep forest green coverlet. With blurred vision, my eyes dashed around the room as I alighted only on confusion. I needed to focus my thoughts and pinpoint my location. My head throbbed again, blurring my vision.

What happened? Did drink last night? No. I was at Lady Salisbury's ball. I found my head yanked back, as finger snaked through my hair. The fog lifted enough for me to scoot away. The edge came too soon, and I fell off the bed. I hit the ground. The pain in my head temporarily paralyzed me. The bed grew before me and shifted in my vision. Turning, I saw a door.

Move.

The carpet beneath my fingers, fine to the touch, grounded me. I strained to focus just on touch. My head felt as if it would topple off my neck if I tried to stand.

"Aren't you going to come back to bed, my lord? Why not continue what you've already started?" Margaret's cousin leaned over the edge of the bed and crawled toward me.

Bugger my head.

I stood up backing away, and my feet faltered beneath me. A chill crossed me. Only my shirt and drawers covered my body. Fuck. Clothes. I looked around, spotting them in a pile. I put them on. I fastened my eyes to Miss Rose, backing away again.

"We did nothing. I am leaving. Now." The words barely made it past my heavy tongue.

"But, Alexander, you know we did." She rolled over. With her hand to her chest, she cried out, "My reputation. You must do the honorable thing and marry me. I'll be locked away from society forever if you don't." She pulled up the sheet in false modesty. A tinge of desperation clouded her eyes and a sheen of sweat covered her brow.

I didn't do anything with the girl. But, how did I end up in the room? With the power of a locomotive blasting every other thought aside, grey eyes pierced my memory. My heart pounded in my ears like war drums. My fists clenched. A red haze filled my vision.

"Where is Margaret?" I stalked toward Rose, forgetting escape altogether.

For the first time, she looked truly frightened. "She's gone. They've taken her."

She licked her lips and I turned toward the door. Married? Margaret? Get out. I turned and pushed through the door into a rotund stomach. Looking up I found three sets of eyes staring at me, Baron Wellmont, my father, and Lady Salisbury.

"You were in there with my little girl? You, you reprobate. You will marry her, or everyone will know of your crimes!" Baron Wellmont lurched at me, bouncing on his feet in an imitation of closeness. Perspiration licked his upper lip, and his eyes twitched around the room.

I pushed him out of my way. He smelt of sweat and hard liquor. If I had to tear him apart to find her, I would. "Tell me where she is or get out of my way."

"You are trying to save your own skin from your immoral

transgression against my innocent girl." Baron Wellmont's eyes sought out Lady Salisbury's sympathetic gaze.

"Lady Salisbury leave." My father turned to Lady Salisbury, with a soft bow. "I will handle this. Please, enjoy your guests." He swept his hand toward the ballroom.

Lady Salisbury didn't move. "A young lady may need my care." She puffed up, her face reddening as she glared at me. The feather in her hair bobbed and her thin mouth grew thinner. Her gumption was admirable.

"My dear, Lady Salisbury, the chit, in question, lured my son into this room. Followed shortly after by her father with a cloth in his hand, most likely chloroform. Mere moments before he came to get us. This man smells heavily of alcohol and is deep in debt. My son is a rich man. I am a rich man. We could make his problems disappear. He has sufficient motive for targeting my family, but the details are too thorny for your delicate ears." My father smiled benevolently at Lady Salisbury with a light hand on her arm.

Baron Wellmont sputtered, his face turning a violent shade of red. He leaned forward his black waistcoat bursting at the buttons. With a meaty paw, he brushed his hair away from his face. Again, he turned to Lady Salisbury, but this time she didn't meet his eye.

Lady Salisbury looked at me, taking me in inch by inch. Satisfied, she curtsied to my father. "As you wish, your grace. I will make sure no one disturbs you."

We stood staring at each other, and out of the corner of each of our eyes watched Lady Salisbury's bustle retreat around the corner. A collective breath escaped. The Baron raised his fist, and with a loud grunt charged me. I slammed him into the wall. The frames shook. My closed fist made impact with his fleshy cheek, grazing his jawbone. Pain reverberated through my hand, somewhat satisfying my rage. The beast, however, had not quieted. I wanted to beat him to a bloody pulp, for what he'd done to Margaret, and even to his own daughter.

Baron Wellmont spit out blood, jeering at me. A crazed

expression lit his blue eyes. "You're too late, Rocque. She's gone. She'll be married within the day. You won't be able to find her."

The words didn't kill the hope that I would find her. My gun glinted on the hutch in the hallway. I grabbed it and thrust it into Wellmont's robust gut.

He laughed and coughed out blood. "I won't tell you anything. You want to kill me, Rocque. I dare you to end my troubles now. There are too many witnesses. You wouldn't make it out of here, but I would be free."

The beast growled. He was right. I could not throw myself into police custody and help Margaret. But, the thought didn't stop me from knocking him upside the head with the butt of my gun. He crumpled to the floor.

My father looked on in silence. I turned to him. His eyes were blank, and his face expressionless. "Never let your emotions rule you."

"Why did you send me to Cromer?" I stood nose to nose with my father. I was inches from slamming him into the wall by the neck. His breath, which smelt of tobacco, was hot against my face.

"Only the girl could bring him out. You were too involved," my father said with an unaffected air as he stabbed my heart. With slow, methodical precision he dragged it back out. I should have seen coming.

"Where is she?" I gritted out. I wished he would crumble as easily as Baron Wellmont.

"We lost her, but I have men searching for the Poisoner." My father looked away from me. "The Queen's interests are more important than a mixed-blood girl."

He used her. He set her up as bait. All for what? Greed--for the Opium trade. I looked at the hard lines of his face and wondered how anyone could love him. I could not. Not anymore. I turned away without another word for the man who had always controlled my world and now taken it from me.

My head swam with disorientation as I left the ball. I imagined a ship, anything to reground me. The canvas sails billowed in the wind, the coarse rope moved through my hands and the hot sun beat against my back. I pinched the bridge of my nose between my fingers trying to clear my head. I couldn't be too late. Not again.

Horse.

I needed a horse. My lungs filled with fresh air, finally bereft of cheap punch and smoke. I hailed a Hackney and told the man to go as fast as he could to Belgravia. Home. I fumbled with the key, my hands shaking violently. Using the walls to support me, I fell through the open door of the parlor. Stumbling around, I removed the area rug. My head spun. I paused, breathing through my nose. I pulled open the trap door, took out my two-pistol holster, and buckled it around my hips. I added the second pistol, allowing the smooth, cold, and familiar metal to remind me of my mission.

From outside the room, Mr. Hartridge whispered loudly, "Miss, this is Lord Alexander Rocque's household. I will call the constables on you if you do not leave at once." Margaret?

"My mistress knows Lord Alexander Roque. She's in terrible danger. This is urgent! Life or death, sir. He would want to hear what I have to say!" I listened to the feminine voice starved of Margaret's softer tone. My heart dropped. The woman continued, "I have been waiting all evening to speak with him," her voice broke on the last word.

I walked to the foyer and saw a petite brunette facing off with my butler, Hartridge. "May I help you?" My voice slurred, and I cleared my throat. I had no time for this. I startled both of them apart. The woman looked like she was about to speak, but Hartridge quickly rushed to interrupt.

"My lord, I tried to keep her in the servant's hall. She came at a most unusual and inappropriate hour without a card." He glared at the woman in a maid's uniform. Her face was red and blotchy and dark circles painted shadows beneath her eyes.

"I will hear what the young lady has to say," I said to Hartridge, turning my attention to the woman in question. I realized she was the young maid who told me Margaret was at the Tescher's. "Miss James?"

The woman nodded. "Margaret," the woman paused to catch her breath. "She was kidnapped. I am certain."

I nodded, my throat constricting.

Tears prickled Miss James' eyes. "I heard Miss Rose talking about it with Lady Wellmont. They said she wouldn't be able to say 'no.'" She hiccuped. "I didn't know where else to go. She said you were courting her. Can you find her?" she let out in one breath.

A deafening roar filled my head, like the sound of rushing waves. "Thank you, Miss James. I will do my..." I paused. "I will find her."

I didn't wait to hear what else she had to say. I looked at Hartridge. I should never have let my father hire my servants, but I thought I would be in England for a few months, and certainly not this involved.

"Give Miss James a room and anything else she desires," I threw my words at him.

I raced to the stables, my heart climbing my throat.

"Rocque." I swiveled to my left and saw a large bay horse with Trent. "God, man. You look awful." Captain Trent assessed me. "Are you drunk?"

"I was drugged," I explained, saddling my horse. It was so damn tall. My vision tunneled. I put one foot in the stirrup and managed to swing myself up.

"Damn, mate." Captain Trent's eyes widened. "Here. A swig of water might help." He tossed me a canteen, and I almost missed catching it.

"Thanks." I took a long drink. My mouth felt less disgusting and my head clearer, or at least clear enough. I tossed the canteen back to Captain Trent. "What are you doing here?"

"The police force heard word from your father that we were to find Lady Margaret and with her, we'd capture the Poisoner." Trent sidled his horse next to me. "Where have you been?"

"Cromer," I grumbled, rubbing my eyes. "My father sent

me away." My mind halted as it collapsed again into the mire of drugged sluggishness. "Bait." Pain constricted my chest. I pushed away from the image of Margaret alone and scared. "He used her as bait."

"To capture the Poisoner." Captain Trent nodded.

"Fuck." I pulled my horse in a circle, a thought formulating in my head.

"What?" asked Captain Trent, but my mind was not yet able to fully divulge its thought.

Margaret taken. The Poisoner and the Opium trade. A blond man who controlled a ship filled with Opium in Cromer. The Cannibal club reared its bloody head. On that day, only two men had a connection to the Opium trade, both through the East India Trading Company--Burton and Dr. Francis. Through the same company, the connection to the case for my father and Margaret's grandfather appeared. Yet, the Poisoner could be any number of men in the Cannibal Club or the Company. Other members hadn't been present that day. Who could it be? Perhaps, he wasn't even connected to the Company, but a trader like Jardine, or even someone with Swineburne's proclivities. After all, why would a member of the East India Company be working against the Crown? Why had no one suspected him? Unless...

"I think I know the identity of the Poisoner..."

Captain Trent pulled to a stop. "What do you mean?"

"I think..." I paused, my head light. "Do you know a man named James Francis, he's an ethnologist who worked for the East India Trading Company in the past?"

"Only by name. A few years ago, we clocked suspicious activity on a ship he had some connection with running opium into Vietnam. The cargo had been stolen from David Sassoon & Sons when it left Bombay. We cleared him, however, when the connection seemed unsubstantiated." Captain Trent shrugged. Yet, I knew I had to be right.

With my pounding head, I had little conviction in my interpretation of the facts. Yet, it fell into place in a way nothing else had. Still, the idea that I was missing something, nagged the back of my mind. Why did the Poisoner need Margaret? Why did he need to marry her?

I could not say aloud that Margaret might be dead. A selfish part of me hoped it was truly a marriage, at least, then, she would be alive. But, the end game that circulated in my mind would need Margaret alive. I feared it was my own wishful thinking rather than hard evidence.

I fought a bout of nausea. I had no clue of which way to go. "How many churches are in London? Hopefully, they haven't traveled out of the city."

I had to hold onto hope that marriage was the Poisoner's end game. It was our only lead. I looked at the sky, avoiding the light of the full moon as if it were the plague.

"Alexander, you know the odds. They could be on a ship for all we know. Ship captains can wed people, after all." Trent watched me with concern marking his brow.

"I know. But I must try something. Anything." The leather reins bit into my palm.

Trent nodded. "There are a couple hundred churches, at least. We don't have the time or manpower to visit all of them." His horse sidled closer to mine, and Trent righted me in my seat.

"We have to look for churches with a penchant for illegal activities." I pulled my horse to a stop again, the black night overwhelming.

"That narrows it down to three that have come up of late. I believe there is one on Bow Common, one on Devonia Road, and one on Upper Thames Street. The City Police have been watching them for their money-laundering schemes, abuse of parishioners, and the like."

It was something. My horse tensed beneath me as I move forward without him.

"Devonia Road, that's closest, and then Bow Common," I returned. Trent nodded, and we headed South down Gloucester Lane. One of them had to be the right one. I could not allow myself to believe I was too late.

"We've sent the street boys to look for her too."

The thought that constantly repeated in my head--Margaret. Margaret. Margaret. Street lamps lit the way and we galloped between the rays of light. At that hour, traffic worked in our favor. Only prostitutes, drunken young men, government workers, and the poor laborers wandered the vacant streets. The cobblestones clacked loudly as I urged my horse on. I took no chances with shortcuts but went the tried and true ways, barely noticing the scenery passing. My thoughts threatened to suffocate me.

CHAPTER FORTY-THREE

M.

A burning pain in my arms forced me to flutter awake. I unconsciously turned over, seeking to relieve the pain and slip back into the fold of a dreamless sleep.

"Ow." My watering eyes opened. The pulling sensation sliding from my sockets to my wrists brought to life visions of Medieval torture. I sat still for a moment, my eyes shut in pain until the burning sensation faded from my skin.

I opened my eyes again, taking in the cracked and water stained ceiling. My hands, tied tightly behind me to each post of the four-poster twin bed, left me immobile. Scooting myself up to release the tension from my arms, I looked around the gloomy room. The bed had no sheets, and some yellow-reddish substance stained the grey-striped mattress pad.

I had no idea where I was.

What a pleasant thought to wake up to. Panic climbed up my throat and filled my eyes with tears. No one would be able to find me. I doubted anyone was looking from me or even knew they should. A shiver of disgust threatened to heave my stomach upwards. Yet, the dress I wore earlier still draped my body, filling me with a modicum of ease.

Nothing filtered through my memory but the image of a dark shadow standing over me before everything went black. My uncle's face also came to mind, his ruddy red skin, balding head, and malicious smile cutting even in my imagination. Pain beat at my temples. Tears, unchecked, streaked down my face. I didn't wish to cry for the Wellmonts.

I'd have to figure out how to save myself, the thought filled me with crippling anxiety. A shuddered breath escaped my chest, and I squeezed eyes shut. Filling my head with thoughts of escape and possibility, I looked around the room once more.

Sparse and clean in an empty way, the room gave me little new to discover. Shutters bolted with thick nails covered the windows. Only small streams of light floated through the cracks. An eerie quiet filled the space, but for a faint hum that came from outside. Voices muted by running water. The room smelt much like a damp basement--the pungent River Thames, fishy, salty, oily, and briny. London? The farthest they could have taken me--if I had been out for the night--was Reading. Unless they wanted to break their necks avoiding the potholes hidden by the night. I wouldn't hold out the hope that a madman would take such care. I sent out a little prayer anyway.

I yanked on the ropes, the coarse weave burning the flesh of my wrists. Unlike the contortionists at Barnum & London Circus, I could not maneuver out of the rope bindings. My throat begged for water. A spider, which looked suspiciously like a false widow, stalked down the post toward my bound hands. My breath stilled in my chest, and my gaze fixed upon its spindly legs. Just a bit closer. I flicked it away, my eyes shut, and a squeal trapped in my throat.

As my breath returned to normal, my ears perked at the unmistakable sound of someone coming toward the room. Blast. I scooted myself up further to a somewhat dignified position. With each step-cracking footfall, my heart raced faster until it felt like it would tear out of my chest and run away. Pushing myself back against the board, I brought my legs to my chest. I could kick whoever it was if they got close enough.

The door screeched open, at first blocking my view. There a man stood like a marble statue of Adonis. Shy of Alexander's height, he was in his late forties at least, with grey at his temples. His crystal blue eyes watched me with his long straight nose notched in the air. He brushed a hand through his perfectly groomed blond hair. He wore an impeccably tailored black suit of superfine fabric, his black oxford shone even in the dim light, and a waistcoat of burgundy velvet peeked out from under his top coat.

Hope burgeoned in my chest. "Dr. Francis, please help me." I yanked against the ropes for emphasis.

He leaned against the door, shutting it. He watched me with little expression, but a slight smirk on his lips.

"Who are you?" I swallowed. "Who are you really?" I couldn't quite connect the man standing before me to the man who had sweetly told me about my mother and comforted me.

"My fiancée doesn't even recognize me. Should I be insulted?" the man asked the air, circling toward me until he stood a foot away. "After all, I went through to get you to my safe house. You've ignored me for an entire night."

A whole night? I swallowed at the thought, taking in the man in front of me. My fogged brain strained to piece together his admission with what I remembered about Dr. Francis.

"I can see you're trying to work this out in that pretty little head of yours. Perhaps, I should have used less chloroform." Dr. Francis laughed, standing too far away for me to deliver a quick kick.

I glared at him and gritted out, "Well, then enlighten me."

"Tsk-tsk. My, aren't you slow?" The man patted my head as if I were a dog, sending rivulets of revulsion speeding through my veins. If only he moved in front of me, I could kick him. "I could only expect that from your breed."

"My breed?" I pushed out between clenched teeth. My skin crawled and I could barely look him in the eye.

"Jew," he said with little inflection, but for the gleam that filled his eyes. His beautiful face contorted into something truly heinous. His gaze burned with violence and impatience. I could imagine the fires of hell burning blue around his face like a halo. In the blink of an eye, he regained control, which was much more petrifying than his loss of control.

"I am not a 'breed.'" I regretted the words the second they slipped from my lips.

He licked his lips, as if happy for my rebuttal. With quick strength, he gripped my skull as if measuring it with his hands. "Jews are born of the serpent seed. Not even Darwin's theory can account for the ugliness of a Jew's skull. Only one step above a Chinaman's or Negro's."

His fingers moved downward, wrapping around my face so that I was forced to look at him. "You're lucky to have an English father, or you wouldn't be quite so pretty."

"Let go of me," I growled out, close to tears. He only squeezed my head tighter, his nails digging into my skull. He pushed my head back against the headboard, before releasing me.

"Sadly, I need you, darling," he said, as he stepped back. "Your family took something that was rightfully mine and I want it back."

"Ask the Wellmonts," I spat at him. "I cannot help you."

The man turned back to me, the same sinister smile stretching his lips. "You think I haven't ventured down that avenue? Your aunt, dear Emily, knows everything. She always was a jealous girl," he laughed, "it must be from her nature as a daughter of Cain."

Sick dread made me wish I could cover my ears and pretend I was anywhere else. The man didn't give me the luxury as he continued to speak, "Her husband is an idiot and only knows me as Dr. Francis, the academic, family friend, and the man he has lost his fortune," he paused, smiling maliciously, "and wife to."

"Who am I to know you as?" I licked my lips, my palms sweating. This was it. Everything in me wanted to continue fighting against the ropes that wrapped around my wrists, but I needed to wait for another opportunity.

"You already know me, darling." He traced my nose with his finger before tweaking it. "I used antimony on your father. It only left behind heart failure and a terrifying premonition of death. Your mother, though, I saved the best for her. Death by strychnine is truly one of the most horrific ways to die. It begins by causing the victim to feel a sense of impending suffocation. Of course, then, the victim does suffocate. As the poison spreads through the body, the facial muscles are forced into a gruesome grin, a characteristic of the poison. Which is why I chose it. I wanted to see her smile for me."

He laughed as any warmth I had ever felt abandoned me. "Next the stomach muscles harden, tense, and cause the victim's eyeballs to stare as if they are about to pop right out of their sockets. Through all this agony, the victim remains fully conscious to the unraveling horrors." He tapped his chin, his crystal eyes assessing me. I cringed wishing I hadn't spoken. The image would never leave my head for as long as lived. If I lived much longer.

"You are the Poisoner?" I asked for the final confirmation, my voice trembling.

He pulled a chair next to my bed. "You know, Dr. Francis has been a great disguise for me over the years. No one is ever afraid of a mild academic. Everyone underestimates him and believes they can get something out of him. They tell me their deepest desires." The Poisoner ran his fingers through my hair. "My dear childhood friend, a weak sickly child, inspired me to take on the garb when he *fell* down a well."

"You're a monster," I spat at him.

"You think I don't know that? It's been an excellent profession, better than I could have ever done as a member of the Queen's smuggling force in the Orient. Even they utilized my particular skills. Only now am I called a monster."

CHAPTER FORTY-FOUR

M.

"You're pretty like your mother, and equally as defiant. I hoped you wouldn't be the same. Emily told me you're a stupid girl, but, between you and me, she's probably jealous." The Poisoner circled to my other side, his gaze taking in every inch of me.

I scooted to the farthest edge of the bed. It was as if I stared down into an abyss, with hungry wolves at my back. He laughed at my intake of breath. His criminals probably surrounded the place. Would I even be able to escape? Taking a deep breath, I steeled the beating of my heart and wrapped my hands around the ropes binding me in place.

"If you think my 'people' are so abhorrent why would you connect with my," I choked on the word, "aunt?" I questioned him because a part of my brain needed to make some logic of the situation. If I was going to escape it had better be with answers.

"I was satisfied with my vengeance on your parents, and your grandfather for betraying me. You didn't really seem worth the effort." I turned my head away from him, grinding my teeth together. "If I had learned of their breed sooner, they may have had a quicker death."

"Look at me when I am talking to you." He grabbed my hair pulling my face back to his. "Good girl. I knew Emily would follow my wishes and create a little hell for you in her household." My eyes widened, the pain stabbed my heart again. I dared not look down for fear that blood seeped from my chest. "However, the markets have changed, and sadly for you, I learned your inheritance was more than money."

"More than money?" I breathed out. I decided if I were to be stuck with the madman, I'd rather know everything. No matter how painful.

"Emily told me you would the inherit the key to the East. All I must do is marry you, and once I am in control of your wealth, not just the wealth, but also the Opium empire I helped the Crown create, I can dispose of you. At least that's what Emily wants. I don't need her. I quite enjoy fresh faces more than wrinkled ones."

"Why are you telling me this?" I whispered.

"Because your face betrays your every emotion." The Poisoner ran his finger along my cheek, tracing the path of my tears.

"Where is your inheritance?" He cocked his head to the side. "'No' is not within my vocabulary, Margaret."

I shook my head, no words coming out. It must be hidden within the document I found in my grandfather's office. The one Alexander had. I turned my face away from him, but he yanked me back by my hair again. My scalp burned as I sucked in a ragged breath, fully looking at him for the first time. He had smoke in the depth of his eyes and held me imprisoned as if beckoning like the sirens for me to join, for there was something familiar in his gaze. Something about myself I had hidden so deeply I had all but forgotten it existed, yet he wasn't afraid to show it--open Pandora's box and shutter out hope.

"Tell me." He shoved my head back against the headboard. "I know there's a code. What is it? I know you went to your grandfather's office after he sent you that pathetic letter."

"I don't know," I growled out. My head throbbed. "I promise. I don't know. I didn't even know I had any, beyond what my uncle was stealing." Instinctively, I pulled against the ropes, thrashing away from him.

He released me, giving me a shrewd looked, again in control. "Remember the code and maybe you'll live past our wedding night." He flicked out a blade and caressed my cheek with it, just hard enough to draw blood. I stilled completely, my heart stopped mid-beat. "I had hoped by allowing you to London, something would be jarred in that pretty little head of yours. At least you helped me souse out your allies, your dear nanny, grandfather, and even the glorious Duke of Auden, your beau's father." The Poisoner gripped my chin, once more, between sharp nails. "But, now it's time to legally bind you to me. When your inheritance does appear, it will be mine. Our meeting with the Parson's trap is in an hour."

I held back a sob, my breath paused by the exertion. He turned to leave, before gleefully spearing me again. "Oh, I almost forgot. If you try anything that dear friend of yours, what is her name? Oh yes, Miriam. She will feel the pain of a special poison. One less Jew no one will miss."

A sob escaped me, and my breath released in painful gasps, which seemed to bring the pain of a thousand knives stabbing my chest. All the fight seemed to leave my body. I couldn't do anything that would harm Miriam. I had already done too much.

A broad grin crossed the Poisoner's face. "I'll leave you to your thoughts."

He sauntered out of the room.

Once the door slammed behind him, I fully submitted myself to the tears. There was no escape, now. Guilt ate me away, corroding me like a ship lost at the bottom of the ocean. I shouldn't have told my aunt I had been with Miriam. I closed my eyes trying to think of something, anything that could save her. Minutes passed, the door creaked open slightly. He returned. Why? I kept my eyes shut. I didn't hear anything. Had he left? I opened my eyes.

A clean boy dressed in patched clothing stood in front of the door. His thin frame paced in front of the door, just outside of the room. He looked at me, his eyes filled with fear and concentration. His dark eyebrows scrunched, as he scrutinized me.

Finally, he spoke, "You're Margaret, right?" he whispered loudly, hand cupping his mouth.

I nodded. Who was this boy? I cleared the lump in my throat. "Yes, I am," I croaked.

The boy inched through the doorway, giving me a clearer view of him. He nodded and gave me a small smile. Before I could say anything, a loud creak from the hallway startled him. He jumped and flew from the room, leaving the door ajar. I could not have him on my conscience, too.

The next person to enter my prison was Aunt Emily. She smiled cruelly at me as she untied my wrists.

"I've waited many years for this," she laughed, the soberest I'd seen her in my entire life. Even her usual austere style of dress had been overthrown for a bouffant skirt of oriental lace and pink Pompadour foulard.

She left for a moment to drag in a large dress bag. She set it inside the room, closed the door, and came toward me. Dragging me to a stand, she held my chin firmly between her fingers, her nails biting into my flesh. She tilted my head from side to side. "You look so much like my little sister. She should never have tried to take what wasn't hers. Maybe, then I could have loved her." She spat directly into my face as she began to undress me. She roughly yanked the yellowed white wedding dress, several sizes too small over my head. She didn't allow me to wipe the spit from my face, so it dried on my flesh.

She roughly shoved me in front of a mirror and pushed me to a seated position. She pulled a brush through my hair, yanking at the knots, which tore apart and broke with her cruel handling. My scalp burned, and tears filled my eyes. Aunt Emily pulled my hair into a bun, jabbing my skull with a profusion of bobby pins and pulling my hair so tightly that stars danced across my vision. She rammed a veil onto my head.

"Once he's done with you, he'll kill you like he did her." Her eyes were filled with a crazed light as she yanked my hair one last time. I wondered if she knew he planned to betray her too.

"Why are you so filled with hate?" I whispered, astounded by the malignant force that seeped off her thin form.

"I love him," she murmured with a heated frenzy. "Ester

should have stayed away. He should never have known about our dirty blood. She knew what it'd do."

The door screeched open again, but I didn't turn around. His form only visible in the warped reflection of the mirror. A more fitting reflection than the lies told to the naked eye. I closed my eyes.

"Excellent, Emily." He kissed her cheek, and she blushed prettily. "Let us depart."

"Yes, Dr. Francis." Aunt Emily pushed me forward.

He grabbed my chafed wrists painfully, as he led me through the narrowed hallway and down the stairs until we were outside. I blinked false tears from the shock of light and sounds.

The sun shone brightly. A day like that day should have been overcast and rainy. I could see the River Thames, yet I found no comfort that we were still in London. Hope seemed like a bitter foolish thing, something I could little remember. Dr. Francis handed me up into the closed carriage, seating me across from him, as I stared out the window. Aunt Emily waved at us from the porch step and blew a kiss to Dr. Francis.

"Silly woman. She hasn't changed one bit since we were children."

He turned away from Aunt Emily, piercing me with his eyes. "I forgot to tell you, that your aristocrat beau has been taken care of. He was quite a help in leading me in the right direction, but he took too much of your time." Dr. Francis cleaned his nails with his knife, pausing and looking up at me with wide, mocking eyes. "Don't tell me you believed he would be able to save you?"

My ears tingled, and my eyes fixed on his. A slow burning fire raced through my body. The Poisoner, Dr. Francis—evil incarnate—had stolen my life from me. Maybe if I reached for the gun, I could end his pitiful life, before he could harm Miriam, too. I had never once thought about killing anyone before in my life. The thought of holding the gun, its cool steel burning my flesh, held no comfort.

The gun sat on his lap mocking me. I bit my lip and looked at him. He looked out the window. I slowly scooted forward on the seat, keeping my eyes fixed on his face. I made a reach for the gun. He looked over at me. I feigned nonchalance, smoothing my dress until he turned away again. I pushed up from my seat, my fists angled toward his perfect face. His mouth broke into a smile, and before I could put my hands up in defense he knocked me on the side of the head.

CHAPTER FORTY-FIVE

A.

My nose bled into my cut lip, as I knocked down the last of the men who had ambushed Trent and me. We would have been done for if only we hadn't stopped at the city station for reinforcements after John Kiles told us of the Poisoner's plans. Everyone wanted to take part in bringing down the Poisoner.

I wanted that too, once.

The glory of it was compelling. Now, all I wanted was to have Margaret safely in my arms. I rolled my shoulder free of tension. My shot wound all but healed, other than twinges now and then. We rode all night and could not find a trace of her. The dawn reminded me of my failure. I leaned my head back and pinched the bridge of my nose to stem the flowing blood. I wiped my face with a handkerchief, my bottom lip all but numb.

We visited both the churches on Devonia and Bow Common, but no wedding ceremonies had been set to be performed. Our last hope--gone. Shaking my head, I dislodged the thought remembering we had one more chance. One of the police officers came toward me on his horse and I swung onto mine. The men circled me, five in strength, waiting for my directive. Hopefully, we would be enough. Considering the ambush, the Poisoner expected resistance and was not taking any chances. I just needed him to make one mistake.

"Where to, my lord?" the officer who approached me asked.

"Upper Thames Street." I turned my horse around, and we set off at a gallop. After that, I didn't know. She had to be there. She had to.

We trotted into Upper Thames Street, near the river--not a single church in sight. I looked to Captain Trent, but I found his attention focused elsewhere. I followed his line of sight and saw a boy with patched clothing standing next to a tall red-haired man. Both stood, talking to a Constable. Captain Trent, the officers, and I sidled our horses closer.

"I seen her da, right. She were tied up. It were 'er, all right, she said so. She didn't 'ave an 'appy look." The small boy pulled frantically at his father's cuff. The man stood and looked awkwardly around, trying to shush his son.

"Button it, Johnny. I'm sorry for botherin' you, Bobby. Children and their imagination." The man frowned at his son, looking like he'd rather be anywhere else.

"It was Margaret o' my name's not Johnny-Boy Carter. She was all tied up, she needs help. Fry my hide. I swears it, da," the boy yelled in frustration pulling at the officer until his father drew him off.

Could it be my Margaret? I jumped off my horse and walked up to them. Captain Trent followed suit. Looking to the officer. "A young woman has been kidnapped. Can you help?" I directed my question to the boy.

The officer's eyes looked over my shoulder, and he noticed Captain Trent. "Oi there, Trent. What are you and the bloody lot doin' in these parts?"

"We are assisting Lord Alexander Rocque to find a missing woman, Lady Margaret Savoy. We have reason to believe she has been kidnapped. We'd be grateful if you could help us out, Edwards." Captain Trent came forward, shaking the officer's hand.

"O' course, what can I do for you two?" Edwards looked at us.

"This young lad works for me," Captain Trent said.

The officer patted the boy on the shoulder, "Hoof it ahead, lad."

Johnny inspected me with distrust. His little face scrunched up and his arms crossed over his small chest. "You're someone to 'er, then, eh, gov? She seemed like a nice lady. I don't want no geezer 'urtin' 'er. Do you swear that you are?" He looked at me with the most honesty I had seen all day. Its innocence comforted me, through the blackness and the beast that surged within my chest.

"I promise you this, I would never hurt her, but the man who has her will. I swear this on my mother's grave." I put my hand out to him.

He looked at it as if confused by the pretense of my outstretched hand. "Not bad. I believe you. Me mum is dead, too." His small hand firmly shook mine.

"Thank you, Johnny. Can you tell me what the lady looked like? I'll know then if it's my Margaret," I asked. My feet itched to run out and search for her as if I were one of my father's hounds in pursuit of a fox.

Johnny nodded his head, importantly, puffing out his chest. "Yes. She's right pretty. She's taller than some girls are. She 'ad dark brown curly 'air and grey mince pies. She were wearin' the ugliest dress I 'ave ever seen in me entire life." Johnny made a face. "There was also a mean lady there with her, with a nasty pinched face."

That must be her aunt, Lady Wellmont. I looked at the officer, "That's her," I looked back to Johnny, "Do you know where she might have gone?"

"Oh, yes, the bloomin' bad man were takin' 'er to the church right on this 'ere street. I'll get out me spoons. It's a wee ways up from 'ere." He nodded pointing up the street.

I looked to Captain Trent, and we nodded to each other, "Thank you, Master Johnny Carter." He tossed the boy a shiny coin.

I looked to the surrounding officers, "We need to split up. I need some of you to contact the Duke of Auden to bring in more men. The rest, who do not remain with me, need to go to the building where Lady Margaret was held. There you need to arrest Lady Wellmont and any of the other accomplices."

The men nodded in response, and we split up.

The officer patted Johnny on his head, looking up to Captain Trent and me. “Ride on ahead. I’ll cop my ‘orse, and I’ll follow after you and Captain Trent, milord.”

I nodded, and we headed off, the officers a bit behind us. With the knowledge of Margaret’s potential location, a calm settled over me like that I had felt on many Navy missions. One-step closer.

CHAPTER FORTY-SIX

M.

Suddenly we stopped, causing my body to fly back against the seat. I lost my chance for the gun, as he got out of the carriage and dragged me down with him.

Someone shrieked my name, and my soul went into free fall. Miriam flailed against a brute that held her hostage. In this neighborhood, no one would think twice, even if someone called out "Bloody murder." Wisps of her blonde hair played around her reddened face, and her lavender gown had a ripped sleeve. We stopped in front of a dusty brick church with decrepit steps. I never thought the Poisoner already had Miriam in his talons. As always, and like many before me, I had underestimated him. With the dawn light behind Miriam, I had failed.

"Insurance." Dr. Francis smirked down at me, hauling me toward the church. As I was pulled past Miriam, our fingertips brushed.

"I am sorry. I love you," I whispered to her. The brute holding her gripped her arm and tugged her behind us.

"I love you, too. Everything will be all right." She gave me watery smile. The bruise forming on her temple swamped me with guilt. Never had I been filled with so much hate. The feeling overtook all other thoughts until it marred me in blackened tar.

Dr. Francis walked us to a wizened priest, with beady eyes like a rat, gleaming with hunger. Money passed between him and Dr. Francis, as we stood before the altar. The brute discreetly showed me the gun that pressed to Miriam's back, so I didn't do anything. I took a deep pull of the musty air, praying to the God who always seemed to fail me.

BANG.

I turned around as the door crashed open behind us. It was my uncle. His face ruddy and his shirt pit-stained.

"Not a peep from you," Dr. Francis whispered in my ear, his hot breath like a hint of hell. My uncle came to stand beside us. "If you do I'll put a bullet in your friend's pretty little head."

I stared at Dr. Francis, too afraid to even move. Even without the edict, it would have been unlikely for my uncle to help, even if I pleaded with him. It had never worked before. He discarded me as if I were less than a piece of moldy bread.

"Where do I sign? I need to get back to my club. My luck has changed. I can feel it," he spoke, his breath labored, and his forehead dotted with a feverish sweat. Buttons on his waistcoat threatened to pop, as he pulled against the hem. He looked around near the priest, avoiding any contact with our direction. He sported a split lip and a bruise on his temple.

I didn't feel sorry for him.

"Also, we have a pesky problem with..." My uncle came forward finally looking in our direction. Dr. Francis looked over him with cool calculation. Uncle Matthew stumbled backwards down the steps, pulling at his collar.

"Yes. Yes. Sign the goddamned papers." The doctor picked at his jacket, looking up with a smile. "Did I say that in the house of God?"

Dr. Francis pushed my uncle toward a table next to the altar, before coming to stop, a foot away. I could see his ears twitching like a hellhound. His face a frozen mask, as he frowned breaking the perfect image.

"Wait, what do you mean we have a problem?" his voice projected a deceptive calm. A calm that my uncle didn't even recognize as fake.

My uncle refused to look at me. He twisted his hat in his hands and seemed to shrink within himself. "He got away. Lord Alexander Rocque got away."

My heart slowed to a stop, a glimmer of hope infusing my blood with warmth. I looked to Miriam. If I could get her out alive, I didn't care what the Poisoner did to me.

Dr. Francis laughed, and the unforgiving cold returned to my veins. "Well, of course, he did. You, stupid son of a bitch." The doctor knocked my uncle to the floor. "Greedy bastard sign the paper." He towered over my uncle, his voice hard, but calm. "You will pay your debt, and I am considering your life."

I could not help but feel a morbid sense of satisfaction as my uncle succumbed to the same terror he had put me through my entire life. In the same thought, I was reminded that when the ink dried on the paper, I had been traded by abuser for another. I flinched when the doctor kicked my uncle in his ribs. My Uncle, wailed, clutching his midsection and crawling away. Blood dribbled down his fleshy chin.

"You're lucky I sent my own men after him, but you'd better hope he's dead, or I will destroy you and your family like I did," Dr. Francis nodded his head to me, and my uncle looked at me with horror.

Alexander could not be dead. I squeezed my eyes shut, no longer caring about my uncle's fate. I turned to Miriam, she gave me a weak nod and I took the sentiment, holding it close to my heart.

"But, but," My uncle lay, sprawled on the floor rubbing his head, "what if I gave you my daughter Rose? She's a pretty piece. How about it then? I have no debt?"

What a bastard. I should have realized what he was that ages ago. Instead, he beat me into submission, making me believe he was invincible and that I was worthless. I should have realized what Aunt Emily was too. Their cruelty had nothing to do with me.

"I don't need your strumpet of a daughter." Dr. Francis advanced on my uncle, forcing him to scramble to his feet. "Sign the paper and get out of my sight."

"Yes, y-yes," my uncle responded, voice shaking, as he signed my life away. Then the coward ran out of the church like the Erinyes were on his heels. I hoped that they were.

The Doctor smoothed his blond hair back with his hand

and smiled at me. “Apologies, my darling. Let’s start.” He gripped my hand painfully, reminding me of our first meeting and forcing attention back to my unfolding doom.

CHAPTER FORTY-SEVEN

M.

The priest droned on. I stared at Miriam, who stared back, with a small smile that could barely hold onto her lips. The disarray of her blonde hair around her shoulders framed her red-rimmed eyes. Dust motes floated languidly through the air, the floorboards creaked, and the priest droned on. I looked around sightless, voiceless, and soundless. Stillness echoed through me in a haunting refrain. I had to think of something, but I found my mind stuck in a dark and twisting maze.

"Does anyone object to this marriage?" the priest said. A finite end crashed around my shoulders and sucked the air from my lungs. Tears welled in the corners of my eyes as the severity of my new life mantled me with dread. I searched the room again through clouded vision, looking for anything.

"Bloody hell, why did you say that? I paid you a pretty sum of cash, so no one could object," Dr. Francis bellowed at the diminutive man. "Continue to the end, and be quick about it, you blasted fool."

"Apologies, sir. Force of habit. I'll get to it right away, sorry." The priest trembled, trying to right himself.

The door slammed open again. We all turned around, Miriam was the first to see. Her gasp echoed through the church. I opened my eyes expecting to see the rotund figure of my uncle bearing down on me to enact some further cruelty of fate.

"Alexander," I inhaled, my voice barely reaching a whisper

as if it were painful to utter a single word. My lungs fought for air. I could only breath him in. Alexander's eyes locked onto mine as he walked down the aisle, his gun securely fixed on Dr. Francis. Behind him, stood Captain Trent.

"Release her, now." Alexander moved closer, ever so slightly. As if assessing a battlefield, Alexander's eyes traveled the small church, every step he took a calculated move. Cold metal pressed firmly against the back of my neck, shuttering any amount of hope that threatened to well within me. Alexander stopped, and the barrel of the gun remained fixed to my neck.

"Come any closer, and they both die." Dr. Francis pushed me forward with the barrel of the gun, only a step or so, but enough to prove his veracity. Miriam yelped as she came under the same treatment by the brute that held her captive. I realized the warning was for my sake, Dr. Francis needed me alive, but he didn't need Miriam. "My men will be here in a matter of moments, and you will be dead, too."

"Your men are dead, Dr. Francis," Alexander said.

I was surprised he knew the Poisoner's identity. Dr. Francis must have been too, for his breath rushed against my neck.

"Police officers surround us. You kill her, and you won't walk out of here alive. The game's up," Captain Trent spoke inching closer.

"The game's never up." Dr. Francis's voice told me he smiled, but I could feel him tense. His hand faltered on the gun, the barrel shaking slightly on my neck.

Alexander glared at the doctor, before turning his gaze toward me. "Margaret, stay calm. Everything will be all right."

"How touching," Dr. Francis said, malice filtering through every syllable. The cold touch of the barrel left my neck, moving toward Alexander.

My heart rushed forward before my mind could catch up. I fell into Dr. Francis, who wavered with the sudden weight of my limp body. His arm loosened just enough for me to slide out of his grasp around my waist. I turned around under his arm, elbowing him in the ribs and stomping on his foot with my heel, remembering Alexander's advice. With both of my hands, I pushed his wrist inward, causing the gun to point toward him. He came at me with his other hand, the one that held me up, but my strength shocked both of us. Our eyes locked. The gun blasted.

CHAPTER FORTY-EIGHT

A.

"I hear the girl's alive," my father said, staring at me over his golden spectacles. He sat behind his desk, leafing through correspondence.

"No thanks to you," I gritted out as I remained standing. The room smelled heavily of cognac and all, but ashes remained in the fireplace.

"Occupational hazard." My father flicked his hand through the air in the same manner he had discarded Margaret's life.

"Is that what mother was?" My shoulders tensed, I hadn't spoken of her to him in several years. Never even breathed her name, Mary Kathryn, in his presence or remarked on her favorite flower--lavender. He couldn't even bear to hear news of Dorset, my mother's ancestral home.

Only the sound of crunching paper and a glass hitting wood filled the space. He stared at me, the paper shrinking ever so slightly as his fist tightened. "She..." He paused, visibly swallowing, "That is not the same."

"Is it not?" I was testing my luck. The beast inside me, hummed with excitement. It wanted me to push the limit and make him snap. Margaret. I blinked away the red.

"Alexander." He cautioned coming to a stand with a white-knuckled grip on his desk.

"What are you going to do?" I cocked my head, moving forward. "Fight me? I am the younger man, father. One, you trained well." I stepped back again, perusing his books and leaving the "You're lucky I have something to lose," unsaid. I wasn't interested in his countless volumes of horticulture, but any clue to where he kept his safe.

My father returned to his seat and ran a hand through his steel-grey hair. "The girl might still be of some use. I know you're..." a look of distaste, or perhaps disbelief, filled his face, "fond of her."

Use--that's all people were to my father. Anyone could be a little pawn to move around the game of life. Economic favors. Brute strength. A pretty face. Tactical intelligence. An heir. "Did you use me?"

He looked up, folding his hand in his lap. "Of course." My father was never one to mince words, but even I was surprised by his easy admittance.

"How?" I wondered if he would tell me, but more than anything, I wondered if I wanted to know. Yet, I needed to know, to understand, and to fully embrace his methods all to keep Margaret safe.

My father's eyes narrowed, considering me. He leaned back in his chair, folding his arms over his chest. For several minutes, I believed he wouldn't tell me. "You're the third son, you can move about society with less notice than I can or even your brothers."

He whittled my importance to merely a scrap, but it didn't hurt as it once did. "Is that all?" I asked with a bored tone, once again tracing the bookshelf with my gaze. I needed to get into the safe.

"I knew I could trust you. Perhaps not to ruin the case, but also to not betray me to the Poisoner. I've lost too many men to bribery."

"Did you know Lady Margaret's connection?" I asked, energy burning through my veins.

"I suspected when you found the code." I watched his gaze move to the bookshelf. My suspicions were confirmed. "I worked with her grandfather and Dr. Francis in the East India Trading Company." A distant look filled his eyes, and he turned toward the maps that lined the walls. "It was all so long ago, or I might have remembered Dr. Francis. An oversight on my part, I'll admit it."

"Do you want her dead, like the Poisoner?" I pushed the words from my lips, carefully masking the disgust from my tone.

"No. The Crown has much to gain if we uncover what her grandfather hid. I should never have doubted Heman." My father chuckled, taking a long sip of brown liquor from his crystal glass. "Now that we have Dr. Francis, or rather now that he's dead, so too is the Crown's largest competitor in the East."

"The Opium trade has much to gain." I gave my father a terse smile. Again, I walked too close to the edge, but the rage that simmered within me had not erupted since my mother's death.

"You do too, son. This Empire is backed by the money made by Opium, by the legacy I helped create. Our social programs the women so covet, the infrastructure from the Romans, and our great bounds in scientific discovery are kept alive by that trade." My father stood, sweeping his hands across the room in a grand gesture. A gross gleam entered his eyes. "The greatest Empire the world has ever seen deserves nothing less. We can become greater still."

"What about the Chinamen? Those addicted to Opium. It's lost public favor."

"You've been reading those leftist newspapers. They sensationalize." My father dismissed my words with a careless flick of his hands. "The second the Opium money disappears; the people will be begging for its return. What's a China man's worth compared to good English stock?"

I gritted my teeth into a forced smile. Abroad I had served with too many different men not to value every human being's life as equal. Sir Hornby had taught me more than my father ever could other than the cruelty of man. "As you say." I nodded, looking at the bookshelf again when my father turned away.

"It might be good to have the girl in the family." My Father returned to his seat, lighting a cigar.

I returned my eyes to his. "What do you mean?"

"Like I said, I know you're fond of the girl. Marry her, then she along with her inheritance will be easier to control. No one will have to know she's a Jew." My father sneered. "If we need to get rid of her at a later date, so be it." He blew a cloud of smoke in my face, its overwhelming scent seizing in my lungs.

I couldn't find the words to respond to my father's cutting pronouncement. The rage had been blasted away by an enveloping numbness. Could a fire stay alight against a man so cold? Luckily, I was not required to respond as the door crashed open.

A man ran in, his face red, sweat dotting his forehead, and his breath sounding heavily around the hollow room. "Your Grace." The man bowed.

Frustration marked my father's brows as he came to stand. "Gads speak man."

The man took a deep breath and wiped at his forehead with his sleeve. "The Crimson Crown Society has attacked one of our ships."

A complete stillness filled my father as his gaze became thoughtful. "They've never attacked on English soil. Not in years at least," he mused.

"Who?" I asked. Something had changed.

"Anarchists." He moved from behind the desk to the man in the doorway. "Take me to the docks immediately." With that, he was gone.

My lungs sought the air, taking it in until my head felt light headed. This would be my last and only opportunity. I returned to the bookshelf re-reading the book titles. Nothing. Until I caught the title *Lavandula: A Case Study of Lavender from the Canary Islands to Egypt.* Could it be? I pulled out the book and a click sounded. Behind the book, I found an open door on the bookshelf. Careful to remember the books' order on the self, I removed several more books to fully see the newly revealed compartment.

A safe.

A Chubb's Lock Safe with a Detector lock. Only a Mr. Hobbs at London's Great Exhibition in '51 had cracked it successfully. The lock had an Anti-lock picking mechanism, which would cause the lock to seize if I made even the slightest wrong move. I did not have the skill nor the patience to create another "Great Lock Controversy." I needed to find a key.

If my father connected the location of the safe to my mother, then perhaps I could find the key the same way. Unless he kept it on his person, it was somewhere in the study. I looked around taking in the room, the desk, the velvet settee, and the fireplace. Then I remembered the needlepoint chair out in the hallway. The one Margaret had sat upon. Until my mother's death, it had been housed in her parlor. She had carefully embroidered the cushion with a sprig of lavender in her youth. Out in the hallway, I looked under the chair. Affixed to the wooden underside of the seat was a small linen bag. I removed the contents, finding three keys of about the same size. Damn. If I used the wrong one the lock would be unusable. Each key had a set of number, which I first mistook to be a serial code. Yet, one had the exact date of my mother's birth engraved along the side. I returned the other two keys to their bag.

With a bated breath, I slid the key into the lock and turned it. Click. Click. Click. The safe popped open. Air rushed out of my lungs. Inside, I saw several velvet jewelry boxes, folders, and a golden wedding band. I set the key aside and leafed through the folders. The code sat on the very top of the second folder. I took it without hesitation, replacing it with a forged replica. My father would eventually know someone had taken it. I just hoped he would suspect me last. Making careful considerations to precision, I returned everything to its natural order. With a thudding finality, I left.

CHAPTER FORTY-NINE

M.

I woke with a start, gripping silken fabric in my closed fists. My breath released through my clenched teeth, and I realized that I had been holding it for quite some time. Red wallpaper with thin gold vertical stripes covered the wall in front of me and above me a deep maroon canopy. I took a deep breath taking in the smell of roses. At the foot of my bed was a vase of yellow roses on a hutch. Miriam. I lay back against the pillows.

A shadow grew over me, and I reflectively flinched away, almost falling off the other side of the bed. "Margaret, good God. You're awake."

I opened my eyes and took in Alexander, willing my heart to slow in my chest. He smiled hesitantly, righting me on the bed and pushing back his tousled hair. "You were mumbling and shaking in your sleep."

I yawned and stretched, gathering my thoughts and trying to ignore the chill sweeping down my spine. "Was I?"

His expression shuttered, and he straightened his rumpled clothing. "How are you feeling?"

Sitting up and bringing the rest of the room into focus, I glared at Alexander. "Where are we? Where's Miriam?"

"Aunt Bita's home, in London. Miriam is safe. You'll see her yourself this evening." Alexander sat on the edge of my bed. "How are you feeling?" he asked again.

A warm surge of relief crashed over me. I had saved Miriam, myself, and even Alexander. Unless... "What happened after the gun blasted? Where's..."

"The Poisoner's dead." Alexander watched me with soft eyes. Eyes I didn't want. "Please, Margaret, are you all right?"

"Alexander, I am fine." I turned away from him. "How long have I been asleep?"

"Two days. You were out cold. The doctor who came in said you needed sleep. The maids dressed you in a nightgown and did their best to clean you up. I hope you didn't mind?" Alexander took my hand.

"Two days." I shook my head in wonder. For two days, everything disappeared. "I don't mind. I wouldn't want to sleep in bloody clothes." I paused, thinking about the white thing. Its suffocating scent made me want to vomit. "I hope you burned that dress."

"I did." Alexander nodded a gleam of satisfaction in his gaze yet worry lined his face. "Do you need to talk about anything? Anything at all?" Alexander took my hand in his, but again I escaped its grasp.

I opened my mouth but instead shook my head. My mind swirled with images of the Poisoner's face, the Duke's face, and finally Alexander's until they all became one

"If that is your wish." The worry didn't leave his face. "I am here for you, always."

I nodded hesitantly, without full compliance. A part of me wished he would leave me alone to my thoughts, while another part yearned to confide in him, even trust him again. Too much remained unsaid.

"Is there anything else you need?" Alexander asked. "I can send up a tray of food."

"A real bath. I would like a bath," I whispered. My skin crawled and I could almost imagine blood staining my hands--viciously, unmistakably red.

Alexander stood and sidled awkwardly back and forth, something clearly troubling his mind. "I'll leave you and send the maids in with a bath." He paused again, a thought poised on his lips. "You'll need to eat," he finally said.

"I'd like to eat at a table I think. What time is it?" I asked, knowing I should have been hungry.

"Past 1300 hours, I mean, one o'clock," Alexander headed to the door, watching me carefully. I ignored his gaze and he finally left.

I threw off the covers, my legs shaking from their prolonged inactivity. I splashed water on my face and looked at my reflection in the mirror. I should look different somehow. I killed a man after all. I pulled at my face, but still, I stared back. Grey eyes, dark hair, straight nose.

A stream of light splashed across my eyes and I turned to the window. The closed velvet curtains suffocated me with the imprint of imprisonment. Freedom. I looked at my hands, stretching them out before me. My own hands saved my life. With surety in my step, I threw open the curtains. The sun broke through the shadowed bedroom. I pressed my cheek into the warmed window which saturated my person.

The window faced the street, and just in front of the house, I noticed two men dressed in black looking up at me. They were out of place in their stillness, and their gazes were fixated upon my window. A chill crawled up my spine, and I held onto the velvet curtain for support. A sad smile spread across one of the men's faces, and he tipped his hat to me. The other man waved leisurely before both men turned away slowly walking down the street.

A knock, quick and professional, sounded at my door.

"Come in," I responded, gripping my nightgown.

The door to my room opened with little sound. I turned around and plastered a smile on my face. A young maid entered, her face hidden behind a bouquet of brilliant red poppies. She set them on the sideboard, before curtseying to me and leaving. Trembling, my fingers traced the delicate petals. Within the sea of red, I noticed a white card.

"It is not the man who eats the opium, but the opium that eats the man."

- *The Crimson Crown Society*

I leaned against the sideboard, speared to my place. My thoughts scurried through the alcoves of my mind, and I ground my teeth to together. Breathing out through my nose, I pushed away and moved back to the window. On the street, I couldn't see the men, but I knew they had sent the message. My fingers clenched the window ledge as a blistering hum of determination shot through me. If I was going to hell anyway, I wanted answers.

The End

Acknowledgments

Thank you first and foremost to my mom for encouraging me to write and for reading many terrible early drafts. This project started when I was only thirteen and has been a part of my life for over a decade. Thank you to my beta readers and critique partners over the years, Kayla Goldstein, Andrea Walker, Shamala Williams, and Dianne Freeman who gave me invaluable critiques and kept me writing when I felt like I couldn't.

Made in the USA
Columbia, SC
25 June 2025